Noel Streatfeild

Twayne's English Authors Series

Lois Kuznets, Editor
San Diego State University

TEAS 510

Illustration by Ruth Gervis from *Ballet Shoes* (1936), by Noel Streatfeild. Reproduced by permission from Penguin Books Ltd.

Noel Streatfeild

Nancy Huse

Augustana College (Illinois)

Twayne Publishers • New York
Maxwell Macmillan Canada • Toronto
Maxwell Macmillan International • New York Oxford Singapore Sydney

Noel Streatfeild
Nancy Huse

Twayne Publishers
Macmillan Publishing Company
866 Third Avenue
New York, New York 10022

Maxwell Macmillan Canada, Inc.
1200 Eglinton Avenue East
Suite 200
Don Mills, Ontario M3C 3N1

Library of Congress Cataloging-in-Publication Data

Huse, Nancy Lyman.
    Noel Streatfeild / Nancy Huse.
        p. cm.— (Twayne's English authors series; TEAS 510)
    Includes bibliographical references and index.
    ISBN 0-8057-4515-7 (alk. paper)
    1. Streatfeild, Noel—Criticism and interpretation. 2. Children's stories, English—History and criticism. I. Title. II. Series.
PR6037.T77Z697 1994
823'.912—dc20   94-18997
                                                                                          CIP

The paper used in this publication meets the minimum requirements of American National Standard for Information Sciences—Permanence of Paper for Printed Library Materials. ANSI Z39.48-1984. ∞ ™

10 9 8 7 6 5 4 3 2 1

Printed in the United States of America.

For Dale S. Huse,
another devotee of the arts.
It's all been Sir Garnet.

Contents

Preface

Noel Streatfeild achieved popular success with her children's novel *Ballet Shoes* (1936), the first of many books exploring the family as a site of artistic or career development, especially for girls. Many of her subsequent children's novels were reprinted in the United States and retitled as "Shoe" books. For example, her Carnegie Award book, *The Circus Is Coming* (1938), was reissued as *Circus Shoes* in 1939. Later titles such as *Party Shoes* (1945, 1947), *Movie Shoes* (1949), *Skating Shoes* (1951), and *Dancing Shoes* (1957, 1958) drew on the success of her first book for children as well as its distinctive themes and structure.

Streatfeild had entered the world of children's literature somewhat unwillingly and unwittingly, responding to a proposal from Mabel Carey, children's book editor at Dent, that she write a book for children about the stage. She drew much of her material from the outline of her first novel for adults, *The Whicharts* (1931), adapting it in ways that continued to be significant for a career as a children's writer that spanned half a century. The prolific and enterprising Streatfeild examined successful families challenged both economically and emotionally. She explored history and described technique and commitment essential to vocation in the arts and other fields. Humor, ranging from nonsensical to satirical and ironic, enriched most of her children's books.

In steadily producing adult novels and plays throughout much of her career as a children's writer, Streatfeild necessarily developed a conscious perspective on childhood that she employed to defend child/adult boundaries while sharpening story forms. At the same time, her multifaceted talent admitted new subjects, character types, themes, and information into the children's book because she assumed competence and intelligent curiosity as the basis of children's contributions to the family and to society.

Although her family novels entered a children's book tradition traced to E. Nesbit and also to earlier sources such as Maria Edgeworth, Charlotte Yonge, Louisa May Alcott, and Frances Hodgson Burnett, Streatfeild demonstrated slight formal knowledge of children's authors until after she had become an established figure. Her own childhood, however, was enriched by her mother's reading aloud from such classic British writers as Dickens, Stevenson, and Scott and by her father's read-

ing of Nathaniel Hawthorne's *Tanglewood Tales* and retelling of Bible stories. Though Streatfeild remembered disliking writers like Scott selected
for Sunday afternoons at the family's vicarage home, this early experience shaped a novelist who assumed children's ability to take in detailed
description and to identify with characters marked by economic need
and varying degrees of virtue and skill. Equally important influences
were Streatfeild's role in her genteel but poor vicarage family and her
struggle to earn a living in the theater. In that struggle she gained a
knowledge of Shakespeare that informed her children's novels in unique
ways—as a basis for numerous child careers, as a foil to more interesting
pursuits, and as a means to understanding ballet and other art forms.

This literary and extraliterary context also contributed to Streatfeild's
versatility as a children's writer. Though famous for the "Shoe" books,
she also wrote with originality about Britain, the arts, and ancient history—works that drew on and elaborated on the concept of childhood that
informed her novels. For example, in one of the last books she wrote, *The
Boy Pharaoh, Tutankhamen* (1972), she stressed the meticulous work of
archaeologists preserving data even as they make exciting and dramatic
discoveries. Like her contemporary Arthur Ransome, she assumed children find work fascinating. Her conservative upbringing, rebellious
youth, and complex relationship to her family through two world wars
provided material for her novels, and her later writing includes three
memoirs that dramatize the Victorian family as it produces a daughter
who tried its patience and proved its resilience in her long life.

Though born into the upper middle class, Streatfeild was able to
chronicle the perspectives of different groups (albeit filtered by her own
class background) through her memories of warm nannies, harassed
governesses, and responsive though august headmistresses, coupled with
her later work experience in Cockney neighborhoods plagued by unemployment and then by bombing. Exploring the tensions of heredity and
environment in both adult and children's books, Streatfeild anticipated
many contemporary questions about the role of women, the structure of
the family, and the implications of the class system.

This study focuses on Streatfeild's novels, nonfiction, and memoirs for
children, especially those of her 80 books that have received or deserve
further critical commentary. I discuss her books for adults in order to
explain her concept of childhood, literary techniques, and desire for artistic expression. One of the ironies of Streatfeild's reputation is the fact
that several of her adult novels read well today yet are not widely available because her publisher's inventory was destroyed in the bombing of

London. The war, in a sense, determined that her reputation would be mainly in the field of children's literature, even though this war, like the one that preceded it, challenged the premises on which her children's books were based. The security of home, especially as typified by an old house, becomes more difficult to achieve in such war novels as *The Children in Primrose Lane* (1941; published in the United States as *The Stranger in Primrose Lane*) or later novels such as *The Growing Summer* (1966; published in the United States as *The Magic Summer*). An understanding of Streatfeild's work also requires an examination of her public life as a "national monument."

One question of special importance to criticism of women writers is how they gain voice or authority. With her persistent use of autobiographical material in her fiction as well as her manipulation of this material in her memoirs, Streatfeild offers a significant example of a rebellious daughter. But she treasured and exploited her connection to a family that enriched her perspective while making her acutely uncomfortable in financial and other ways. Her century saw, among other events, women's struggle for suffrage and for entrance into the professions and the end of a colonial era that had underpinned the childhood of which she wanted to write. Streatfeild used the poverty of women and their work in the domestic sphere to link the public with the private worlds shaping children.

Streatfeild's need to earn a living—and her mother's surprising support of her unorthodox choices of the theater and of writing—was a major challenge for her. Ambivalence toward her mother, in particular, supplied the varied female perspectives of her fiction. This aspect of Streatfeild's work has been little noted in previous studies. Children's literature is often characterized as placing parents into background roles, yet many important adults, especially mother figures, are essential to the "Shoe" books and to Streatfeild's other work as well. Likewise, her ultimate admiration for her father's vocation as an Anglican clergyman informs her description of productive and yet humorous or ironic work lives.

This examination of Noel Streatfeild's work suggests some meaningful ways to evaluate the family novel, the role of a children's novelist in preserving and constructing a historical record, and the implications of formulaic patterns that derive from female experience. The impact of two wars on the development of a woman writer, and her impact on children's literature, suggest Streatfeild's importance in the literary record as a chronicler, critic, and artist of the twentieth century.

Reiterating the economic basis of the contemporary family, Streatfeild demonstrates how children's literature has been one important way for women to challenge conventional wisdom. And though many of her books do use male characters, Streatfeild's fame as the author of *Ballet Shoes* and its successors offers a challenge to the status of "girls' books," described in most criticism as ephemeral or constituting a category separate from "great books." Few of the children's books that fascinate twentieth-century critics or receive the label of "classic" have been either identified primarily with a female audience or singled out from among a large set, such as Streatfeild's many "Shoe" books. Yet her work constitutes a critical challenge precisely because of its formulaic nature as well as the appeal of its contemporary themes and traditional values.

Acknowledgments

Angela Bull's 1983 biography of Noel Streatfeild has been invaluable in my work, especially for its focus on vicarage life. Lois R. Kuznets's 1984 discussion of Streatfeild in *Children's Literature Association Quarterly* provided a critical context, raising questions about the patterns, range, and impact of the "Shoe" novels; as my field editor she has thus been a superb counterpart. Women's Studies, as it draws from and reconstructs the study of literature, is a third source for my analysis; in particular, the work of Sara Ruddick acts as a beacon.

Without the excellence and thorough support of the Augustana Library I could not have undertaken to read all of Streatfeild's work. Individual librarians—especially John Pollitz but also at various times most of the staff—provided help. Rosemary Copeland did the difficult work of locating numerous out-of-print sources. The Faculty Research Committee, chaired by Don Erickson, awarded a sabbatical grant. Bea Jacobson, who had read *Ballet Shoes* to her daughters, took a vital interest in the project at every turn. The University of Iowa's Center for Advanced Studies provided added support. I thank Jay Semel for this valuable environment.

Many friends and family members helped, too; I thank all of them by singling out my sister, Agnes Lyman Ireland, who looked after my education as Noel Streatfeild looked after her sister Richenda's.

Chronology

1895	Mary Noel Streatfeild born to William and Janet Streatfeild on 24 December in Frant, Sussex, England, the second child of six.
1902	Family moves to St. Leonards-on-Sea.
1910	Noel Streatfeild is expelled from Saint Leonards Ladies' College.
1911	Family moves to Eastbourne. Noel Streatfeild is confirmed at her father's insistence.
1913	Sees Ninette de Valois dance with "Lila Field's Little Wonders."
1915	Her youngest sister, Richenda, is born.
1916	Works at Woolwich Arsenal producing munitions. Produces parish plays.
1919	Enters the Royal Academy of Dramatic Arts.
1920–1922	Tours British Isles with the Charles Doran Shakespeare Company, using the stage name Noelle Sonning.
1923	Kitty Barne Streatfeild produces a pageant in Eastbourne.
1925	Acts part in a children's pantomime. Begins correspondence course in writing; is urged to write for children.
1926	Meets Daphne Ionides, a close friend and literary mentor.
1926–1928	Tours Australia and New Zealand with repertory company.
1929	Her father, newly appointed bishop, dies suddenly. Streatfeild returns to England in November.
1930	Finishes *The Whicharts* in autumn.
1931	Charles Evans of Heinemann accepts *The Whicharts* for publication. Vic-Wells Ballet Company and Sadler's Wells Ballet School are founded.

1936   Mabel Carey of Dent persuades Streatfeild to write a stage novel for children. *Ballet Shoes* is published and sells out 28 September.

1937   *Tennis Shoes* is published. Streatfeild visits the United States.

1938   *The Circus Is Coming* (*Circus Shoes*) is published. Streatfeild visits the United States.

1939   Receives Carnegie Award for *The Circus Is Coming*. Begins writing romances as Susan Scarlett.

1940   Procures mobile canteen; works with Women's Voluntary Service (WVS).

1940–1942   Keeps diary, *London under Fire*.

1941   Flat at 11 Bolton Street is destroyed in bombing. Works with PEN; produces WVS newsletter.

1946   *Party Shoes* is published. Streatfeild moves to 51A Elizabeth Street.

1947   Visits the United States; sees Margaret O'Brien filmed in *The Secret Garden*.

1948   Constructs garden on the bomb site at Elizabeth Street and Chester Square. Meets Margot Grey, who becomes a close friend and companion.

1951   *White Boots* (*Skating Shoes*) is published.

1953   *The Fearless Treasure* is published.

1960   Abandons writing of adult novels.

1961   Helen Hoke Watts suggests a vicarage memoir.

1963   *A Vicarage Family* is published.

1966   *The Growing Summer* (*The Magic Summer*) is published.

1968   Suffers a partial stroke.

1972   *The Boy Pharaoh, Tutankhamen* is published.

1974   *When the Siren Wailed* is published.

1976   *Gran-Nannie* is published.

1983   Receives the Order of the British Empire.

1986   Dies on 11 September in a nursing home.

Chapter One

Difficult Daughter
as Family Writer

"It will all be Sir Garnet." This comforting if nonsensical statement—suggesting a romantic rescue from suffering—uttered by the nannies in many of Noel Streatfeild's family novels encapsulates the major concerns and strategies of the writer's long career. Spoken by women who provide for children's material and emotional needs in early childhood—and whose influence often continues into their nurslings' adulthood—the "Sir Garnet" phrase comforts in its duality. The nursery phrase recalls the age of chivalry as well as pre–World War I England in which one's place was assigned from birth according to carefully constructed class boundaries. These boundaries also kept women and people of color confined within a moral, political, and linguistic order enjoying widespread public support. But Streatfeild's life spanned a transition in British culture from the reign of Victoria to the age of Margaret Thatcher. Paradigms of race, class, and gender became crucial to the work of historians and literary critics during a century marked by the decline of empire, two world wars, and women's suffrage.

The ironic dimensions of "Sir Garnet" seem obvious. Yet the nursery phrase also represents the coherence of family life, to which the nanny gives partial voice. Children in Streatfeild's novels recognize that their families can cope with the various economic and emotional stresses from within and without. Yet they also recognize that Nanny is playing with reality, appealing to an imaginary and even silly figure of male authority, wealth, and competence. How things work out for Nanny's nurslings most often depends on the complex interplay of luck and hard work in a world where church and empire offer a benevolent start even as their premises are called into question by children who are their own authorities and who flourish in that process.

While the nanny's voice conveys her importance as a loving figure, its appeal to the past and to literature suggests a reason beyond affection for the success of various Streatfeild protagonists, who are usually girls gaining competence in the arts or other professions. Streatfeild experienced the turbulence of the century. Forced to earn a living (although women in her family's long recorded past had lived as gentlewomen), suffering the immediate effects of two wars, and seeing much of her own work discounted in the wake of a new realism in the children's novel, she coped with loss and disappointment by creative work that enhanced her self-esteem and gave her a whimsical authority and power not unlike that of her many nannies, governesses, and teachers who fuse the worlds of private affection and public performance. "It will all be Sir Garnet" is powerful in part because it is not true and Nanny and the children know it. Streatfeild continually drew on the myths of continuity even as she confronted and validated changes in the world and in herself.

Books were important in Noel Streatfeild's early life; she was entranced by *Peter Rabbit* and other stories. Yet her works suggest that experience as a middle child—what she described as a "misfit" in the family of a saintly vicar—and as a girl maturing in a time of transition, may count more than traditions in literature as a genesis for her work. According to Carolyn Heilbrun, "Misfits are often our most gifted children and, for girls, those most likely to require a different story by which to write their lives."[1] To the extent that Streatfeild invented a "different story," it is one focusing on the family as a site for women to become whole in possessing both the powers of love and the rewards of career. Departing from the traditional romance and its dependence on the marriage plot, she imagined a world in which more than one destiny, and many possible identities, welcomed girls who knew on some level that they themselves would be "Sir Garnet." Many kinds of love become important to Streatfeild's plots.[2] Showing how a mix of relationships and interests define happiness, Streatfeild enlarged the scope of the twentieth-century children's writer. She confronted one of the three major taboos of children's literature (sex, money, and death) with novels that depict the family as the site of threatened but not impossible economic power.

Childhood and Youth: Circe and Victoria

Noel Streatfeild consistently drew from her family history to create stories, manipulating a body of facts within a resonant pattern in various systematic ways. A basically happy family with a number of close siblings; a need for money, often brought on by the absence of a parent; creativity exhibited by one or more children; movement from a spacious house threatened or necessitated; emphasis on hard work, even on vocation; and a spectrum of female figures who provide different parts of children's nurture, of whom the nanny is often the most successful and the mother the least, are some of the key elements of the pattern.[3] All of these apparently formulaic elements figure in an account of her life drawn from her siblings' and her own memories and in her fictionalized autobiographies. Little that she wrote can be described as not, in some way, about herself, a characteristic she claimed children's writers hold in common.[4] How the basic elements of the pattern became available to Noel Streatfeild as a writer constitutes in itself a family story.

To recover this story, biographer Angela Bull used records left by Streatfeild's siblings as a balance to the author's speeches, autobiographies, letters, and diaries. Though she views Streatfeild's autobiographies as novels rather than "objective" accounts, Bull in her own account supports them in most respects.[5] Recent critical work on autobiography as a genre offers ways to value and interpret the construction of real-life narratives, all of which involve omissions and emphases selected by their authors. The life Streatfeild imagined for her characters and for her fictionalized self is an interesting amalgam of fact and desire. Thinly disguised as "Vicky" in the autobiographies, the difficult daughter internalized family as her subject—a family dependent on her creative gifts to record it and celebrate or critique it as she willed.

Streatfeild's parents met when William Streatfeild interned as a curate with Janet Venn's father. Their families had a long history that included, on the Streatfeild side, life as gentry in rural Kent. William had grown up in a household of 10 children, under the care of a devoted nanny as well as his own parents. But Janet's mother died when she was four; she and her sisters never felt completely comfortable with their Scottish stepmother, and stories about Janet's deprivations—especially with regard to clothing and toys—were passed on in the family. The issue of how to mother, and what relationship those skills have to economic status and vocation, thread their ways throughout Streatfeild's work—part of her reaction to her mother, to Janet's strained childhood, and to William's relatively content one. When Janet Venn met William Streatfeild, she was 17, and they married when she was 21 and he 28.

The second daughter of William and Janet Streatfeild, Mary Noel Streatfeild was born in Frant, Sussex, on 24 December 1895. Before she was two, her father accepted the vicarage at Amberley, where she lived her preschool years until moving to St. Leonards-on-Sea and later to Eastbourne. Her birth date, coinciding with a major religious festival overshadowing her own importance, and her birth order helped to fuel her later sense that she was a misfit in her genteel family. Her older sister, Ruth, and her younger one, Barbara, were delicate; another younger sister, Joyce, died at two. Her brother, Bill, was a well-adjusted boy who thrived despite being sent away to school at six. Twenty years after Streatfeild's birth, Janet and William had another daughter, Richenda, whom their second daughter would identify with and protect. But among the bevy of older girls, Noel Streatfeild alone had good health. Ruth's asthma caused the family to send her to Kent, to the home of William's parents, where she was nursed by her father's old nanny, known to the children as Gran-Nannie. Streatfeild used this woman as the prototype for her novels' nurturing figures, and in *Gran-Nannie* (1976) she depicted her father bringing each of the three daughters to be nursed back to health at her hands.

Separated from her older sister, Noel Streatfeild at two became temporary oldest child until Ruth joined the family at St. Leonards, deemed a healthy enough climate for her. At six, Ruth could read all of *Little Women*, while Noel was slow to read, by the family's standards, not learning until she went to school. Her difficulty with learning to read seems to have been the earliest concrete evidence that she was a problematic daughter. But the fact that she was a daughter and not a son, possessed of a stocky, large frame and unusually good health, may have affected the way her parents treated her. Certainly she was not a candidate for their concern in the ways that her more fragile sisters and young brother—the only son—would have been. Her younger sister Barbara looked like their pretty, dark mother, a distinguishing characteristic; their father often praised his wife's beauty. But even her place as second daughter was ambiguous; with Ruth away, learning to paint at her grandfather's side at Hoseyrigge, the ancestral home, Streatfeild was for an important period the first child at home.

Streatfeild's earliest years were marked by imaginative play, often in the care of her nanny or young nursemaid. Though the family did not have much money, a cook, maids, and nursery staff were viewed as indispensable. An early memory involved walking with the nursemaid as the latter pushed Barbara in the pram; details of Streatfeild's green velvet outfit remained in the writer's memory for use in many stories focused on children's need for special clothing, usually for their creative work. Another important memory was of herself acting out the role of Circe in the nursery, after her father had read the story in *Tanglewood Tales*. Streatfeild's passion for self-dramatization and for drama itself are embodied in the Circe anecdote; acting and putting on plays was both a source of her self-esteem in childhood and a subject for her novels after a career in theater itself had waned. Circe, with her disruptive female power, was a role especially suited to a daughter growing into a rebellious child. Centering attention on herself by giving commands, asking unpleasant questions, and even engaging in violent behavior—throwing an inkwell at a servant—she caused her father to pray on his knees for guidance in dealing with her.[6]

Another memory was Queen Victoria's funeral procession; as William held her up to view it, he told her never to forget the sight. In strong contrast to his reading of imaginative literature was William's careful injunction to honor authority, to observe ritual, to identify as a British citizen with the nation's institutions. Though Streatfeild often said she was bored by her vicarage childhood, she made good use of her family's conservative commitments in novels that celebrate stability. In her nonfiction as well, an appreciation of tradition and of careful detail reflect the training the vicar gave her. Attributing greater understanding of her "difficult" nature to her father than to her mother when it came time to write autobiographically, Streatfeild nonetheless conveyed a dread of his remedies for her behavior, especially the early Confirmation he prescribed for her. William's devotion to his calling, however, seems to have provided a key motif for Streatfeild's work. Typically her child characters use spare minutes to practice ballet or plan pageants, much as the vicar always had in mind some devotion or some parish event.

Janet Streatfeild also read to her children, and when she needed to she could brilliantly synthesize material that outlasted the attention of her audience. She displayed little aptitude for parish work but sustained a meticulous interest in studying and gathering flowers. When mother and daughter went on flower-naming expeditions they got along well, and Streatfeild continued all her life to fill in her mother's copy of Bentham and Hooker's wildflower book whenever she found a new specimen.[7] Moreover, the hobby provided important outlets from the heavy rituals of Good Friday, when the vicar's family left him to officiate at services while they found flowers for Easter Sunday.

Janet Streatfeild, a dutiful and apparently adored wife, resisted the High Church atmosphere her husband reveled in. Unlike the Streatfeilds' Anglican and Kentish roots, hers were in Evangelical traditions. Though like William she came from a vicarage family, she found ways to undercut the emphasis on churchgoing, or to modify the children's required Bible recitations. When Streatfeild wrote about her childhood as a misfit, she emphasized her troubled relationship with her mother, noting that Janet preferred daughters more dependent than she was. Yet just as numerous as the recorded slights and harshness (e.g., sending Noel back to school after an influenza epidemic while extending Barbara's time in her care) are subtle references to the ways the mother made space in a constricted life for alternative ways of spending time. And in the same book (*A Vicarage Family*) that appalled her family with its jealousy of Barbara and dislike of Janet, Streatfeild credits her mother with major career advice based precisely on the misfit's feistiness.

The vicar's daughters learned from their mother when Noel was 13 that they would have to earn their own living. This came as a surprise, according to Streatfeild's account, though Ruth already wanted to be a painter or illustrator. In *A Vicarage Family* the mother agrees that the eldest daughter will be an artist, the youngest will marry early, as each hoped, but for the middle daughter "it will be nothing ordinary for you. You will be the one to surprise us all" (*VF*, 179). Streatfeild had already "surprised" the family with her expulsion from school in St. Leonards, yet she had exhibited writing talent. William's transfer to Eastbourne had kept quiet the news of her disgrace. Much later Janet Streatfeild supported both career choices of her difficult daughter—first to become an actress and then to change over to writing.

Both parents sensed that Noel was creative; the best evidence came from the parish theatricals she wrote and organized, which was the one way her nonconforming style seemed to earn their approval because it furthered the family's commitment to William's work. Finding money to educate Streatfeild at what would become the Royal Academy was not easy for Noel's parents, and they both assumed that their sacrifice would result in professional security for her. In a profession in which it was so difficult to become established, an added factor would be the toll of the depression. Like her many child characters whose families pooled their resources—including siblings' allowances—so that they could dress for auditions or buy equipment for their craft, Streatfeild received support for her ventures because her family expected her to earn money to keep herself. They would provide a launching place for each child. In Streatfeild's novels, however, the family continued as an economic and communal unit long after the discovery of vocation.

Novels like *Ballet Shoes* suggest that advice and financial help from siblings and teachers provide for the success of the child star, who in turn maintains the group so that all will continue their intermingled lives, usually in the birth home or one resembling it. This plot deviates from but comments on Streatfeild's experience. It is true that her siblings were important to Streatfeild; she and Ruth fulfilled a childhood dream when Ruth was selected to illustrate *Ballet Shoes*. Barbara and Bill were especially close and provided a model for several pairs of siblings in their sister's work and a way that she would explore creativity. She kept Richenda from feeling displaced and unloved when the family decided, after William's sudden death, that a 13-year-old belonged at her mother's side. Noel Streatfeild cabled from across the world to insist that the girl be allowed to stay in the school where she had been happy. And in the childhood theatricals Ruth and Barbara performed well under her direction. She visited Bill in Bangkok (like many Streatfeild men, he served in the empire's farflung bureaucracy), and, when he and his family were interned in Japan during World War II, she pulled strings to get messages to them. She also provided a transitional home when they returned.

As in most modern families, however, Noel's siblings assumed their new family units would replace the childhood family. In this she differed, dreaming during her first career that she would find a second at her father's side, difficult no longer, assisting in his work while becoming a writer. Instead, her father's death in 1929 ended the vicarage life. Bill executed the estate, establishing Janet in her own house. He arranged one year's housing in London for his sister. She would have just that long for a transition from actress to writer. Her mother was provided for, if displaced; but even inheriting Hoseyrigge had not meant that William's adult children would be financially independent. Her imposing clan provided Streatfeild with memories rather than money.

To an imaginative child like Noel Streatfeild, the fact that her original ancestral home was a castle—vacated by the family two generations earlier in favor of a smaller yet commodious mansion and then in favor of a newer place the grandparents built and called "The Little House"— must have occasioned daydreams. Both her adult and her children's novels focus on large houses, usually with separate nurseries like the one her father's nanny had run. She depicts Vicky, the difficult daughter of *A Vicarage Family*, relaxing at her grandparents' house, puzzled about why she "was so much nicer here than she was at home" (*VF*, 100). The mature narrator explains her feelings not in terms of the physical environment but the emotional one: "But what, quite unconsciously for all their children and later their grandchildren, both Granny and Grandfather had exuded was faith in them. Because they believed sincerely that every child in the family was doing his or her best, there was a feeling of ease and happiness in the house, and they all tried their hardest not in any way to offend. Even Victoria behaved well, arriving to meals clean and tidy and never arguing about anything" (VF, 96).

The grandmother in A Vicarage Family—a prototype for several mothers-in-law, just and unjust, in the novels—singles out each child for loving advice about the family as a system. For the difficult daughter, the advice is to assist her father in his work because he loves her best and she is good at helping him. Vicky protests about the look of pain she often sees on her father's face when he hears that she is again in disgrace with her mother or her teachers, but the grandmother says they have a great deal to give each other. This interventional grandmother provides a buffer between the troublesome child and her mother in the autobiographies; in the fiction she sometimes interferes with nearly fatal consequences in the daughter-in-law's affairs. The power of the maternal fascinates the writer, even as she asserts herself the father's most beloved daughter.

The actual "Little House" had six bedrooms and servants' quarters the children never saw. Four servants and an unmarried daughter ran the house. While the autobiographies give relatively little description of this house, other than that the family's beautiful possessions had been stored in favor of the numerous gifts brought back from foreign service by the uncles, Streatfeild goes into more detail about the effect of physical environment on the vicarage family. At their third home, Eastbourne, "there was nowhere to lay out a game and leave it for another day. No room in which to be noisy and, on occasion, fight" (VF, 105). The children's only common area is to be the garden. The lack of a nursery signals the end of their closeness in play. In some sense "The Little House," with the sons' gifts strewn about, had the ambience of a nursery in its entirety. The preservation of space for developing talent and for creative play became an issue in many of Streatfeild's books; it was in the nursery at Amberley that she had discovered her own imagination, and she remembered that in re-creating the family idylls and conflicts.

A final part of the system of memories at Streatfeild's command was the range of servants, including cooks and governesses, who supply various kinds of support or danger in her plots. If her nannies bear no resemblance to Mary Poppins, her cooks often do, sometimes bringing a colorful past that makes them appreciate talented children. The cook in A Vicarage Family always separates Vicky's Christmas Eve birthday from the family Christmas; she is transformed, in Tennis Shoes, into a transcendent character who helps turn Nicky Heath into a star performer. Servants in Streatfeild's books almost always are glad of a home and invested in the family's fortunes (sometimes quite literally, as in *Ballet Shoes*). Biographical evidence suggests how anxiously people like Janet Streatfeild looked for just the right help, and the enormous changes resulting from the war. Yet Noel Streatfeild was able in adulthood to surround herself with staff that helped her to keep writing well into old age. In her fiction and her life a household was for Streatfeild a place of mutual prosperity for its members the more they believe in the creative lives at its center.

Educated as a day student in boarding schools, Streatfeild locates her stories in the home rather than at school. But schoolmistresses such as the ones Vicky and her sisters encounter are a major link to her storytelling. The difficult child succeeds in holding their attention and in getting their advice. They are overall benevolent, despite Streatfeild's protestations about her hatred of school and her misery at being at the bottom of her form. More than once she played pranks. Her sister Ruth remembered well one that involved organizing the "Little Grey Bows Society" at St. Leonards. Each girl lost marks when she was polite to a mistress. In the autobiography Vicky forms the society to retaliate when a teacher tears up something she had written. The difficult daughter resisted lessons about keeping a stiff upper lip, though she knew well that doing so was expected of her.

Finding an outlet for her talents in drama often kept Noel Streatfeild from being more disruptive at home or at school. Child performers—"Lila Field's Little Wonders"—fascinated her after a special outing in Eastbourne. She carried her love for performing into school, parodying teachers to win attention from other girls. Entering into new roles and forming community through shared jokes and language, she partially countered the social restrictions imposed by her mother about those the girls could play with and the religious dogma William never submitted to discussion in the household. She made stories and dramas out of nearly all of her childhood memories, using a slight from an aunt, a cup of soup from her father's nanny. They are movable pieces in a game of storytelling modeled on a plot outline in which the family finds its difficult or unwanted child the one who maintains it beyond expectations. According to her biographer, "She burned with a desire to make life more dramatic" (Bull, 41). Like many women writers seeking to move outside conventional plots yet remain intelligible and accepted, Streatfeild found even in childhood that performative strategies enabled her to describe and invent simultaneously and safely. Enacting Circe and observing the queen's funeral, a misfit daughter could say and do a great many forbidden things while maintaining the environment that gave her voice (Frye, 11).

Actress Daughter

Streatfeild's life as an actress is interesting for the ways she maintained her links to the past while skirting some dangerous situations (she accepted gifts of money from the men she dated). William's connections provided ways to further her exposure to art and history. She would use her experience as an actress in her children's books to elaborate on the need to earn enough money to buy food, clothing, and shelter; to stress the worth of hard work even by those of relatively little talent; and to present as a taken-for-granted condition of childhood the ability to participate in the production of culture and the creation of art.

During her teenage years, attending Laleham school in Eastbourne, Streatfeild acted in theatricals and sometimes wrote scripts; hearing about the ballet, she yearned to see it but could not afford a trip to London with her school. With the war fashion and hairstyles changed at the vicarage, as did the girls' church attendance. But sexual mores did not change. In *On Tour* (1965) Vicky's fear of becoming an unwed mother—observed firsthand in the parish—keeps her from experimentation. Streatfeild also mentions repeatedly that their mother did not discuss sex with the girls, although in some ways she held more advanced views than their dedicated and conservative father, who did not allow the girls to greet the Pankhursts when they lectured. The outspoken and experimental daughter could no longer speak of her "real self" to her father. But the birth of Richenda in 1915 brought shared confidences among mother and daughters; they were initially appalled at the pregnancy. Richenda's childhood, however, suggested to Noel a model of children's connectedness to the adult world that gave a new structure to the nursery idyll she preserved from her grandparents' house. Sophisticated children, not sheltered ones, would people her nurseries.

After leaving school Streatfeild took a course at the Eastbourne School of Domestic Economy in domestic science, perhaps because she recognized her mother's ineptitude in managing the household. It is not clear what she learned, for she always insisted she could not cook. Still, her books are replete with dresses to be hemmed and meals to be prepared. When Streatfeild's soldier cousin was killed in Normandy in 1914, she had become involved in Red Cross work suited to the family's class. She also produced plays to support the war effort locally.

Eventually the war precipitated her leaving home to work in a munitions factory, shocking her family. She lived among Cockneys, whom she would later write about as people who, though harmed by unemployment, had their own culture and survival patterns to share. Her good health, however, was tested by her time away from home, and she was sent home with colitis to face a decision about her future.

When Noel Streatfeild announced to her parents that she wished to become an actress—a decision that would have shocked them in their youth—they expressed complete faith in her. Although the war had made the theater respectable for women, the life of an actress was still considered a morally dubious one. Her father used his connections to find out where she should train, and she applied to the Royal Academy of Dramatic Arts. There, for the first time, she worked hard as a student, regretting the years she lost in avoiding serious study. Though too tall for ballet and already 23, she was proud to discover an aptitude for the classic discipline she had admired as a teenager. She received an award as an improved student but did not find work on graduation. Meanwhile, her parents expected her to be self-supporting. In *On Tour* Vicky's mother had even given up the little sister's nanny as a way of financing her training. The melodrama in her situation may have escaped Streatfeild at the time, but the suspenseful and stressful aspects of it would be recorded in her stage books.

Streatfeild was an attractive woman, described by her sister Ruth Gervis as "a honeypot for men" (Bull, 58). She had a flair for wearing interesting clothes, which may account for her luck in finding a job through an agency: the misfit had grown into a woman who fit well into the flapper era. She went on a five-week tour under her stage name, Noelle Sonning, then found a good job with the Charles Doran Company doing Shakespeare in repertory, including roles as Titania and Audrey. For the first time she understood and responded to Shakespeare. Like her growing knowledge of perfection in ballet performed by dancers like Ninette de Valois, her firsthand work with literature affected her deeply. Many of her child characters would share her early dislike for Shakespeare and come through rigorous obedience and tenacity to understand the lines they were speaking.

Slow to read, slow to become a real student, Streatfeild seemed finally to comprehend what was implied in her father's vocation and his insistence that she never forget the spectacle of a nation mourning for the queen. What she had always understood intuitively—the power of emotion and the force of words and gestures to work magic—she had now reconciled with the attractive, incomprehensible wholeheartedness of her father's steady yet inspired work.

One of Streatfeild's links with her father was an idealism that sometimes blinded him to his family's needs. Without understanding the possible consequences, she helped to instigate union activities among the actors. Angela Bull finds this an example of her naïveté and even of her shallowness. Losing a job for union activities, however, is not necessarily without its admirable side. Rather than count on a benevolent authority, Streatfeild assumed that actors should determine their work conditions. "Sir Garnet" was not Charles Doran. But her acting career did not recover from this incident, though she continued to hope she would achieve fame as well as earn a good living through her craft.

She acted in a light comedy, *Yoicks*, worked as a model, and seemed more interested in worldly friends, clothing, and gifts from men than in serious work at her profession. Her description of Vicky in *On Tour* implies that she was puzzled about the hold her vicarage family held over her. But at this same time she was helping her friend Christabel Russell elude the press during a famous paternity suit, seeing a side of marriage and family not discussed at home, even though the complications of childbearing and economics were obvious in Janet's history too. Since Richenda's birth Janet Streatfeild had become a more agreeable mother. She had more energy now than when her other children were young. In this way she may have been important as a role model to an actress daughter becoming depressed by her failure to get major parts.

Nearing 30, without distinction as a performer and not interested in marriage (like other women of her generation, marriage precluded career in her thinking), and also without a clear picture of how she would survive as both a vicar's daughter and a sophisticated professional, she was compelled in 1925 to take a job she dreaded. She played the part of a fairy queen in a children's pantomime at Newcastle. With her usual ability to become fascinated with spectacle and with her memories and desires, the comedown in fact became an inspiration. A troupe of child performers, "The Manchester Mighty Mites," played in the show. Watching their training and discipline, noticing the class and economic issues implicit in their work and their dress, she regained the excitement of her youth in Eastbourne when "Lila Field's Little Wonders" held her spellbound. Her interest in children and fantasy seemed a possible escape from a life becoming more and more unsatisfying.

It is hard to say what might have happened next to Streatfeild if she had not come from her particular family. The "Mighty Mites," working-class children, had won her admiration, even envy, for the competence their lives had given them. Perhaps she might have started writing children's stories at once, or even begun to work at her acting career in a more determined way, if the head of a touring company had not decided that using the bishop's daughter as the female lead in his productions would lend prestige to his group. Without understanding how her special treatment would earn her the enmity of the other actors, she accepted, touring in South Africa, and returned to the vicarage disheartened by the experience. One aspect of the trip had gone well—her father's introductions to Anglican families who entertained her and deepened her ability to read her surroundings. Though at times she wished to forget that her father was a bishop, unpleasant relationships within the company confirmed her as more comfortable in some ways as a daughter than as an actress.

With her mother's encouragement Streatfeild began to imagine herself a writer, taking a correspondence course and eventually publishing a story in a children's magazine. It was based on growing up in the wrong environment—a rabbit exchanged for a daughter—but it had a happy ending. This tentative beginning was abandoned when another invitation to tour abroad was given. She left for Australia, determined to keep a diary in order to work out possibilities for becoming a writer when she returned to the vicarage. Though she notes that the diary seems lacking in introspection, Angela Bull traces in it the dawning of an important understanding that would provide a range of material to the writer.

Through an intense friendship with Daphne Ionides begun aboard ship, Streatfeild discovered her attraction to women. After a painful separation from Daphne, Streatfeild read *The Well of Loneliness* (1928), Radclyffe Hall's tortured, Freudian-influenced examination of her lesbianism. While there is no evidence Streatfeild had sexual relationships with women (or with men, despite frequent dating and rumored affairs), she was deeply moved and disturbed by Hall's book. But she was also possessed of a friendship that would be significant to her self-esteem and social and literary stature. Daphne would engage Streatfeild in volunteer work, put her in touch with a literary agent, and otherwise enrich her life. Perhaps she would also deepen the writer's interest in women as subjects for her fiction. Though many of Streatfeild's fictional children do have fathers as well as mothers who further their careers and general well-being, they are surrounded by women servants and teachers whose various perspectives make life more fun and make child actors successful.

Angela Bull devotes a good deal of thought to Streatfeild's reasons for not marrying, deciding that she was asexual. Unlike Streatfeild, Bull seems to assume marriage as the real norm for women. Yet in a country where three million women of her generation remained single in the wake of a major war, Streatfeild's situation was not unusual. Moreover, by observing Victoria but being Circe, she may have found her own way to construct a woman's life. She would shape her own "Mighty Mites" before long.

Writer and Worker

Her father's death in 1929 marked a major transition for Noel Streatfeild. The new bishop died suddenly, at 61. Streatfeild was unable to return for the funeral. She completed the Australian tour and then visited her brother in Bangkok. Before reaching England, she resolved to give up acting. Within a decade she became a prolific and acclaimed writer for adults and children. She also established London as her home and embarked on volunteer work among unemployed Cockneys in Deptford. Most of her accomplishments depended on the work habits acquired as an actress and on the contacts she made through her family and friends, especially Daphne Ionides. Depicting herself in *Beyond the Vicarage* (1971) as "knowing nothing and ridiculously full of self-confidence"[8] about her writing, Streatfeild used her father's old typewriter to produce *The Whicharts* (1931). This novel—about three fatherless daughters abandoned by their mothers and raised by their dead father's former mistress—drew directly on Streatfeild's theater years and indirectly on her family life. The father—"which art" in heaven—provides the playful title, and a mother role divided among various female figures (guardian, nanny, and teachers) provides the structure for the three girls' quests for work and money in a rather sordid world. Quite different from her imagined life in the bishop's residence, the adventures of Streatfeild's characters nonetheless validated commitments among sisters and a home maintained by different kinds of maternal presences. Streatfeild imagined a dangerous but amusing alternative to the refuge promised by her father's presence.

The wit and freshness of Streatfeild's writing impressed Ionides's friend, the writer Roland Pertwee. He in turn passed the manuscript on to Charles Evans, his editor at Heinemann. Evans decided that Streatfeild was a major new talent and helped her continue as a writer by paying her to do book reviews so that she would have a steady income. Meanwhile, she had developed her own method for focusing on her new career. When she found that theater friends were a distraction, calling her during the day and assuming that she could not be serious about being a writer, she decided on a ruse that she then made an actual practice. She began to tell callers that she was still in her pajamas late in the day and so could not see them or go out. Before long she had acquired the habit of returning to bed after breakfast, doing her writing in longhand and establishing a lifelong habit of writing daily for about six hours. Late afternoons and evenings were free for ballet and theater, turning Streatfeild into an observer rather than a participant in those fields. She missed her theater friends and acquaintances, but other relationships and obligations partly took the place of her old life. Charles Evans, her editor, was a frequent visitor to her flat. Characteristically, she turned nostalgia for stage life into a theme for her writing. She also tried her hand at playwriting.

During the years when Noel Streatfeild was producing adult novels in quick succession—*Parson's Nine* (1932), *Tops and Bottoms* (1933), *A Shepherdess of Sheep* (1934), and *It Pays to Be Ignorant* (1936)—she wrote plays for adults which were produced, briefly, in London—*Them Wings* (1933) and *Wisdom Teeth* (1936). Impressive as it was, however, this work did not mine her talents for moving characters through exemplary roles and for giving vent to children's desire for competence. Despite a certain stiffness, her work of the period she least valued—plays collected in *The Children's Matinee* (1934)—exploited these despite their stiffness. Designed for children to perform but adults to attend, the plays have awkward moments when children misinterpret adult language in order to create double entendre. Years later, people remembered the excitement of staging these plays under Streatfeild's direction, and her notes to child readers indicate how seriously she took children's acting talent. These notes have an excitement and resonance the plays themselves lack.

Empathy for children pervaded Streatfeild's life and imagination well before she became a children's writer. For one thing, she had assumed a protective role toward her young sister Richenda, choosing her clothes and taking her to plays in the wake of her mother's bereavement. "As if it had broken her spine" (*BV*, 28), the death of the bishop left his wife somewhat infantilized. She turned to her once-difficult daughter for emotional support, but Streatfeild was better able to empathize with the displaced teenager than with the bereaved wife. She had realized how "sculpted" into her own soul William's Christianity was; the closeness to her father she had yearned for now seemed accomplished through her internalizing of his commitments. Soon after his death she found herself reciting a prayer from the evening service the family never attended and decided her father's knowledge of the prayer had found voice in her. William's sense of wonder and his faith in his work did seem to have infused Streatfeild's writing life. Unlike the loneliness of the theater tours and her disdain for people she met on them, life as a writer provided company more to Streatfeild's liking. It also enabled her to preserve her sense of home and family by exploring them in memory even as she visited her mother and kept in touch with her siblings.

Returning to the tension between her parents' restrictive yet centered world and her nursery enactment of whimsical and seductive sorceress, Streatfeild's books frequently deal with the perspectives of children. Even a book like *A Shepherdess of Sheep*—which caused readers to beg for a sequel so that the governess protagonist could marry at last—was praised for its child characters, "real flesh and blood little mortals, neither imps nor angels."[9] Although the stage children of *The Whicharts* were among Streatfeild's most important creations, the varied personalities of the tribe in *Parson's Nine* likewise suggested the importance of children's ideas and preferences.

By 1936 Streatfeild had begun an ambitious novel—*Caroline England* (1938)—amounting to both a panorama and a satiric portrait of class constraints as women, in particular, experienced them. Alternating between anger and nostalgia, this novel, like other Streatfeild novels, today seems as important for its treatment of women's lives as for such other concerns as changing tastes in the theater. Before this book could be completed, however, an editor at Dent, Mabel Carey, intervened to propose that Streatfeild write a children's novel about the theater, combining her two great subjects for a new audience. Unlike *The Children's Matinee*, the book, she was told, need not appeal to adult notions of humor; like it, it was agreed that the illustrations would be done by Ruth Gervis, Streatfeild's sister. According to Angela Bull, having Ruth as illustrator again was the only appealing part of the proposal (Bull, 136). Streatfeild did not want to write for children. Such a step seemed a comedown—the kind of thing one did to gain exposure as a writer but not the act of someone so well established. The offer intrigued her nonetheless, and she set to work rehashing *The Whicharts*.

When *Ballet Shoes* appeared in September of 1936 it attracted little attention. But Christmas reviews changed everything. Streatfeild later described the book as a gift to her child-self, because it offered a milieu of glamour and accomplishment rather than the restrictive round of Sunday ceremonies and daily rules in the vicarage. It caused a sensation. The writer was amazed to see it featured in the window of a famous London bookstore, Bumpus's, surrounded by ballet shoes, including those of Tamara Karsavina (Wilson, 23). She discovered the the novel was rationed—one copy to each buyer. So easily written, yet hailed as "original," "real," and functional in its inspirational impact, the book earned, in Streatfeild's mind, far too much notoriety. With little knowledge of the current state of children's literature, Streatfeild had touched a resonant chord for reviewers tired of stereotyped school and adventure books (Bull, 138). Parents and children, too, responded with enthusiasm to the story of the three girls' success.

Prompted by Mabel Carey, Streatfeild continued to make room for her new "sideline." She produced a self-portrait in *Tennis Shoes*'s Nicky Heath, remembering a time she seemed good at nothing and yet offended others by insisting she was special. This time she was pleased with the book and its success, but she left London as soon as she sent in the manuscript. Her dreams were not about writing for children; she wanted to write Hollywood scripts. So a longtime plan of going to the United States finally was realized with some of the money from her successful children's books. Streatfeild's inquiries and contacts did not earn her a place in the California sun. At home, however, Mabel Carey had a new topic in mind—the circus. A reluctant Streatfeild agreed to do a third children's book, motivated at first by her new flat, complete with housekeeper, and by a desire to travel again. Then she found herself caught up with the story of children badly educated but desiring the hard work and satisfaction of a circus home. Much of the writing was done on Streatfeild's second trip to California in 1937, after she had completed observations of the Bertram Mills circus as it toured England.

When *Circus Shoes* (published in England as *The Circus Is Coming*) won the Carnegie Award, Streatfeild was in the south of France working on an adult novel, *Luke* (1939), and toying with the idea of writing about Aimee Semple McPherson. Yet the signals that she was a children's novelist were becoming clearer. She began to lecture about children's literature, doing research to fill in her lack of knowledge about such writers as E. Nesbit. The war put an end to travel, however, and made writing just one of her daily activities in the midst of chaos. It also grounded her more deeply in the culture of the city.

Destruction and Continuity

When Streatfeild wrote about her travels in the United States in *Beyond the Vicarage* she characterized herself as something of an inept scatterbrain in the efficient world of New York taxi drivers and Los Angeles storekeepers. Yet the war at home brought out Streatfeild's most impressive powers, personal and literary. For seven years she had been working on the Care Committee in Deptford, doing volunteer social work at Ionides's invitation and using some of her experiences there in her writing, especially in *Tops and Bottoms*. When the air raids began in 1940 she helped to evacuate families, returning to her own neighborhood to sleep in shelters or—when her flat was bombed—to stay in a friend's basement. There she continued her writing, earning money to live on. Her war work intensified; as a member of the Women's Voluntary Service (WVS), she organized a mobile canteen for shelters in Deptford, using her father's strategy of lobbying the powerful and affluent to get it equipped. Insisting on autonomy, she kept control of the van even though she ran it as part of WVS and the Housewives' Service. In the tradition of her father's great-grandmother Elizabeth Fry, a prison reformer, she demonstrated the importance of the domestic as the basis of civil life.

Streatfeild's flat was bombed on 10 May 1940. In *Beyond the Vicarage* she describes the devastation she found when returning, with an ambulance driver, from bringing a casualty to a first aid station: "They fell over Victoria's front door which was in the middle of the road. Somehow they climbed over obstacles to reach her sitting-room which was clear to the sky, both the ceiling and the roof had gone. There was a little piece of her white carpet left; they sat on it together and finding miraculously two bottles of beer unbroken drank it while they watched the German planes being chased by the searchlights" (*BV*, 150). Loss of her prized white carpet and brocaded curtains seemed to free Streatfeild further into a gallant and energetic mode. She now brought the comforts promised by "Sir Garnet" long ago—the well being promoted through the hostels, bands, war libraries, salvage efforts, and children's parties she helped to organize. Satisfactions her father had derived from his wholehearted dedication were now hers. In addition, she retained the power to criticize, satirize, and romanticize that her mother's varied attitudes had suggested long ago.

During the war years Streatfeild produced four adult novels, five children's books, a diary (still unpublished), a series of WVS newsletters, and a number of stories, articles, and radio scripts. Moreover, to her "sideline" of children's novels, she added another—the romance serial. She wrote nine of these under the name Susan Scarlett, eventually doing 12 in all. Writing had become a necessity, financially and psychically. In the adult novels *The Winter Is Past* (1940), *I Ordered a Table for Six* (1942), *Myra Carroll* (1944), and *Saplings* (1944) she chronicled the devastation around her. In *Saplings* especially she depicted its effect on children. The "stiff upper lip" of her childhood training and the continuity made possible by owning land and ancient houses are the enabling factors when the modern family is split apart by the war and its aftermath. Though several of her books received good reviews, their existence—like much that Streatfeild wrote about—was imperiled. Paper shortages and the bombing of warehouses meant that few copies of the novels remained to circulate.

The children's novels included three inspired by the war. *The Stranger in Primrose Lane* (*The Children in Primrose Lane,* 1941) uses the threat of fifth columnists for a thriller plot; *Theater Shoes* (*Curtain Up,* 1944) uses the war as emotional and physical backdrop; and *Party Shoes* (*Party Frock,* 1945) draws from her family's experience of rationing. In each novel self-dramatization by child characters, competent performance, and the security of family life enrich the wartime experience. In *Party Shoes* a whole community enjoys coming together, much as Streatfeild had transformed her father's parish with her Eastbourne theatricals.

While she alternated between adult novels, children's novels, and sentimental romances, Streatfeild was not without ambivalence about her role as a writer. Eventually she would embrace her life as a children's author when it became clear that it gave the widest range to her powers and enabled her to be heard by an appreciative audience. But she always suppressed the Susan Scarlett novels on official bibliographies. For example, Barbara Ker Wilson's 1961 monograph does not mention them.

After the war Streatfeild alternated between children's books and adult novels for more than a decade. She reestablished her household at 51A Elizabeth Street, next to a bomb site. In a gesture truly resonant with her optimistic and energetic personality, she planted a neighborhood garden at roughly the same time she produced an adult novel—*Grass in Piccadilly* (1947), set in bombed-out London. The bishop's daughter, hampered in youth by pressures about money and good conduct, turned her parents' bequest of gentility into a monument to good luck and changing mores: she paid for the garden with money she won in a horse race.

Children as Audience

Beyond the Vicarage devotes only two chapters to Streatfeild's postwar
life, finishing with an upbeat note after describing 1968 as a year of
loss—of family, friends, dog, and health. The decades before and after
this watershed year were prolific ones during which the writer thought
of herself as a traveler and a speaker. The dominant image from her
biographer, however, is of Streatfeild "writing away," buttressed by a
loyal staff. Such an image is necessary to explain how Streatfeild managed to write and edit such a large number of books and to vary their
themes and format enough to remain both popular and respected. As
the war years had proved, Streatfeild left behind the slender and glam-
orous Titania in favor of a sturdy, cheerful British version of Mother
Courage.

Once the threat to England was over, Streatfeild became a kind of
ambassador for the country's culture and values. The Circe who delight-
ed in ordering about her nursery companions and the little girl solemnly
taking in the sight of Queen Victoria's casket became merged in the role
of children's writer. Perhaps her self-naming as "Vicky" in the autobiographies flowed from this same strand of memory and identity. Much of
Noel Streatfeild's late adulthood and old age was taken up with speaking
engagements. By the early 1970s she presided frequently at Puffin Club
gatherings, where children greeted her with enthusiastic requests for
autographs and sequels to her books. How she accepted and expanded
the role of children's writer constitutes her postwar biography. While her
friendships, family, and social activities meant a great deal to her, nothing
mattered as much as finding ways to enchant her audience and engage it
in her story, in the pageantry of past and present English childhood.

The period after the war required reestablishing a home and a routine. With the usual good humor and slightly ironic self-description
Streatfeild used in her autobiographical writing, *Beyond the Vicarage*
describes the difficulty of finding such ordinary comforts as a mattress
and such extraordinary ones as a housekeeper and a cook. The government recognized her literary and wartime achievements by sending her
to Alderney to put on a pageant and to the Netherlands to lecture about
the Housewives' Service. Travel to the United States—this time on a
long sea voyage to allow time for thinking about her next steps as a
writer—included research for a children's book about Hollywood (*Movie
Shoes*, 1949; published in England as *The Painted Garden*). She could not
recapture her prewar interest in Aimee Semple MacPherson; now she

was interested, she knew, in what had happened to England. On the way back from California she began *Grass in Piccadilly*. The habit of alternating an adult novel with a children's book persisted until the late 1950s. *Mothering Sunday* (1950), *Aunt Clara* (1952), *Judith* (1956), and *The Silent Speaker* (1961) showed that she retained her abilities to tell a witty and probing story, but that her interests were not in literary modernism or even in postwar realism. In deciding to abandon efforts to be a novelist for adults, Streatfeild responded in part to the sense that she was out of fashion. *Beyond the Vicarage* suggests that she thought the novel as a form might well be dead—at least the novels she liked to write and read. She tells herself, "You never belonged to the great. So give up writing novels here and now. It's not as if you had not more work than you can handle in the children's world, so why struggle with the new tastes of the 1960s?" (*BV*, 196). The language is instructive. Even in her sixties, Streatfeild relished work as the focus of each day. Her creative mind used work as a way of giving coherence to life, and the children's book world offered many roles and opportunities for which she was ably suited, and about which she did not have to agonize or struggle. She could continue to transform her personal experience into narratives that engaged a community.

Streatfeild's personal life had taken on some new aspects. After visiting Ireland as part of a PEN conference in the 1940s, she returned each summer, staying on the western coast with her friend Rachel Leigh-White. Eventually she would write the children's novel *The Growing Summer* (1966; published in the United States as *The Magic Summer*) that voiced her delight in those summers and perhaps pictured herself as an eccentric old aunt with an understanding of life's more important issues. Leigh-White described Streatfeild as "extraordinarily unpractical, even in the most ordinary things of life. I wouldn't have left her in the kitchen to boil an egg! Not only was she the most unpractical, but she was physically the most clumsy person I have ever met. Everything got knocked off tables, got lost or broken. . . . She did care about her looks, clothes, etc., just as much in Ireland, but being without her maid, the results were sometimes funny. . . . In some ways she never quite grew up" (quoted in Bull, 233).

The visits to Ireland complicated Streatfeild's life in ways other than depriving her of her maid and making her more responsible for daily domestic life. They also meant she could not have a dog, unless she found someone to share it. Until her mother's death Janet and she "shared" a dog, with Janet keeping it and Streatfeild visiting frequently.

The family dog, especially the dachshund Agag in *Tennis Shoes*, figured in her writing and satisfied some of her needs for intimacy and nurturing. So an arrangement with Margot Grey, a somewhat unconventional friend with a seaside house, allowed Streatfeild to share her residence with both her flamboyant friend and the small black poodle, Pierre, they jointly trained and cared for. Pierre stayed with Margot when Streatfeild traveled, but at other times she doted on him, making him part of her daily routine and taking him for walks in the park when she had completed her writing for the day. Since Pierre was her child substitute, she tried out on him some of her theories of childrearing, maintaining that he did daily chores that kept him alert and interesting. To her family's consternation, she and Margot invested in racing dogs—a situation she satirized lightheartedly in *Aunt Clara*.

Until 1968 Margot and Pierre were part of Streatfeild's home life; that year Margot died, and Streatfeild, recovering from a stroke, decided to have the aged dog put down. In addition to the pleasure she took in their company, her life with Margot and their dog yielded several story lines. Margot's unknown origins—she was apparently the illegitimate daughter of a gentlewoman—became the basis of spunky Margaret Thursday, a character in two Victorian tales.

Streatfeild claimed to enjoy middle age and even old age far more than she had enjoyed her childhood. Being middle-aged freed her from what she described as the boredom of nightclubs and being taken somewhere after the theater; it also freed her from whatever pressure to marry she may have felt. During what she called her "speaking years"—the 1950s and 1960s—she came into her own as a children's author, finally assuming the kinds of responsibilities members of the royal family carry out: "She spoke to an audience of some sort at least four afternoons or evenings each week. Heaven knows how many prizes she gave away in those years; she reckoned that the bouquets received (her only payment) if put end to end would have stretched for many miles. . . . As well as prize givings there were church bazaars to open. . . . Then there were the luncheon clubs" (*BV*, 200).

Streatfeild adds that she had to give up female luncheon clubs because the long local speeches before her own made her unable to enjoy her food. Excesses in eating acquired during her life with Margot filled out Streatfeild's tall frame so that she was in her last years a very large woman. Frequent travel and clothes buying sometimes meant that she spent more than she earned, fueling the rapid writing and willingness to take on editorial and anthologizing tasks between novels and speaking engagements. But she had no difficulty finding paid work, and she enjoyed her numerous pleasures with what we might describe as gusto.

Variations: Themes, Forms, and Genres

The variety of Streatfeild's work life was remarkable. Her decision to concentrate on children's books meant increased fame and stature in at least three major new areas. She created a radio serial about the Bell family and their vicarage life that proved immensely popular during the late 1940s and early 1950s, as had been the "Children's Hour" dramatizations of *Ballet Shoes* in 1947. The opportunity to do the Bell series—one of her most humorous pieces of writing—arose because Streatfeild was willing to lobby or "network" other professionals her social connections afforded her. She had mentioned to May Jenkin, producer of the "Children's Hour," that she had an idea for a radio series after she marveled at how well *Ballet Shoes* transferred to that medium. Jenkin remembered her interest and called six months later with an offer.

A second new genre, the informational book, allowed room for Streatfeild's ideas about childhood in England and its potential richness if children have access to culture and the arts. Putting together anthologies on manners (*The Years of Grace*, 1950) and confirmation (*Growing up Gracefully*, 1955) enabled the kind of combined social and professional contacts and events she enjoyed, as well as bringing income and making her a virtual authority figure for adolescents, especially girls. Her secretary called her a "devil for work" (Bull, 211), and during the 1950s she produced outstanding books like *The Fearless Treasure* (1953), a social history whose central focus she evolved from a memory of her father (Bull, 211), and books on the ballet in which she was able to promote her own views on how Britain should build its dance traditions. While writing these Streatfeild continued with her fiction, numerous editing jobs, and calendar or birthday books. Her enjoyment of research and respect for detailed, exacting work—carried out in her hobby of searching out and recording wild flowers—inspired one of her best nonfiction works, *The Boy Pharaoh, Tutankhamen* (1972), after her fiction had begun to receive bad or careless reviews.

A third triumph came in the 1960s, when Streatfeild took up the suggestion of Helen Hoke Watts that she write about her memories of the vicarage. She had entertained her American publisher with these stories at some length; once again her social skills yielded valuable professional success. The trilogy about the vicarage made Streatfeild one of a new company of autobiographers writing for a young audience. The same daughter the vicar prayed for on his knees became the daughter pronouncing the way to live as an English child of the late twentieth century. This transformation meant creating a kind of picaresque character for herself that conformed to her optimistic and self-affirming personality. While the trilogy caused some consternation among her family because she seemed to seek revenge on Janet and Barbara, no severe rupture occurred. The family simply avoided the party to celebrate the book's publication. A final book about the Streatfeilds' past, *Gran-Nannie*, eased some of the wounds, ending with a pronouncement by Streatfeild's sisters, "It will all be Sir Garnet."

Her family was not alone in resisting some of Streatfeild's appropriations of lives and material for her versions of the truth. Doris Langley Moore was offended by what she considered Streatfeild's opportunistic use of discoveries she had made too late to include in her biography of E. Nesbit (1951).[10] But Noel Streatfeild had charmed Nesbit's daughter into sharing the papers with her, and she gave Moore credit for the discovery in the introduction to her own book on Nesbit (1958).[11] While her circle of close friends narrowed—Ionides and another woman, Theodora Newbold, had parted company from the writer—Grey, Kitty Barne (another children's writer), and her staff provided the companionship she needed between her writing hours and her speaking engagements. The ability to enjoy theater and dance performances gave Streatfeild continuing pleasure—one reason that she so strongly advocated children's access to art and other fields requiring concentration, practice, and perfection.

In some respects Streatfeild confounds notions of human development that assume loneliness and despair are the dangers of old age. Whatever dangers her later life held for her, none seemed to equal those of the days she accepted money from her dates to buy food. The vicarage had succeeded at last in giving its feisty daughter the prized "stiff upper lip" that males of her class practiced at the expense, at least in her fiction, of their childhood and family life. In her old age this survivor of two wars and one of the key figures of children's literature counseled herself about how to maintain the equanimity that had sustained her since the bombing of her home. She jotted down maxims involving restraint, privacy, and politeness as a way to "make a good job" of old age. She would not discuss her health or go to parties when too ill to laugh; she would not criticize younger people; she would continue to go to church regularly, to get God's help in being pleasant as she aged; and she would have as a motto "Keep right on to the end of the road" (*BV*, 202). The last rule served well when she began to receive mixed reviews, such as those after *Dancing Shoes* (1958; *Wintle's Wonders*, 1957) and most of her books of the late 1960s. She relied on her great popularity with children, turning out some of her best books after her seventy-fifth birthday.

Even books that seemed mundane to critics—such as the series on Gemma Bow, a child actress—showed how Streatfeild could recognize change and yet preserve the emphasis on theater, music, and dance that gave meaning to her characters' lives. No nanny presides in the small suburban household where Gemma experiences herself for the first time as a member of a family—a cultivated yet somewhat financially straitened family that manages to produce a bevy of talented children. In this family the shallow movie-star aunt, Gemma's mother, supplies money for vacations essential to her daughter's understanding of British life. Tolerated and even enjoyed for what she is, the aunt reaps the benefits of having a conservative, albeit talented, brother-in-law and a sister who is an expert at mothering. Somewhat like Streatfeild herself, the distant aunt helps the children realize their genetic heritage, and they in turn create a wholesome and deeply nurturing environment for her daughter.

Accused of an accumulating tawdriness in these books,[12] Streatfeild depicted plastic costumes and improvised music as some of the world's good things—part of the stage world of Shakespeare and of Mozart. Her philosophy in old age—that "a world of interest" was still to come— made her able to imagine childhood in these terms. Some would say that she herself was immature[13] or that her repressed sexuality was a deficiency (Bull, 127). Another way to look at Streatfeild's life, however, is to recognize that other paradigms than Freud, other plots than romance, are richly human. She found in her creative processes and in her sense of wonder an indisputable sense of harmony.

Although Streatfeild had overcome the effects of her serious stroke in 1968, a series of smaller ones in 1979 resulted in her decision to enter a nursing home. She tried even there to continue her writing, but she could not. She did, however, manage to get out to the Royal Palace to receive the Order of the British Empire in 1983. Dame Streatfeild died on 11 September 1986, at 91. To the end she received letters from the Puffin Club sounding much the way letters about *Ballet Shoes* had sounded in 1936.

Chapter Two

Family Novelist for Adults, 1931–1938

Although Noel Streatfeild's first novel, *The Whicharts* (1931), and four subsequent novels of the 1930s were not written for children, each showed her empathy with children and her understanding of their central role in culture. Even her dramatic writing—in such plays as *Wisdom Teeth* (1936)—explores childhood and youth affected by historical contexts and gender, race, and class.

Streatfeild had been keenly aware of the way female experience was evolving in the twentieth century even before Mabel Carey recruited her as a children's author. The convergence of traditional female roles and sexuality with capitalism's mixing of women of all classes in the workplace fascinated Streatfeild. With irony, humor, multiple perspectives, and a relentless yet playful validation of "a new woman" imagined outside of or in spite of the pressure of the "marriage plot" common to most novels, Streatfeild claimed the dual satisfactions of love and work for herself, her readers, and her characters. In doing so, however, she resisted and redefined the patriarchal nuclear family, questioning the idealization of motherhood and the assumption that high culture is the unchanging heritage of the privileged.

This complex and paradoxical redefinition process begun in novels and plays for adults touched centrally on the lives of children who read Streatfeild's popular and acclaimed early children's novels. Shaped more by her experience and her theatrical ear for dialogue and eye for action than by literary predecessors, Streatfeild's fresh perspective and witty narrative form are comparable, among writers for adults in this decade, to those of Rose Macaulay (Bull, 118). Among works for children, Streatfeild's family stories offer forms unique in posing problems for analysis and potential for enrichment.

Angela Bull emphasizes the idea of vocation, rather than career, and successful characterization as selling points of 10 million copies of *Ballet Shoes* (Bull, 143). Placing these features into a larger context of women's history and the changing social needs of readers underscores the long-range implications of Streatfeild's work.

The Whicharts

Popularity sometimes seems incompatible with literary achievement. But the popularity of novelists may mean that the aims of the genre have been met. The novel's task is to be flexible, to summon readers' energies toward "eternal re-thinking and re-evaluating" (Frye, 22). Some critics have argued that women novelists who alter literary forms also alter women's lives. The popularity of a novel with a new form may suggest that it matches readers' desires or yearnings for change and that it functions to make such change possible. As a source for *Ballet Shoes*, *The Whicharts* is fascinating; its first page is nearly identical to the first page of the children's book.

The differences between the books, however, are even more exciting. The main difference is the suppression of sexual content in the children's book. Yet that issue is not simply a matter of Streatfeild's bowdlerizing her work. Like the other differences between the Whichart sisters and the Fossil sisters, the writer's strategy results in a literary continuum moving from flippant irony to suspenseful optimism. Streatfeild depicts the family as a successful institution *and* one subject to a continuing process of questioning and change. Questions about the family as an institution—which are also central to the liberation of women—include the challenge of imagining nonoppressive family relationships, of identifying children's real needs to mature into healthy adults, and perhaps of considering the possible benefits of some forms of sexual repression.[1] Streatfeild's first decade as a writer can be seen as a deep-rooted and playful raising of these questions in her adult novels and as an equally deeprooted and playful response to them in her children's novels. Streatfeild's playfulness moved these questions into new conceptual space. By depicting the diverse and active lives of children engaged in productive work in a "real" world of economic necessity and an "ideal" one of artistic expression, and by exploring the family's permeable boundaries within the larger society, her novels redefine adulthood as well as childhood.

Like many first novels, *The Whicharts* is autobiographical. The presence of three sisters plays out some of the tensions in the relationships of Ruth, Noel, and Barbara Streatfeild. For example, the eldest Whichart,

Maimie, goes through a religious phase similar to one Ruth experienced, while the middle sister, Tania, resembles Noel, who for a time was unwilling to be confirmed. Tania, hating (like Noel's mother) the ostentation of High Church ritual, knocks a cross onto the floor when Maimie erects an altar in their room. Talented Daisy occasions Tania's jealousy when she secures a major role in a play. Unlike Tania, who is forced to dance in an absurd troupe called "Pansy's Peaches," Daisy enjoys mild fame and a relatively easy life. Since one of Streatfeild's major childhood crises was her mother's preference for Barbara during an illness of both daughters, it is ironic that the three Whichart sisters are depicted as loyal to one another, in particular showing the older and younger willing to sacrifice their own happiness for the middle sister.

As a playful construction of family relationships that are nonoppressive, at least to the children, The Whicharts employs humor to remove the father of the family and ascribes virtue to a most unlikely candidate—his first mistress, Rose. Though she had succumbed to the charms of a lecherous man, "the Brigadier," in her young adulthood, her training to be a woman means that she accepts charge of the three babies his successive mistresses bear, naming each after her mother. He has bestowed a house on her and an income for her lifetime, but Streatfeild depicts Rose acting from feelings for her past lover when she offers to adopt the baby of Maimie. "There must be something of the Brigadier in the baby. It didn't show, but it must be there."[2]

Maimie shows no sign of attachment to her baby Maimie; she is eager to leave for her home in Scotland. Like Streatfeild's mother, Maimie is the daughter of a minister and is very beautiful. Tania, the second pregnant mistress, has Russian royal blood as well as English wealth behind her. She loves the arts and is extremely sensual but cannot express herself well. She allows Rose to bring up baby Tania only because of this; thus Streatfeild endows the middle daughter with a loving, though silenced, mother. Daisy, the third mistress after Rose, dies in childbirth. Her parents at first want no part of the baby, and the brigadier appears on Rose's doorstep to implore her to take yet a third child. Though Tania is welcome in the nursery as a companion for Maimie, little Daisy—suspect as the child of a show girl—is the proverbial last straw, for Rose as well as for Nanny. But Rose accepts the third child, and the brigadier dies shortly thereafter. With these degrees of parentage and mothering (Maimie and Tania leave their names and addresses for the babies, Maimie unwillingly) Streatfeild establishes the relative merits and destinies of the Whicharts.

The family name draws on Streatfeild's punning sensibility as well as her memories of long prayers and rituals in the vicarage. The older girls tell Rose, when they are enrolled in kindergarten, that they must have a name, and it is obviously "Whichart," for "our father whichart in heaven." For reasons not discussed by any characters or within the narrative, Rose wishes to conceal permanently the name of the girls' father. The conclusion the girls draw is humorous but supports Streatfeild's other tales of this decade. Girls and women create intricate lives with one another, and adult women are essential to the nurture of females' creative and professional abilities. While the father's money and sexual desire are at the base of the family, the family survives only because of his absence. By implication, had the brigadier not died after Daisy's birth, his nonmonogamous and preemptive emotional behavior would have harmed the daughters by confining them to genteel femininity while draining away finite capital and energy.

An important factor in the Whicharts' story is the search for economic self-sufficiency. Attaining this is equated with emotional well-being. Rose, who works in a factory during the war (like Streatfeild), cannot support the children once men return and separate gender codes are reestablished. Taking in boarders—which is Nanny's idea, and one approved by the barrister in charge of the brigadier's estate—relieves the pressure for a time. It also enables Streatfeild to construct an extended family with important resources for the children. The boarders—a young married couple, two women professors, and a third woman who is a dancing school teacher—prove serendipitous. Tania learns about cars and machinery from the young husband; the dancing teacher proposes that the girls be educated to earn their livings on the stage and works out a financial arrangement with "The Madame Elise Academy." The activity, routines, and humor involved with these arrangements meant that Streatfeild was not confined to a retelling of the Oedipal drama. Parents do not devour children, nor children murder their parents in her narratives, because the immediate family is intricately connected to a set of other vital relationships that in turn help it to survive.

Rearing children in nonoppressive families and leading them to healthy adulthood requires that they take part in commerce, that they share in their own reproduction. Otherwise children's dependence invites domination over women as well as children. At issue in *The Whicharts*, however, is whether sexual relationships can be acknowledged as part of the economic arrangements of women who have social responsibility. Rose, proving her gentility to the lawyer by the way she talks of her mother role, upholds the standards of traditional feminine conduct even while planning for the girls' autonomy. She and Nanny exhibit tolerance for Maimie's sexual freedom and Daisy's class origins; they reconceive the notion of family to include a wide range of behaviors and connections that keep it healthy. For example, taking in boarders results in an unexpected emotional benefit when the dancing teacher helps them to find a reasonable vacation cottage in Sussex. Like many events in this novel, the healing time in the country is drawn expressly from Streatfeild's own family memories.

Maimie (somewhat like Streatfeild herself) is suspected of exchanging sexual favors for money when she cannot get work on the stage. Tania refuses to accept this money even to keep the household together after Rose's death. Yet she too crosses into what Nanny regards as tawdry behavior, pawning Rose's jewelry when money must be found to outfit Daisy for an audition. Maimie's philosophy—"I don't care how I get money" (*W*, 85)—is countered by Tania's: "We can't let you be mauled about for the lot of us" (*W*, 153). Though Tania by herself might be seen as upholding conventional sexual rules for women, her "mauled about" (*W*, 10) contrasts with the proud assertions of her birth mother about her own relations with men before the brigadier.

The fact that each daughter is named for her birth mother suggests that young Tania resembles her behaviorally as well as physically. Just as Maimie keeps relationships—except with her sisters—on a superficial level, and Daisy eventually disappears from the Whicharts' daily routines when her grandparents claim her, Tania is on a quest for experience and adventure. She differs from her birth mother only in the crucial valuing of a centered home. Though the novel ends with Tania's telling her mother she'd rather have an airplane than a husband, her ability to express such a wish derives from finding her mother and sensing herself at home even as the two journey together.

Often tongue-in-cheek about the tawdriness of stage life and the economic underpinnings of the Whicharts' household, Streatfeild nonetheless creates a sympathetic set of characters. Maimie, for example, is so loyal to Tania that her questionable involvements seem irrelevant to her virtue. The faithless brigadier has the not unlimited loyalty of Rose, whose complete commitment to the girls is the moral center from which Tania's difference can be made the symbol of a new order. Tania's affinity for flying and her admiration for women pilots like Amy Johnson evoke Virginia Woolf's *Orlando* (1928) and also look forward to a time when feminist literary critics would propose that writers create characters more like Amelia Earhart—that is, move to more self-determination and ambition in female figures (Donovan, 77).

In terms of an ongoing examination of the family by feminists, Streatfeild's first novel represents a merry escapade paradoxically freeing women and children abandoned by men from domination by them. It depicts positively an explicit need to earn money by means that had, except for working-class women, been considered damaging to female security and status. Tania's interest in flying for itself, and not as a metaphor for sexual conduct, was Streatfeild's way of making space for change.

Tania is the central character of the novel, despite the writer's frequent presentation of other points of view. Her search for meaningful work and for a home repeatedly complicate and enrich the narrative. She has the least aptitude for dancing—the work the girls are trained to do—and her ingenuity and luck—she wins a car in a raffle—provide her with both the home she needs and the opportunity to train as a pilot, her childhood dream. From the outset she differs from the other sisters in the most important ways: her genes are aristocratic, and she is loved by her birth mother. Though all of the girls receive careful nurture from those who rear them, only Tania has a mother she can reclaim when she must move beyond the invented Whichart family.

Tania's emergence as a main character, though useful for Streatfeild's story of work and family, represents the author's inherent conservatism as much as it does her spirited questioning. Tania's ability to read Shakespeare, for example, is the key to her unfolding as a character with a quest of her own, just as Streatfeild's family connections enabled her to achieve independence. While Streatfeild does not suggest that the family existed in order to produce Tania, she focuses the ending on her in a way that reimposes codes of individualism current in twentieth-century culture. Yet the mother-daughter story makes the quest different from many novels emphasizing individualism.

Streatfeild's first novel established her in a new vocation. The combination of family memories and theater experience amounted to a cornucopia of character types she would continue to use in her storytelling. For the large questions about family relationships, childrearing, and sexual mores in the twentieth century this first novel sketched out a working pattern: the best families incorporate diversity and are maintained more by women than by men; children flourish when they have significant responsibility combined with steady approval from several sources, including each other; linking the family to other networks is crucial for survival; and, finally, sexual freedom has its limits. Young Tania seems to have sublimated, thanks to economic necessity, the urges that her mother ultimately found boring. More than a redirection of instinctual desire, this sublimation transforms that which cannot be put into words into consciousness.[3] Such a definition links the process to preverbal experience and thus to mothering. Desire for experience is cast in social, rather than in simply instinctual, terms. Streatfeild's description of the family addresses a central concern of feminist cultural theory and practice. Conceptualizing alternative family arrangements is a socially crucial literary process.

From this promising start Streatfeild moved to further reshapings of the family and, especially, of female experience within it. Her first novel had refused to disconnect the family from the workplace as literary forms separating public from private do.[4] Her subsequent novels for adults continued to present thematic structures rooted in the complexity and variety of family relationships, especially as family survival affected female artistic expression. During this decade Streatfeild presented several alternatives to the "love story" typically expected in realistic novels. She also demonstrated some of the constraints on her thinking imposed by that dominant plot structure. In fact, the writer's move into children's literature was simultaneous with her increasing adherence to the conventional adult romance narrative. Writing for children offered an alternative outlet for an artistic vision that conventional treatments of marriage would confine to an ironic mode. But rather than retreating to children's literature because she had failed to engage an adult audience, Streatfeild wrote for children because she found an opportunity to represent the pageantry of the theater and other art forms as liberating, without distorting the historical truths of women's circumstances in the family.

Parson's Nine

Streatfeild's second novel drew on vicarage memories to describe the Churston family. An idealistic parson father and an independent mother indirectly cause one daughter's evolution as a writer, in the context of war. Like Janet Streatfeild, Catherine Churston is ambivalent about mothering but lives to regret spending time away from her three sons, casualties of the war. The writer-daughter, Susanna, completes the book left behind by her twin, Baruch, who kills himself to avoid fighting. Susanna writes in order to continue Baruch's life and justify her survival—a theme replayed by Streatfeild in her autobiography. The novel also emphasizes the importance of sibling relationships and economic resources. Unlike the Whicharts, and more like the Streatfeilds, the Churstons have two father figures—the parson and his old father. Codes of church and gentry are frameworks for behavior, though the mother resists some strictures. Notably, she limits her number of children to nine, having matched her husband's original list of biblical names, and knows how to recognize changes in the class system.

The war kills the three interesting sons, leaving three who lack imagination. Each of the three daughters, however, achieves distinction in adulthood, though their education by a hapless feminist governess offers amusing and sharply poignant incidents as each girl seeks to elude her plans. Miss Crosby recognizes Susanna's gift for writing first; along with the "church pussy" (a parish worker) Miss Love, she is a new addition to the roster of female helpers common to Streatfeild's domestic novels.

From nine points of view, one for each child, *Parson's Nine* shifts to a sole focus on Susanna. This complex strategy displeased some reviewers, but, as in *The Whicharts*, Streatfeild's examination of childrearing leaves room for female artistic expression. The narrowing focus demonstrates how a daughter's creativity results from loving acceptance by a mother and her female servants and from sublimation of sexual passion within a family. Children's games and their sibling conflicts create the basis of the narrative, with a circular framing device to show how small rituals that once seemed absurd become inspiration for Susanna's writing. Moving from dependence on Baruch's writing through a stage of writing "a hotch-potch of legs, breasts, beds, drugs, and drink,"[5] Susanna acquires an editor-mentor who helps her to discover her own muse in domestic life. Unlike a Victorian novel, however, this partnership ends not with marriage but with meta-narrative about childhood.

The only portrait of a writer in Streatfeild's many novels, Susanna may be a fictional model for the autobiographical self Streatfeild would call Vicky in *A Vicarage Family* and its sequels. Just as Streatfeild wove her own experience as Shakespeare's Titania into Susanna's story, Susanna may have been rewoven into an embellished tale of Noel herself. In a telling move, Streatfeild supplies Susanna with an economic motive based on Catherine Churston's deliberate falsehoods—lies designed to offset her daughter's emotional paralysis at Baruch's death. Needing money, whether based on actual or invented circumstance, constructs a daughter as an artist.

Tops and Bottoms

Streatfeild dedicated her third novel to Charles Evans, her own editor-mentor. Like Susanna of *Parson's Nine*, Streatfeild had connections, like those with Daphne Ionides and Roland Pertwee, based on class privilege. Not unaware of how class affected her career, Streatfeild used this theme in her next three novels. Partly because of her social work in Deptford under Daphne's sponsorship, class became as important a focus in Streatfeild's work as theater or the other arts. Her 1933 novel merges three groups—country gentry, Cockneys, and theater performers—in an examination of heredity and environment.

A pastoral theme is subordinated in *Tops and Bottoms* to urban survival that simultaneously allows continuity in a family of actors and forbids sexual and economic autonomy for a Cockney girl, Beaty, adopted by a genteel spinster, Felicity. Both Beaty and Felicity are affected by the vitality and force of the Timpson dynasty Felicity's sister had married into. A more powerful mother than Felicity, the grandmother-actress Marie Timpson enforces the continuity of the theater family by arranging a marriage for Beaty when she becomes pregnant by a Timpson grandson. Beaty's daughter inherits the performers' talent and drive; ultimately Beaty must relinquish a dream of living in the country house inherited from Felicity so that the child's gifts can be developed. Life on the stage—complete with its flashy and tawdry side—is preferred to pastoral contentment.

The novel's title invokes its structure. From the "bottom," her graphically depicted slum origins, Beaty moves to the "top"—being adopted by the spinster Felicity after the child wanders into the spinster's garden during a school outing in the country. Beaty's Cockney stepfather is astounded that Felicity wants to be a mother by means of adoption; "to him children could only be procured by one method."[6] But Felicity's connection to children is underscored by her duty to her dead sister's brood of Timpsons; those who conceive children are differentiated from those who nurture them. The struggle to rear children is another form of "tops and bottoms," like playing "Snakes and Ladders," "through no fault of your own stepping on the head of a snake and sliding to the bottom again" (*TB*, 139).

In Streatfeild's drama genes seem to triumph when a compliant Beaty sacrifices a way of life Felicity wished for her so that the Timpson child can train for the stage; yet Felicity accedes to the child's prior claim on

Beaty's loyalty. Inherited class privilege, via Felicity's estate, is less important than agreeing "the show must go on." The Timpsons are more fun than either the gentle Beaty or the moral Felicity; in Streatfeild's aesthetic they are the "tops," possessed by their own gifts and their approach to money—make it, spend it—as opposed to the conserving of property for the future.

A bittersweet, debatable ending contrasts with the freedom of Tania Whichart and the expressiveness of Susanna Churston, unless the reader chooses primary alliance with the anarchic, carnivalesque Timpsons. The parody of motherhood offered in a duet by Marie Timpson and her prodigy granddaughter bores Beaty but delights a theater audience. Laughter and tears, sudden and grandiose self-consciousness, become the test of female strength, its "top" acknowledged by Felicity but barely understood by Beaty, at "bottom" a victim of others' desires.

A Shepherdess of Sheep

In Streatfeild's fourth book (1934) she extended her use of family themes such as plural motherhood, children's needs and rights, and sexual sublimation using a governess figure, Sarah Onion, to complicate the idea of maternal sacrifice. Sarah's apparently futile sacrifice of her own chances for home and motherhood to safeguard the child of another woman made many readers uncomfortable. Naive and oppressed by an unexamined class structure, Sarah Onion is presented in frame chapters as a victim, a governess destined for increasing poverty. Yet the body of the text resists this presentation, depicting Sarah's bond with Jane, a disturbed child of her dying employer, the strong-minded Ruth Lane. Using allusions to *Alice in Wonderland*, Streatfeild suggests that the illogic of loving a threatened child may be the purest form of logic. While a context of war ironizes the battle for Sarah's soul waged by Ruth (so that Sarah will continue to rear her children) and Sarah's suitor, Doctor Lewis, Streatfeild skillfully depicts Sarah's private commitment as a heroic one.

Another issue threads through the narrative as well: Sarah's competence and satisfaction in her work. One more mother-by-adoption in a string of governesses, nannies, and guardians in Streatfeild's later work, Sarah is different from the compliant Beaty and the dashing Rose of previous novels, more self-conscious in her courage but without the economic resources of mothers-by-choice in *The Whicharts* and *Parson's Nine*.

A progression in the novels suggests that Streatfeild's affirmation of the family could not always accommodate women's safety, even when it was congruent with their morality.

The Children's Matinee

Between her third and fourth novels Streatfeild wrote a set of short plays for a charity performance. Other than a short story published before *The Whicharts*, these plays are her first writing for children. In the preface she advises young readers to skip certain chapters and directions, but she claims that at least one play, "The Thirteenth Fairy," was written so that child actors could enjoy dressing up in costumes. As Angela Bull notes, however, the plays have disappointing aspects, including the jokes based on children's lack of experience with sex (Bull, 129). The preface seems more insightful than the scripts. Noting that children will act in the plays but adults will produce and attend them, she reveals her preoccupation with pageantry and delight in the process of staging plays.

A heritage of Streatfeild's parish childhood, pageantry and ritual were of crucial importance to late Victorians. In fact, the need for ritual was an overriding cultural truth of the late nineteenth- and early twentieth-century British character.[7] Virginia Woolf's *Between the Acts* (1941) acknowledges and uses this feature of the society she too lived in. Since Noel Streatfeild, more than any other writer, linked children to this heritage of the British, these plays for child actors record her deepest imaginative source. That she was uncomfortable with the distinction between child and adult that the plays maintain (she urges children to omit what does not interest them) signals another of her writing standards. Once she began writing novels for children, she posited equality between authorial presence and child audience (Wilson, 25). The preface to these early plays depicts children as indispensable partners of the adults who would produce the matinees.

It Pays to Be Good

1936 was a full year for Streatfeild. She had a play produced; she was invited to write a children's book; she looked forward to a future as a historical novelist; and she drew on her interest in child stars to produce one of her finest, Flossie Elk. Flossie moves successfully on the "Ladder" by avoiding the "Snake," the sexual involvement that prevented Beaty's rise in *Tops and Bottoms*. In the tradition of *Pamela* and the Harlequin romance, Flossie happily uses men to acquire wealth without damaging her reputation. This ancient and seemingly callous plot is filled out by Steatfeild's skill in describing class differences, her empathy for women, and her mischievous liking for the theater and its intrigues. In particular, Flossie's parents are presented with humor and irony, the mother subverting the father's forbidding of stage training. War changes gender arrangements; the father's absence unleashes the mother's determination. Streatfeild's liking for this mother, Fanny, seems connected to Fanny's subtle resemblance to another inept housekeeper, Janet Streatfeild. Fanny is further endorsed by a character who might be a self-portrait, Mouse, who is a paid guide for Flossie's ascent to the stage and to the peerage.

It Pays to Be Good pushes against the codes of religion and respectability by endorsing Fanny, if not Flossie herself. It is less concerned with the personality of the child actress than with the glamour of the theater and the counterpoint of women's friendships. Few readers would endorse the father's hope for Flossie of early school-leaving and helping Mum at home; the mother's ironing of Flossie's clothes seems a more just action than the father's rule-giving. An unresolvable love story in the subplot merges with the structure of the family story. Unlike Streatfeild's earlier work, no one character becomes the unique focus; instead, the many voices of the novel are in process throughout, suggesting that no centered home, only reenactment of the multiple small satisfactions, can exist.

Wisdom Teeth

While Flossie Elk's story brought out Streatfeild's humor, her first serious attempt to write for, rather than about, the theater used the thematic formula of the novels—diverse mothering, children's needs, and sexual repression—in a brisk plot about divorce, remarriage, and the growth of children. A governess who marries the father of her charges after their mother abandons them for a lover demonstrates the constancy of motherhood-by-choice. Her reserved style contrasts with the effusiveness of the mother, who tries to reconnect with the children when they are in their late teens. Knowing she must allow room for moral choices, the governess proves a more skilled mother. In this uncluttered example of her interests, Streatfeild seemed ready to validate the traditional family as it is constructed in the twentieth century. Unlike her increasingly ambiguous novels, the drama allowed the creation of relatively uncom-

plicated characters. The play indicates Streatfeild's need to write truth-
fully, yet to depict women as strong and free—a challenge her adult
novels seemed unable to meet.

Caroline England

Streatfeild's long 1938 novel, planned before she undertook her children's novels, struck one reviewer as having its "back broken beyond
repair" because the vibrant Victorian child of the first half grows into the
utterly conventional wife of the second. Caroline England—her name a
pun for Streatfeild's attempt at chronicling English history—treasures
her version of the past more than her husband's monogamy. Streatfeild
here combines the story of Caroline's childhood home in the country
with the decadence of the theater. Issues of sexuality and respectability
divide the characters, and Caroline's compromise—preserving her marriage to a promiscuous actor in order to continue her hopes of preserving
the manor—seems like a mistake. The book is a prolix family saga, contrasting styles of child care. Streatfeild captures the point of view of a
child who moves from a world of terror to one in which a number of
people, including her father, begin to pay attention to her. His stories
about the history of the family home mark her identity formation. But
Caroline's elopement with an actor causes disruption in the family history, including the ruin of her governess and miseducation of younger siblings. "England"—country and husband—disappoints. Streatfeild makes
an unconvincing move to hold the novel together through an emphasis
on rituals and traditions. But the family's decline coincides with
England's prewar aura: too much emphasis on its inner workings, too
little involvement in larger human narratives. As Streatfeild completed
this story of childhood lost and womanhood wasted, she had already produced the work that would make her world famous, shifting into her
dual role as writer for adults and children and surpassing in the children's novels the verve of her adult novels.

Chapter Three
Family Novelist for Children, 1936–1938

Mabel Carey persuaded Noel Streatfeild to write for children by suggesting that she could adapt *The Whicharts* for a new audience. One mark of greatness in a formulaic writer, according to John G. Cawelti in *Adventure, Mystery, and Romance* (1976), is the ability to offer variations of archetypal patterns by employing specific cultural materials to suggest both security through the familiar and excitement through new perspectives.[1] It is possible to argue, as Lois Kuznets has, that in *Ballet Shoes* Streatfeild combined the theme of apprenticeship with the family formula common to many children's books and achieved a fresh approach unique among her many novels (Kuznets, 149).

Ballet Shoes

With more than 10 million copies sold and still circulating from children's libraries after more than 50 years, *Ballet Shoes* has a status it shares with few books one might think of as "girls' books." In fact, only *Little Women*, among English-language children's literature, is both a recognizable "classic" (e.g., a book much written about and rewritten by various authors) and a "girls' book." Surprisingly, *Ballet Shoes* is not particularly well known in the United States.

Streatfeild's strength as a writer, as Cawelti's theory suggests, rests not on a one-book achievement but on the exploitation of contemporary materials over an extended time period in ways that satisfy an audience's deep needs. While it is true that the classic status of her first children's book affects a critic's reading of it—each page does indeed seem alive and fresh—this vitality is characteristic of much of Streatfeild's other work. Trying to account for her attraction to contemporary audiences, Kuznets comments that the family story per se appealed to public nostalgia for the Victorian family and possibly contributed to the "feminine mystique" of the 1950s. The apprenticeship theme, Kuznets suggests, matches the psychological needs of the child during the latency period to

learn to use the tools of a society (Kuznets, 149). The two appeals—one
to women, one to children—combine in *Ballet Shoes*. Writing for a child
audience, Streatfeild was able to set aside the unresolvable part of her
equation—the need for women's sexual repression—and in order to support this system she concentrated on depicting diverse kinds of nonoppressive mothering and sibling relationships and on children's need to
experience competence and material sustenance as interrelated, satisfying parts of daily experience.

How Streatfeild could set aside the erotic components of childhood
may be explained by her vicarage upbringing. In contrast to recent discussions of Victorian children, especially girls, and the ways they were
appropriated for the sexual needs of adults, Streatfeild's life-long venera-
tion for her saintly father seems to have convinced her that children were
safe within their homes. Curiously, however, a key component of many
of the books in which girls learn competence and independence is the
absent father-lawgiver. To the extent that an absence is a presence,
Streatfeild's autobiographical books would later demonstrate her father's
crucial role in her moral and aesthetic development.

The idea of Streatfeild as a particularly skilled auteur, or formulaic
writer offering elements of surprise within the tried-and-true, is not
quite satisfactory. To some extent all writers work with patterns previously used. Moreover, if Streatfeild—as Kuznets suggests—is one of
those writers whose skill is at the macro, or structural level, but not at
the micro, or linguistic level, then it is hard to explain why her dialogue
remains vivid today. While this is partially explained by the idea that
children's literature often depends on a kind of transparent language
with few surprises, it is also possible to claim that Streatfeild's being
steeped in both the King James Bible and Shakespeare had formed her
linguistic habits along the lines of clarity and effective repetition.

Unlike some writers who alter their sentence structure for the child
audience, Streatfeild's transition to the new audience involved few
changes in her language. Yet that language is lively despite its relative
deemphasis of metaphors and other consciously poetic devices. Theories
of the novel like M. M. Bakhtin's that emphasize dialogic processes supplement Cawelti's structural framework, explaining the excitement of
the text's exchanges among various social groups within a household or
extended family system.[2] Feminist dialogics such as that offered by
Joanne Frye help to pull together the family theme and the apprentice
theme noted by Kuznets. Frye claims that readers who engage with
Doris Lessing's Anna Wulf or Toni Morrison's Claudia MacTeer "learn to

recognize female strength, accomplishment, and responsibility" (Frye, 199). Designed for first-person narratives, Frye's explanation must be placed into its general emphasis on reader-response theory, especially that developed by Wolfgang Iser. If novels this culture values call on readers to change, as Iser claims, and if girls and women are generally still surrounded by messages about female incompetence, as research among young girls suggests,[3] then the attraction of Streatfeild's novels of vocation becomes clearer. Her work responds to the condition of twentieth-century women and girls, suggesting that accomplishment is an explicit capacity of women in relation to the total human community. In that sense—as part of the dialogical truth of the novel as a genre—the playful fairy tale frameworks of Streatfeild's children's books also encompass social realism of a most important kind.

While Streatfeild seemed to admire women like Caroline England who valued the past, she was unable to depict them as competent. At the end of her first decade as a writer, childhood became the subject, and children the audience, of her best writing. Holding up a standard of happiness achieved through competence, she offered her readers a potentially profound advantage in coping with loss and change. She was prodded into her new work by Carey, and she grew into her vocation as children's writer gradually. Yet from a historical perspective it is no wonder that she found this task worthwhile. As an extremely competent woman, she may have enjoyed creating female characters to share the wonders of the culture without having that culture enclose them in the marriage plot.

The readers ready to find zest in competence were children, especially girls. Streatfeild's preface to *Ballet Shoes* addresses them directly, explaining the specifics of the girls' careers, each amazing yet presented matter-of-factly: Pauline is now in Hollywood making films, Petrova hated acting, but her heart was in the air, and her name may be famous one day; and Posy—not yet 12—"if you are a balletomane, watch for Posy; dancers such as she is are not born every day."[4] As she had in the preface to *The Children's Matinee*, Streatfeild assigns to the child reader the identity of participant in the arts. In place of details about sexual relationships and about the girls' birth mothers in *The Whicharts*, the children's novel is replete with descriptions of acting, dancing, and filmmaking.

Other differences support the book's function as a female novel about success in relationships and at achieving competence. Pauline, Petrova, and Posy Fossil in many ways match the three Whicharts. Pauline/Maimie's parents are unknown, and she is blond and reasonably pretty and talented. Petrova/Tania's origins are Russian, and she is dark and attracted to automobiles and flying. Posy/Daisy is the daughter of a working-class dancer. In a passage that suggests Streatfeild's mischievous transposition from adult to child audience, the brigadier becomes Great Uncle Matthew (Gum), who Pauline thinks is like the stork in the fairy tale: "He very nearly did bring us in his beak" (*BS*, 8). Storks—or baby bringers—were always called "Gums" after that in the Fossil nursery.

The family is literally a collection of Fossils placed in the care of Gum's great-niece Sylvia and her nurse, Nana, in a house of six floors and large rooms Gum had purchased to hold his fossils. It happened that, in collecting these, he had also managed to find the babies, in succession. Bringing Pauline to an irate Nana and a compliant Sylvia, Gum protests, "I thought all women liked babies" (*BS*, 13). Nana is won over when the baby coos, which she signifies by asking, "Which rooms am I to have for my nurseries?" Streatfeild uses the nanny as a powerful figure whose code will not permit her to reject an infant but who otherwise stays well within her sense of what it takes to live an ordered life. Though the second baby is welcome as a companion for Pauline, Posy "caused an upset in the nursery." Posy, like Daisy before her, is pictured lying face-down on Nana's knee, being powdered and disapproved of until the possibility of an orphanage is mentioned.

The Fossils' Nana speaks without Cockney inflection, but her opinions are similar to the ones expressed in dialect by the Whicharts' Nanny. When it comes to naming the girls, Petrova's good memory for details serves them. Gum had sent a package to "The Little Fossils"— necklaces of turquoise, pearl and coral, one for each. Showing herself the successor to Tania, possessed of a fine brain as well as the most expensive necklace, Petrova remembers the address label. While a strange name, as Nana observes, "it's as good as another," even if it was what "the Professor called all those dirty stones he brought home" (*BS*, 23). Nana is generally able to be reasoned with, drawing her boundaries at just a few conventions that help to sustain respectability for the girls.

Likewise, the girls construct their own self-histories, as the Whicharts do; theirs are rooted more securely in respectable guardianship and private property. The Whicharts pawn Rose's gifts from the brigadier when they need money, but the Fossils are endowed with birth gifts of their own. The necklaces become an important plot device, ensuring that Pauline will have a dress to audition in and thus begin to earn enough money to keep the household going. Nana agrees to pawn the beads, but Petrova's mentor, the boarder who teaches her about mechanics, intervenes. He "buys" the necklaces, and Pauline scrupulously buys them back. The need for both protection and challenge is met constantly by the range of family members available through the device of taking in boarders and recording the servants' commentary and connections.

Despite certain clues that Petrova's difference marks her as a better person, *Ballet Shoes* weaves the situations of the three sisters throughout the story. We do not in this book see the dark-haired sister emerging as the author's double. Even in the nursery Posy is consulted about taking the name Fossil, and she is not ridiculed (as Daisy is) for her class origins. In fact, Posy dances her way through the text—even on subway platforms—always working out her routines and certain that her dancing is of first importance. While Streatfeild should be recognized for creating in this character a very intriguing child prodigy, she should also be cited as constructing an image of sibling equality within the story. Each girl has her high drama—Pauline's becoming too haughty and needing to recognize the rights of others, Petrova's discovering her talent for machines, Posy's searching out a great dancing teacher when Madame Fidolia becomes ill. While Pauline's working is crucial to the plot, and her decision-making about money supports both the theme of female autonomy and the pleasures of that autonomy, Petrova is working, thinking, and demonstrating both care and creativity throughout. And Posy is able, at 10, to comment on the quality of the dancing in *A Midsummer Night's Dream*. She often insists on the girls' "vowing" ceremony, a birthday promise that they will make their names famous.

Early in the book's history illustrators' work suggested the family as diverse and connected to a larger world. (Current editions do not have illustrations.) The first edition, illustrated by Ruth Gervis, Streatfeild's older sister, and the 1937 North American edition, illustrated by John Floethe, offer two such presentations. Gervis depicted Posy on her pointes as the cover design. Throughout the text, however, each girl is usually seen with the others or with one of the adult characters. The three are kept quite distinct, showing their various ages and interests. Gervis depicts the girls during their vowing ritual, making Christmas tree chains together, and asleep, with Nana watching them. Posy's abandon is caught in one sketch, as she cavorts in a bath mat, her derrière exposed. Pauline and Petrova are shown as Mytyl and Tytyl, their first important roles, and all are shown in various ways at dancing school.

The Floethe edition, using two-toned illustrations in yellow and orange, merges the girls' ages and does not place the pictures to intersect with the text as Gervis does. Floethe does not represent the vowing ceremony but creates a tableau in which Pauline gazes into a mirror, Posy puts on her ballet shoes, and Petrova stands reading a script and wearing a boyish haircut and trousers. Fewer pictures of the girls together appear in the American edition. In the Gervis edition important characters such as Mr. Simpson and the two women professors who board with the family and coach the girls in Shakespeare are depicted. One of the women teachers wears a necktie.

Winifred, a child who understudies Pauline and offers an important subtext about children's needs (she must support an entire family, while Pauline and the others are preparing to support themselves) is depicted twice. Garnie (the girls' name for their guardian, Gum's niece Sylvia) appears, as do the cook and the maid. In all, Gervis's opportunity to illustrate her sister's book allowed 37 illustrations, conveying the importance of the text and yet offering a careful interpretation of the girls' emotional states throughout. Floethe did 21 illustrations, which include no pictures of Nana or the other supporting characters and no pictures of the girls doing their paid work. Streatfeild was pleased to hear that her sister would illustrate her book, and the importance Gervis (and her editor) assigned to the extended family and the stage scenes is indicative of their empathy for Streatfeild's perspective.

The time span in the book is relatively short, especially in contrast to the span of *The Whicharts*. But the number of points of view supplied is extensive. Sylvia, like Rose, suffers from the pressures of maintaining the household on little money. Unlike her, Sylvia lives to carry the plot beyond the ending; she will travel to Hollywood with Pauline, while Nana will go with Posy to Czechoslovakia. Like Tania, Petrova has her fears of displacement, but her future is predicted by Pauline, who constructs a new ritual for their separate birthdays. She says that she and Posy will vow to "help in any way I can to put Petrova into the history books" (*BS*, 291), indicating that a film star and a dancer will not have that distinction. Posy learns the ritual by enacting it in dance, as she always responds to new knowledge.

Like Streatfeild, told by her mother that she would be the one to surprise them all, Petrova faces an uncertain future. But Gum returns. Petrova will live with him and the cook and Clara the maid—more of the old home preserved for her than for the others, with the newness of Gum's presence. Petrova, however, articulates the importance of the three sisters to the readers: "I wonder—if other girls had to be one of us, which of us they'd choose to be?" Had Tania asked this question, the answer would have been unanimous; Petrova's question evokes three answers, at least.

The *New York Times* reviewer, less excited than the London audience, objected to the mass of detail in the latter half of the book, contending that it obscured the original and humorous mood of the first chapters.[5] In England the book had become instantly synonymous with the ballet newly thriving through the efforts of exiled Russian teachers. Irina Baranova, at 14, and earlier Ninette de Valois as a child ballerina were fresh in Streatfeild's mind and in the experience of many Londoners. In December 1936 the writer was startled to see in the window of Bumpus's bookstore in Oxford Street piles of her book. Around the window hung several pairs of pink ballet shoes; Tamara Karsavina's shoes were the centerpiece. In another store the books were rationed—two to a person—and even Streatfeild could not buy more.

To girls who took ballet lessons, and apparently to a great many others, the tedium of practice was part of the authenticity of the book. From a developmental standpoint, children during the middle years are known to insist on detailed and accurate information, asking for nonfiction when presented with fantasy and fiction. Streatfeild, like Tania/Petrova in her savoring of the mechanics of motion and reflecting her own arduous training for the stage, would continue to write books for children that assumed their need for and interest in clarity of detail.

One theme involving important details is the girls' training to act in Shakespeare plays. Through this motif we can trace the importance of pageantry and theater to the idea of an extended life, especially for girls. Rather than viewing Shakespeare as rarified fare for the few, Streatfeild admits the difficulty of learning to appreciate his work without giving the impression that it is of small consequence to do so. Much of the second part of *Ballet Shoes* concerns the struggle of Pauline and Petrova to live up to the task of acting Shakespeare. The sign that they have learned their craft, constructed themselves as professionals as they have invented themselves as sisters, is their active seeking of parts that challenge their abilities but meet their needs for economic independence, success, and potential fame.

Petrova's private fantasies of flying are also nourished in the context of staging Shakespeare. Representing the highest achievement for a British actor, one that Streatfeild herself had to struggle to accomplish, the three Fossils encounter Shakespeare first within the family of boarders. As the particular passion of the two women professors, Dr. Jakes and Dr. Smith, the ability to understand and enjoy Shakespeare seems related to their own crossing of gender codes in their life-styles and professions. Even Posy, the future ballerina, takes part in this intellectual rigor and sophistication when she critiques the dancing in a play; Sylvia, who admits to a poor education herself, is astounded at Posy's confidence in her judgment and ability to participate as an observer with clear standards about the arts, much as the two professors do.

Dr. Jakes, the literature professor, is crucial to the novel. During her first conversation with Pauline, Jakes elicits the story of the Fossils' self-naming. She suggests that the girls' lack of a patronym means they are potentially well motivated to "make the name of Fossil really worth while" because, unlike her own case, people will not "say I take after my grandfather or something." Pauline is excited by the prospect of making Fossil an important name, and Jakes explains that it would mean "you must have given distinguished service to your country in some way" (BS, 41). Through a clear example of dialogic process—Pauline describing her doubts that the girls can do anything of importance, Jakes responding strongly to the mention of poetry Sylvia had taught them—Jakes proceeds to read aloud the scene between Prince Arthur and Hubert in King John: "There. Learn that. Learn to play Prince Arthur so that we cringe at the hot irons just as he does, and then you can talk about reciting" (BS, 43). She then has Pauline read aloud a speech of Puck. She had never seen it before and halted over some of the words, but she succeeded in getting "a remarkable amount of the feelings of Puck into it."

This significant scene leads to the invention of the vowing ritual in the nursery. Pauline's performance for Dr. Jakes, who made a vow of her own in a joking way—"I'll make a Shakespearian out of you" (BS, 43)—leads to the offer by Smith and Jakes to tutor the children for the pure pleasure in the task. When Sylvia objects that they are not Jakes's children, the professor reminds her that adoption works on many levels. Asserting her claim to help rear the children, Jakes offers support to the idea that another boarder, Theo, will have the girls trained for the stage: "The training will have done them good, and you will at least have taken a step towards trying to make them self-supporting" (BS, 50).

In this scene the girls' five "mothers"—Sylvia, the professors, Theo, and Nana—reach a consensus about the children's needs and abilities; Nana pronounces, "I suppose that Anna Pavlova was a little child once." At other points in the narrative Jakes and Smith support the girls' development in ways that differ from Sylvia's tendency to worry about money and about convention; Jakes agrees when Pauline wants to spend more of her earnings on going to the theater, because she believes the experience will develop her aesthetic sense.

The "Midsummer Night's Dream" chapter conveys both the contemporary ownership of Shakespeare—Nana is horrifed that Pauline as Peaseblossom and Petrova as Mustardseed will be dressed "in their combies" (*BS*, 207)—and Shakespeare's importance to the girls' economic and aesthetic success. In a funny scene Petrova finds it impossible to speak with the right inflections for her part. The struggle is mitigated by the fun of flying in a small harness fitted with a wire. In a typical detail-rich passage Streatfeild explains the technical complication: "They could fly in any direction, because the trolley moved all round the flies; but they could not fly at all except on an arranged cue to an arranged place" (*BS*, 214).

The first performance causes each girl to make clearer to herself what she will do in the future; the sisters talk through these plans, analyzing the play and its technical nuances, moving about the nursery to prove their arguments by demonstrating stage and dance motions. When Nana arrives to scold and tuck them in, the girls finish the argument in the dark, Petrova insisting on her own insight to the end, Posy contesting that she could better identify the dance steps used.

Having learned from the professors, and from Theo, that conventional manners would not always serve their best interests, Pauline and Petrova take the unusual, even somewhat tawdry, step of soliciting parts as the princes in the tower when a fellow actor produces *Richard III*. Challenged about their credentials, Pauline invokes the training of Dr. Jakes. Her listening ear enables convincing readings. But Petrova's ear is not good, and a solitary perusal of the text of the play convinces her she cannot act the part she has boldly asked for. Nonetheless, she analyzes the scene, noting the young Duke of York's tendency to play with words. Encountering Sylvia up late doing her accounts, Petrova finds out that the house must be sold. Even though Sylvia does not want Petrova to act if she is not happy with the work, Petrova pretends to like the work, thinking, "I don't want not to act when we need the money, I'd only like not to act if we didn't need it" (*BS*, 246).

Once Petrova has resolved to keep "a stiff upper lip" (as Streatfeild would later show boys trained to do at school), the realities of the stage keep her from being chosen, and she reverts to candor about Garnie's need for money. Her dilemma emerges in her conversation with the producer. When he offers her the possibility of being an understudy rather than a page, her relief at being simply a page turns to horror, and she and the producer come to a mutual understanding. He tells her, "You are a scream. All right, I was only teasing; I'm not offering you an under-study" (*BS*, 247).

Pauline and Dr. Jakes have extensive conversations about the role, and it leads to a film test. Dr. Jakes is a resource for this, too, since Pauline needs to empathize with a new character. Streatfeild describes the differences between film and stage acting, showing Pauline protected from being made vain and kept from being mobbed by fans through the agencies of Dr. Jakes and Nana. The notion of excellence fostered by Dr. Jakes carries over to the treatment of others; when Posy weeps for her threatened ballet education rather than for the ill Madame Fidolia, her family is horrified. Yet Pauline helps Posy, first by buying tickets to see Manoff dance and then by giving up the stage (her preference) for five years in Hollywood so that Posy can be trained by Manoff.

Pauline's sacrifice for Posy can be read as unfortunate, but that would mean overlooking the interdependence of the sisters and the focus on excellence through Pauline's ability with Shakespeare. Posy's genius must be served, but she in turn, with Pauline, will support Petrova's life as an explorer. Pauline has demonstrated throughout the text a fascination with money, clothing, and the life of an affluent person, and this has been viewed as virtue within the household. In her speech at the end of the novel Petrova has a theatrical role reminiscent of indirect addresses that finish Shakespeare's plays; she thus exhibits her importance as part of the group of sisters.

Though the optimism of *Ballet Shoes* contrasts mightily with the ironic shadows across some of the family-novels for adults Streatfeild produced during the same time period, the adult novels—especially *The Whicharts*—depict the woman-defined family as a space for hope and creativity. By using examples of family relationships and childrearing gleaned from her own life and exulting in artistic excellence while demonstrating that a degree of sublimation of sexual expression benefits the self and others, Streatfeild would in her writing for children find a way to keep faith with her past and enjoy making the kind of contribution Dr. Jakes described to Pauline.

Tennis Shoes

With Mabel Carey's encouragement to write about children other than the "Lila Field's Little Wonders" who partly served as the inspiration for *Ballet Shoes*, Streatfeild produced *Tennis Shoes*, which, according to Angela Bull, is Streatfeild's only self-portrait and one of her favorite achievements

(Bull, 148). Though it is more accurate to say that Nicky Heath may be Streatfeild's most conscious self-portrait in fiction, the focus on Nicky's difficult personality and latent genius offered Streatfeild another way to look at families as the locus of childrearing, and the surprises involved in that process as children develop. Having struggled to perfect her tennis game as a child and envious of more athletic children, Streatfeild used that fund of feelings to allow Nicky an exuberant triumph. Still relatively unread in children's literature after Frances Hodgson Burnett, Streatfeild avoided copying the common plot of lesson-learning and female submission in many children's books of the period.

While the ego-driven youngest child would become a staple character in Streatfeild's novels (Kuznets, 149), Nicky resembles the Vicky of the memoirs more than she does the always-adorable Posy Fossil. With the focus so clearly on herself, Streatfeild explored in a lighthearted way a subject later developed in her nonfiction—her relationship to her father and his landed family. Mr. Heath is a doctor and, before injuring his leg, was a good tennis player. His father, noticing the two older children, Jim and Susan, acquiring skill at tennis, gives them a money box, shaped like a house, so that all of the children can save their share of the fees for lessons. He promises to match their funds if they succeed. This habit of saving, however, conflicts with Nicky's plans to spend her money other ways. Likewise, the youngest boy, David, cannot save money. These two find other ways to obtain it, but Susan, the dutiful eldest child, saves both her share and that of her twin, Jim, who is away at school.

Despite Nicky's attempt to get her grandfather to cover for her negligence at saving money, he sees through her hints and foils her request. Compared to the others—with the possible exception of David—Nicky is so outrageous that she might not be recognized as one of the family. But she has the red hair they have all inherited from the grandfather, so they figure that they must own her. The children's father coaches them and enforces certain rules. One is that they ought not to complain; Nicky and Susan note that their school does not prepare tennis players well. Susan obeys, noting that her father simply does not think girls' schools matter much, and tells Nicky she is not a "true" St. Clair girl— as indeed she is not.

Nicky's outrageous acts begin when she is a baby—when she "got bored, rolled over, and stuck a safety pin in her behind."[6] When her ideas about games are rejected, she spurns the idea of practicing tennis; she is shown reading *The Wind in the Willows* but gets cake on it; she climbs into the ring with the clowns at the circus; she patronizes her siblings when they do well at tennis; and she nearly loses her chance to play at Wimbledon when she loses her temper at a match and her family walks out in exasperation. Nicky's secret practicing, encouraged by the family cook, Annie, makes all of the difference in her life and in the plot. In order to play, however, she must put money into the "Tennis House." So Nicky has the idea of selling the family umbrellas—and she therefore gets no birthday or Christmas gifts so a new supply can be bought.

When Nicky does win, in the wake of Susan's unexpected defeat, "there was absolutely no one to jump about and be pleased with" (TS, 169). Even on the day of her big triumph Nicky causes an uproar when, after she had told the man who bought the umbrellas from her about the Tennis House, he is caught burglarizing the family. As she notes, "A fat lot of spoiling I got" (TS, 207). This account of Nicky's foibles resembles those of Vicky in the memoirs; here, though, Nicky "would do what she liked and never cared what other people thought" (TS, 36), as her brother Jim observes. The intensity of Streatfeild's relationship with her father is transmuted into the tale of a prodigal who must be welcomed even without a chastened spirit.

If Nicky's father does not rule her, then her mother is even less significant. Mrs. Heath is depicted as overwhelmed on the day of Nicky's pin incident and near convulsions, so that "more help" is sought. The family has a kind, efficient governess, Pinny, and a much more interesting cook, Annie. Like the cook of Streatfeild's childhood who always remembered Noel's birthday when everyone else was caught up with Christmas preparations, Annie is Nicky's mainstay and confidante. Fittingly, she is an ex–circus performer, who announces meals by using her trapeze yell, "Whoop! Whoop! Coming over!" Because of Annie, who has a practice board made for Nicky, the girl practices and wins. Annie supplies mythic help as well as practical assistance when she tells Nicky the story of a woman lion tamer who was "corpsed" but could have learned from the champion.

The role of Annie as one of Nicky's mentors/mothers is part of the considerable humor of *Tennis Shoes*, but it also exemplifies the writer's depiction of extended families that include important servants. A middle-class perspective is upheld in this way, but it is also apparent that the middle class, represented by St. Clair's School, has an unsatisfactory view of girlhood. Annie's story of getting "corpsed" unless one sets out to be a champion serves Nicky better than her snobbish school does, and that ironic thread runs through all of Streatfeild's autobiographical writing, even when she finds some good in annoying memories, as she does elsewhere. Although the focus on Nicky is important, *Tennis Shoes* is the story of a family. Susan, though not Jim, receives attention in the narrative; serious Susan persuades the family to invest in Nicky once she sees her talent. But David is a hilarious counterpart to Nicky, singing on the street for money until he can pay his share. He is given a dog, Agag, who is an important character in the book, and one based on Streatfeild's own pets. Agag has his own possessions, personality, and chores. When he is lost on the day of Nicky's first win, David has to sneak into the match late. Despite the hilarity of these adventures, the family functions as a vibrantly connected group. It has enough sternness, enough softness, enough fantasy, to account for Streatfeild's fondness for her own family despite her difficult childhood.

Nicky's most significant need is met by Annie and her practical whimsey and strong expectations, but the grandfather in the background, with his money for tennis club membership, knows Nicky well too. Unlike Petrova and her care for Sylvia, and for everyone in the *Ballet Shoes* family, Nicky is not asked to show care. Her technical expertise and red-haired identity as a Heath are all a talented girl needs. This novel, a joke on everyone who knew the writer, combines the family and apprentice themes without vows of sisterhood. But Annie is a caring woman, at the heart of the book, linked to the food-clothing-domestic concerns of the adult novels and *Ballet Shoes*, and that care is the indispensable foundation of Nicky's apprenticeship.

Circus Shoes

Renamed *Circus Shoes* in the United States, *The Circus Is Coming to Town* (1938) is the third of Streatfeild's Carey-prodded children's books. When Streatfeild returned from Hollywood without having found a script-writing job, she agreed to Mabel Carey's idea of writing a circus novel. Carey arranged to have Streatfeild tour with the Bartram Mills circus, a model of excellence in the field. The result was the most traditionally well-made of Streatfeild's books to date, dependent less on her own personal experience than the previous children's books and more on the combination of writerly skills, knowledge of literary patterns in fairy tales and myth, and Streatfeild's zest for thorough expertise and showmanship.

The book relates the well-worn archetype of two innocents wandering into a world they do not understand and gradually, through help from mentors and their own effort, finding a home. Borrowing the form Shakespeare used in his late comedies, the opening shows a distorted world out of touch with nature; by the end of the book the two children, Peter and Santa, discover their own powers in conjunction with the world of animals, the sea, and fire. In a carefully prepared for yet surprising ending, the children demonstrate that they have become part of the world of the circus, and they are invited to stay by Mr. Cob, the "king" or owner of this world. No loose ends, such as Petrova's open quest or Nicky's propensity for mischief, remain. No ambivalence about becoming circus performers—members of the working class rather than the imitation nobility they had been taught to be—clouds the ending.

With this orderly form, the book has a familiarity about it that Streatfeild's previous children's books do not; yet its conventional form is enriched by excellent scenes of father/son conflict (between Uncle Gus and Peter), festive celebrations involving people from several countries who work in the circus, multiple points of view (Peter, Santa, and Gus), and exciting descriptions of the circus acts, the animals, and the big top being destroyed in a storm. Streatfeild's family theme is altered toward a more communal and shifting set of relationships, but the emphasis on meaningful work learned over time is played out again, with clear descriptions of Peter's instructions from Ben the horse trainer and Santa's from Ted the acrobat.

Unlike the Fossils, the children undertake their work mainly to have something to do that will earn them the respect of the other circus people. Peter and Santa had been raised by Gus's sister, Aunt Rebecca, after their parents died. She trained them to think that they were too good to work. Poorly and snobbishly tutored, they know just enough to find their uncle at the circus rather than be sent to separate orphans' homes when their aunt dies. Santa fiercely tells her newly found uncle, Gus, to run over her rather than to try to separate the siblings. When Gus relents and the children begin learning circus skills, they do not realize the economic implications of their practice until they are very nearly sent to learn office trades. They have no aptitude at all for these, although Gus tries to offer them this conventional way of life out of a sense of duty. In order to have a community they undertake circus work, and in revealing that they have learned their skills they gain all that they had been seeking—a secure home and pride in selfworth now accurately perceived. As a well-made and moving story with rich humor and detail, this book received the 1938 Carnegie Award.

In many respects *Circus Shoes* departs from Streatfeild's customary formula. No commodious house or large family with multiple mothering appears. But children's real needs are met, largely through their determined efforts and the kindness of working people, especially of the male parent figures who teach them skills and the surrogate father who dutifully provides for the orphans while respecting their insistence on not being separated. While Santa's role is that of younger sister who initially looks up to her brother but then grows ashamed of him when he is called "Lord Fauntleroy" because of his shabby-genteel ways of behaving, she grows as Peter does with her struggle to belong to the circus. Learning that, contrary to Rebecca's teaching, it does not take a woman to cook, clean, mend, or otherwise run a home (Gus is independent in his trailer), Santa sees another pattern for being female in the competent child performers, such as Mimi the French girl, and in the women of the circus who care for families and take part in their own acts.

Peter learns the codes of manliness as the workers define it; his mentor, Ben, shows him that eventually his interest in chivalry can be incorporated into a model of skill and competence. While female gender stereotypes are thus confronted, a "true" male gender model is offered. As Santa works with Peter to save the horses and tent during a fire at the end of the book, however, Streatfeild shows her participating comfortably in the realm of bravery and strength, just as Gus is comfortable and skilled in his homemaking. In the sense that only men "mother" in the book, focusing on the children's needs for competence, they do so in order to help the young people find a place in the larger world beyond the nuclear family. Fear persists that Gus will send them away; though he shows some interest in them as they improve in the common sense he finds missing initially, their fear is justified. Only the dramatic ending rescues the children from being sent back to live with one of Rebecca's friends, in part because Gus has only this option and the orphanages to choose from, until Mr. Cob recognizes the skills each child has developed.

At the beginning of the book the children "stopped indoors most of the time, and became green and thin like bulbs grown in a cupboard."[7] Gus is impatient with them because of this pallid quality. When Peter asks why he, an "artiste," puts up his own trapeze, Gus is exasperated that the boy does not understand survival. "You hear that, Ted? He'd let somebody else put his stuff up for him. The boy's a fool" (*CS*, 83).

Speaking in the aphorisms Streatfeild assigned to her nanny figures, Gus is relatively inexpressive and unable to teach children who know almost nothing of the world. Peter's development involves learning to say nothing at times, rather than to break relationships. For example, he allows an animal trainer to get credit for his own intuition that a depressed poodle from Mimi's act is pining for an elephant friend now that the cages have been shifted into a different lineup. The man gives him 10 shillings for his silence, taking the credit that will help him be rehired, whereas Peter has little at stake and could even alienate others by boasting.

Unlike Peter, Santa wants to discuss the plans Gus is making, despite her fear that asking questions will precipitate bad news. She too holds her tongue until Gus introduces the subject. Neither can argue with Gus's decision, yet both cry when they have solitude. The acceptance of the inevitable seems to be one of the tests the children pass successfully; acceptance is associated with the competence of ordinary people and of circus workers.

One of the most humorous and also most poignant motifs in *Circus Shoes* is the life of circus animals. Many conversations with circus people, such as Fritzi's German parents, center on how the animals "speak" German, or French, or English, depending on their trainers' background. They are depicted as "artistes," as personalities, and as capable of friendship. Yet they are bought and sold; in one case Ben succeeds in arranging to have two old horses sold together so that their lifetime partnership will continue. Peter disputes this view of animals, arguing that they simply respond to stimuli, but the circus people view their animals as part of their own family. Their family members, too, must work and train in distant places. The trial-by-fire for Peter and Santa involves not being afraid of the horses, even under desperate circumstances. Far from being pale green bulbs in a cupboard, Peter and Santa have the strength of elephants and the skill of acrobatic poodles.

Circus Shoes defines the family as an earned set of relationships and a system in which children can be trained to excellence defined in resistance to false values of gentility. Motherhood is not a female role in this kind of family; paying attention to the young is important for everyone's survival. Respect for the beauty of the circus is combined with understanding of the daily labor involved in producing it. Extending the circus to a metaphor for an ordered society rooted in nature, Streatfeild's resonant traditional book reveals her profound understanding of her craft and her tendency to be an arbiter of British culture and taste. Still, though, she did not want to be known as a writer for children only.

Chapter Four
War and Its Aftermath:
Adult Fiction, 1938–1948

If Streatfeild's adolescence and young adulthood during World War I had given a dramatic turn to her life and art, her middle adulthood in World War II and its aftermath immersed her directly into the danger, heroism, and sacrifice of the era, turning her into its chronicler in several adult novels and extending the horizons of her children's novels beyond her own experience and national boundaries. Literally homeless for part of the war—sleeping in shelters or in friends' homes after her apartment was bombed—and in need of money though fully employed as a canteen worker, she produced nearly 20 books during the war years. Several of these were popular romances written under the pseudonym Susan Scarlett; five were adult novels examining, as did her children's books, the nature and forms of the family. But novels of this era show how, amid the destruction of war, women's and children's lives are dependent on fortunes and values men ultimately control, even though war opens possibilities for women's reevaluation of their situation in the family.

Five Adult Novels

Early in the war Streatfeild trained as an air raid warden for the Westminster City Council. With the war still somewhat remote—the first phase of the Blitz would not occur until 1940—Streatfeild was able to spend several months in the south of France working on the first of five adult novels she would produce during the war.

Luke

Luke (1939) seems in many ways quite different from the four other novels—*The Winter Is Past* (1940), *I Ordered a Table for Six* (1942), *Myra Carroll* (1944), and *Saplings* (1945). While these treat family life in the context of wartime England, demonstrating both flippancy and tempered optimism in the midst of ironic disintegration and unwelcome change, *Luke* points up some of the flaws in accepted social codes, especially as they impinge on children. This novel uses the reflective lives of children as a key to challenging silences based on exaggerated gender roles. It suggests that gifted children fare badly in the world as it is constructed. More probingly than in any other book she wrote, Streatfeild here acknowledges the dangers to children within the conventional family. Written in the calm before the heralded storm, *Luke* suggests the possibilities for Streatfeild's growth as a social critic—possibilities that often became muted in the later commitments she made as chronicler of her times and standard-bearer for childhood engagement with the arts.

Luke is a mystery in which a murderer is known for what he is by a young stepsister, Viola, who exhibits her terror but cannot name it to anyone. Luke's mother, Freda, and his Nanny may know, but they suppress even to themselves the truth that Luke, 13, poisoned the stepfather who kept him from his music and insisted on a conventional boarding school for the boy.

The novel opens with the mother sobbing and praying over the body of her dead husband. Streatfeild quickly establishes a conflict over religion, sex, and motherhood in Freda's past and present by alluding to the crucifix and Madonna displayed in the bedroom, with its pink nightgown and striped pajamas likewise displayed on turned-down twin beds. George Duncan, the family doctor, notes Freda "could never fail to be moved by a direct order from a man; it made her frail."[1] Throughout the novel Freda's possible motivation for giving her husband poison is examined by other officials, including a detective and a judge. Women who had observed her closely—such as a childless neighbor married to the headmaster of Luke's school and Luke's former governess—are aware of Freda's characteristic dependency; Luke's father, a brilliant musician, had supervised his education until the divorce and remarriage. Alienated by the long wait for a divorce caused by Freda's religious views, Luke's father had gradually cut off all contact with Luke. Freda's second husband ended Luke's contact with the music teacher his father had selected because the teacher was a known homosexual.

Freda's history involves High Church devotion bordering on obsession. According to a priest who was her confessor, she found sexual pleasure in receiving Communion. But only during this phase of her life had she seemed certain of herself, according to the neighbor's account. When confronted with a choice between her religion and her second marriage to Andrew Dawson, Freda abandoned her High Church beliefs. Later she suffered doubts. The priest encouraged her to remain with Dawson, living without the sacraments, as a kind of atonement that would give stability to Luke and to the two Dawson children.

Within this structure of authority, sexuality, and religion ruled by gender constraints that offered no certain place to a woman like Freda, Luke suffered abandonment. Disordered gender/sex relations, resulting in a further imposition of male heterosexual authority to right the wrongs done by an angry father and a teacher feared to be a pederast, are the implied cause of the boy's criminal act. The suppression of Luke's great gift in favor of a presumed normalcy ends with a full range of questions about that normalcy. Though Dawson never appears to have been more or less than "a hearty roast beef sort of fellow" (*L*, 153) subject to no gender-related disapproval such as that pronounced on Freda's perceived weaknesses, an understood disapproval for his intolerance toward homosexuality is implied by the bishop to whom Freda's confessor goes for guidance. The bishop, perhaps a sign of Streatfeild's reverence for her recently deceased father, resists the mind-body dichotomy of his subordinate.

The insights of a boy who deviates from the perceived norms of boarding school in his dress, manner, and predilection for girls' company at playtime, and of his stepsister's, underscore the flawed adult systems for uncovering truth about the murder. Luke's Nanny may have perjured herself to deny his involvement, and the doctor who has traced the evidence—a packet of poison—back to Luke may remain silent about his discovery. The novel validates children's needs and talents without assigning the 13-year-old full moral agency. Rather than using the notion of inherited predisposition to evil, Streatfeild examines the sex-gender norms that make the nurture of difference in children problematic and dangerous. As a contrast to the children's novels in which women of varied class positions provide creative environments for developing talents in the young, *Luke* constitutes a signature by Streatfeild, before the domestic discourses generated by World War II engaged her attention and partial commitment, that gender arrangements in relation to children within the family were of more than passing interest to her. The text suggests Streatfeild's continuing position within a sophisticated set of responses to the shifting gender codes documented by recent critics of modernism.[2]

The subsequent adult novels Streatfeild wrote during the war era depart from the complex critique of gender codes she attempted in *Luke*. While continuing her examination of varied class and age perspectives in the course of telling a story, these novels fit more comfortably the norms of traditional feminine roles and tend to idealize motherhood enacted in the context of war, loss of economic and social position, and personal disappointment. Producing these novels while waiting for the declaration of war against Germany, or while working in the Women's Voluntary Service, and simultaneously writing pulp romances and children's books, Streatfeild varied her writing genres to include the journal. The book she compiled from this personal writing, *London under Fire*, remains unpublished. It represents Streatfeild as a writer increasingly committed to recording the history of her times but able to view her own foibles in the domestic sphere with a good deal of humor. Knowing her daily life threatened by the war, and her survival as a writer dependent on the secretary and cook she employed, she may have found it relatively easy to move to a more conservative ideology in her writing.

Angela Bull observes that Streatfeild's wartime books are an excellent representation of the era, informed by the writer's eye for details of ordinary life and by her wide-ranging inclusion of class perspectives. Besides contributing time and energy as a canteen driver bringing food to the shelters during the bombing of London, Streatfeild lost her elegant apartment in a raid. Homeless until the end of the war, she stayed with friends, in shelters, or in temporary rented quarters, keeping a grueling schedule of virtually full-time writing and full-time war work. After the war she settled into what became her permanent home at 51A Elizabeth Street. This apartment over a garage, in a convenient neighborhood, remained her residence for more than 40 years. The experience of being uprooted, of having to start over, and even of doing so by starting a neighborhood garden amid the rubble, may also explain the valorization of domesticity in Streatfeild's adult novels of the war years. Here she was a product of her times as well. Women's writing about the war generally supported a view of women as willing to preserve the family and home at any cost as war assaulted every institution.

Like her friend and colleague Storm Jameson, who recorded Streatfeild's determined and energized look when war was finally declared (Bull, 160) and who herself recoiled from the pacifism of her youth when England was attacked, Streatfeild moved from her earlier stance as a writer cynical or subversive about family life—the Whicharts and the Fossils being the chief examples of this cheerful iconoclasm—to one more congruent with other women who wrote domestic fiction. These writers created women characters in support of the war effort not to return to an idealized past but so they and their children could redefine home and nation.[3] In the main, such plots resisted the convention of women as passive and inferior; at the same time they showed women's willing participation in a separate-sphere gender system revealed and reified by war. Thus personal reflection by women about the relative value of sexual freedom, self-expression through work, and the continuity of the household, as well as their declaration of loyalty to the nation so that their children could inherit it, form the framework of domestic novels of the period. Home, not nation, is subject to redefinition in these novels (Lassner, 97). For many of these writers, women's new power at home would provide "initiatives to reimagine a nation's fate" (Lassner, 99).

For Streatfeild, the discourse of popular domestic fiction allowed women who faltered as mothers to recoup their energies and convictions. Often the older generation, especially a husband's parents, provided examples and interventions to enable these triumphs. The context of war altered, temporarily, the divisions among the classes in such fiction. It thus became more like the children's books in which Streatfeild overtly depicted the collusion of women of different classes in rearing competent children, and less like adult novels in which governesses and other servants are fated for sacrifice, as in *Caroline England,* for example.

War seems to have enlarged Streatfeild's view of class and allowed the creation of women characters who speak about a different society in which revitalized motherhood will be the foundation of the social order. Men as parents, too, will constitute its chief glory. The inclusion of middle-class men directly in the care of children (albeit in homes with nannies and other servants) seems a code for which Streatfeild was well prepared. Her resistance to, and later acceptance of, her father's guidance and her fascination, described in her later autobiographical trilogy, with her paternal grandparents' home constituted this preparation.

This "all hands on deck" spirit for continuing the nation via family relationships in Streatfeild's novels effectively preserves a newly idealized motherhood without denying the contribution fathers can make to parenting. In terms of narrative structure, the frequent "rescue" by father figures and the women's focus on the needs of men provide a sometimes disturbing counterpoint to the central story of a woman's development in wartime. War had placed men in the foreground of the national consciousness, even as women organized to defend their homes and to shelter evacuees. Yet women who chose men over children, in Streatfeild's war novels, committed moral suicide. Even in her patriotic chronicles, Streatfeild caught the sharp edges of the realities of women's subordination.

The Winter Is Past

The first example of Streatfeild's wartime chronicles, this novel demonstrates how Sara, a "new woman," claims her reproductive powers as a way to make a private peace within the chaos of a changing England. Initially depressed after a miscarriage and tempted to return to the stage (not a real option, she is told, after 30), Sara believes that her soldier husband's disapproval of wartime pregnancy helped to cause the miscarriage. Unlike her mother-in-law, Lydia, Sara does not participate in the "stiff upper lip" ethos Lydia developed during World War I. She shuts herself away from Bill, who eventually recommends that she spend a year in America as he begins to have casual affairs with other women—a revelation he makes at the point of Sara's reclaiming her maternal powers at the end of the novel. Accepting that her denial of sex to him was grounds for his behavior, she is undeterred in her reconciliation: "I want to be able to feel from now on that you've enjoyed every second we've been together. So whatever happens, and even if later on I have to carry on by myself, I've got your happiness inside me."[4]

Bill is absent for much of the novel, involved in the war. The plot that regenerates Sara as a potential mother is reminiscent of *The Secret Garden*, with the important differences that the child kept alive and strengthened through the pastoral setting is a Cockney boy billeted with his mother and siblings at Levet, the manor home Bill will inherit if it survives the war, and that the parent healed and regenerated to continue the family is a childless woman, not a grieving father. A central conflict involves child care issues: How is Tommy to be nursed through the illness resulting from his being lost in a blizzard? Having gone outside to rescue his tulip bulbs from the spring storm, Tommy is rescued through the concerted efforts of his own mother, Mrs. Vidler, to whom frenzy had given "three times her normal strength," and Sara, who sees his scarf in the snow before his mother does. Though Sara falls in the snow and must be lifted by Mrs. Vidler before she can carry the six-year-old to the house, Lydia notes how forcefully Sara responded to the news of the lost child and thus initiates her daughter-in-law into the tradition of Levet motherhood. Sara proves worthy by knowing, even more presciently than Mrs. Vidler and Lydia do, exactly what will help Tommy pass the crisis—the sight of some of the bulbs sprouting. Though Sara is important in his recovery, clearly Lydia's knowledge of nursing, Mrs. Vidler's understanding that her son needs the warmth of conversation, and the servants' diligent efforts all contribute to saving the child.

Sara's triumph in rallying Tommy rallies her. Giving contentment to another, she decides, is the means to happiness. Thus at the end of the novel she offers herself as her husband's comfort, believing that this relationship will suffice even if she does not conceive again.

Streatfeild combined many social issues within this pastoral fiction. Despite her probably inevitable attribution of physical sensation to the Cockney family—Mr. Vidler's sexually active visits from the city are quite a contrast to Bill's choice to sleep in a dressing room—she can be viewed as valuing, in the tradition of Burnett and Lawrence, the ongoing cycles of nature, including reproduction, which these urban dwellers seem to enjoy more than those to the manor born. The hearty vitality of the Vidlers is pronounced good even by Lydia, when she tells her gardener that his offer to adopt Tommy is out of order. "Every decent soul in the land likes to rear their own family" (*WP*, 310). The Vidlers not only engage in life processes; they teach Sara how to respond appropriately to death—by comforting the living. Even after the recovery of Tommy, Sara is aloof when her sister-in-law is grieving for a husband killed in the war; she feels unworthy to speak to a woman who, unlike herself, had made her husband happy. Mrs. Vidler knows that she can tell Sara to break the code of reserve and separation: "It seems all wrong some'ow, that 'e should be killed, and every one take it so quiet" (*WP*, 264).

In addition to an expanded class consciousness and a central focus on relationships as a woman's province, this novel examines generational issues. Although Lydia knows she will be relegated to the background when her daughter-in-law understands her position in the family, she nonetheless brings about a kind of birthing process for Sara. In a world where the Levet estate may no longer be possible, however, Sara helps Lydia to imagine other forms of home, including her own presence nearby as Bill and Sara take over the coach house (soldiers are now billeted at Levet). Nanny will reside with Lydia, standing by for assistance with the hoped-for children.

Contingent yet optimistic, the plans are reminiscent of those that close Streatfeild's stories of the Whicharts and the Fossils. This time, however, the return of the male provider-of-babies has quite different implications—those the Vidlers' conjugal visits have underscored. The "new woman" and her talent as an actress have been exposed as barren. The melting snow and the muck of spring make such images brittle, a contrast to the validation of art and earning one's living characteristic of the earlier novels. War changes landscapes, including those of Streatfeild's novels.

I Ordered a Table for Six

Streatfeild's 1942 novel uses a war incident—the bombing of the Café de Paris on 8 March 1941—as the basis of an ironic narrative showing how war takes lives randomly, killing those who might desire and deserve to live while leaving those who might be judged more deserving of death. Though Streatfeild later denied using the incident in her fiction, her diary indicates that she seized on it as an opportunity (Bull, 181). Doing so enabled her to market a book somewhat removed from the usual domestic fiction, although related to that genre in valuing the family and the domestic.

Of the six characters assembled at the cafe by Adela Framley, three die—Meggie, Adela's innocent and rather neglected daughter; Andrew Bishop, a young pilot whose own family has slighted him; and an American named Gardiner whose philanthropic dream is to create urban centers on the order of settlement houses to renew the bombed city and create a harmonious society. Three people live—Adela Framley, whose coldness toward her daughter, Meggie, is entwined with hatred of her criminal son, Paul; Noel, an acquaintance of Paul who is himself a fraud and an egocentric; and Claire, the upper-class shelter worker who doubts purpose in the universe even as she tries to alleviate the effects of the bombing on the populace.

The flawed personal relationships within Adela Framley's family add to the irony of her status as a war worker; she has engaged in war relief, founding an organization called "Comforts for the Bombed," largely to seek her own comfort in the wake of her family problems. Her son's conviction, to her horror, is known to American friends, the Gardiners. Though Gardiner believes Paul can be rehabilitated, Adela is convinced she has given birth to a monster. Her daughter is cared for by relatives in the country, and by Adela's middle-class secretary; Meggie, too, believes in Paul, just as the secretary, Letty, disapproves of Adela's mothering and yearns to start her own family.

While Claire is the only survivor of the bombing who seems to bring some hope for a decent society, her questioning mind does not offer the stability other characters not invited to the café represent. In addition to the conscientious secretary, Streatfeild offers a philosophic perspective via, once again, a Cockney who values the struggles of families to survive decently. Bill views the shelters differently from the way Claire does, for Claire despises their squalor as much as she is energized by the challenge of the raids. For Bill, the details of ordinary life have meaning: "He saw in the shelters the comic, if it were not tragic, effort to carry on the tradition: the newspaper spread on the bench, and the odds and ends the housewife had managed to buy, between sirens, laid out for the family tea; the murmur, which was almost shamed, which rose from the women: 'I don't like 'em to come 'ome and not be able to give them so'thin' 'ot.'"[5]

While Claire is fatalistic but inclined toward leftist ideas, Bill is fatalistic in his conservative views. He holds that everything is planned, "even this war, and there's more shape to things than what you think" (*OTS*, 119). Undercutting Bill through the senseless bombing at the café, the narrative leaves Claire to find out why she was spared and Adela to face her unacceptable son. While the odds of success at these life tasks seem to favor the charming, honest Claire, Adela's life does not look hopeful. Streatfeild seems to offer failed motherhood as a parallel to the senseless and random war while suggesting that working at the maternal offers the only valid life. Bill's memory of his mother's work to rear him supplies a focal point in Claire's conversations.

The narrative also undercuts the satisfactions of making a home by describing Letty's frustration at delayed marriage and her lost efforts to guide Meggie. Through its open-ended irony, this novel allows the reader to supply a possible ending: Are Claire and Bill potential lovers? While unlikely, this resolution is part of Streatfeild's clever use of the wartime event to produce a novel both within the parameters of typical domestic fiction in its valorizing of family and interesting for its challenge to that premise through the inexplicability of war. As another turn of the screw, Streatfeild offers no explanation for Paul's behavior; though Adela is cold, she is not the monster she (perhaps accurately) believes her son to be. The "fathers-to-the-rescue" motif represented by Bill and Gardiner are not necessarily able to sustain Claire, or Letty, as they have not sustained Meggie or Andrew, the dead youths.

Myra Carroll

While *I Ordered a Table for Six* has been cited as one of Streatfeild's more enduring adult novels (Wilson, 31), *Myra Carroll* (1944) is considered by Angela Bull a low point in Streatfeild's career, along with certain children's books (*Harlequinade* and *Curtain Up*) produced near the end of the war when Streatfeild was beginning to view her writing as a chore (Bull, 183) rather than the central focus of her life. The contrast with the previous novel is startling, for *Myra Carroll* seems close to a "chapbook" offering a behavior code to housewives, as Nancy Armstrong has characterized domestic fiction.[6] In this case, again valorizing motherhood,

Streatfeild uses a standard narrative frame—a day spent sorting furniture and mementos in an old barn—to offer a retrospective explanation
of the life of the beautiful matron Myra Carroll. The coldness and maternal deprivation of her childhood, complemented by the forceful rearing
of her "ice slide" of a governess and the manipulation at the hands of an
unwise aunt and uncle, create Myra's resolve not to love wholly. Her
youth involved only one unmitigated love, for her small dog, Fortesque.
Using a potpourri of events from her own life, Streatfeild constructs a
credible case for Myra's resistance to bonds with others. Rather than
leaving the text in its ironic mode, however—seemingly successful "mère
de famille" is actually constricted by the codes of beauty and class that
have constructed her—Streatfeild chooses to add the optimistic "Sir
Garnet" element.

Thanks to a cheerful man she marries because, she says, "I like him
but not too much," and whose affection survives Myra's "Oh, do leave
me alone sometimes"[7] as well as her adultery and virtual abandonment
of her children, Myra accepts at length the subordinate position in her
marriage. Thus, sorting mementos, Myra's reminiscences end with the
certainty that her family loves her. In a final flourish of mother-as-
Cinderella, Streatfeild brings Myra's youngest daughter to the barn to
urge reestablishment of their Devonshire household, since Myra is the
bow, the family the violin, and her presence is necessary to them all.

In a war-torn country, the personal war within a woman hurt in childhood is triumphantly resolved through the enduring institution of the
family. The code of submission earns status and respect through Myra's
tears, when she returns to ask for a divorce but is moved by memories of
her husband's kindness to her beloved dog Fortesque. Streatfeild's placing the seemingly absurd constellation of feelings in the dog is a link to
other books in which she draws on the importance of family pets as a
way of healing division and pointing out the human relationship with
nature. Successful because they acknowledge limited love as a workable
tradition, Myra's family may be seen as part of the wartime rewriting of
the maternal Streatfeild participated in rather overtly.

Saplings

Pamela Hansford-Johnson has called *Saplings* (1945) Streatfeild's
"best book to date" (Bull, 182). Certainly it has more in common with
earlier books than *Myra Carroll* does. Rather than focusing on one person's perspective, *Saplings* explores the minds and values of several mem-

bers of a family whose father dies in the war and whose mother succumbs successively to grief, alcoholism, and the paternalistic requirements of a new husband. The novel's opening depicts the father, Alex, as the involved parent of the four children—Laurel, Tony, Kim, and Tuesday—who range in age from three to 11.

Covering a four-year span and including several members of the extended family and key servants as well, the story traces the children's gradual loss of home, security, and potential. Streatfeild's enduring theme of continuity, however, brings closure when the paternal grandfather comes to bring Laurel home when she has run away from school, stolen money, and turned to her former governess as a last resort. Irony is retained because the protection of the grandfather may conceal the sufferings and disintegration of the family and, by implication, the society. The children are not the same persons they would have been with the presence of Alex and the stability of home and school, and nothing can make up for the war's destruction of their family and home.

Besides the familiar rescue-by-patriarch, the novel uses several other Streatfeild staples: a talented stage child (Kim) who alone thrives in parental absence; a sensitive girl who feels herself lacking in special qualities but who innocently blunders into knowledge of her sexual powers (Laurel); and other well-sketched individual children. Also present are a "Sir Garnet" reference like that in *Ballet Shoes* (here more ironic, however), a poor but loving parsonage family with the most satisfactory mother in the book, and an indispensable puppy.

The novel employs the wartime context of domestic fiction admirably, making the children's homelessness despite their patrician connections a gradually revealed sadness. Lena is one of the least successful mothers in Streatfeild's fiction, yet she is presented as both likable and understandable. Dedicating the book "'For my mother'" may have been an ironic gesture, as indicated by the quotation marks, yet both the parsonage mother, Sylvia, and Lena's good intentions after her husband's wartime death have some resonance with the way Streatfeild described her own mother. The dedication highlights one of the most interesting features of the novel—the effect on children of father loss and the effects on a society of war, as well as the fate of a "good-enough" mother who prefers to be a wife.

Lena resents Alex's desire to "switch things" so that the children's development rather than their erotic life is the center of the couple's existence, and she wishes to send the children to the United States when the raids begin. Alex refuses to be separated so drastically from them, and he compromises by having the children kept by relatives in the country while he spends his nights with Lena in their city residence. Lena finds her sexual appetites fed by air raid signals; later, after Alex dies in the bombing of their house, her strong sexual passion is said to "coarsen" her. This judgment, by an American lover who recoils from marriage, highlights what Streatfeild portrays as the war's destruction of what had functioned as an excellent family despite Lena's not being centered on the maternal role.

Lena struggles to meet the demands of her new role as provider, planner, and disciplinarian rather than adored and decorative center of attention. Streatfeild uses material details—her welcoming flowers and puzzles when the children return on school holidays—and the children's perspectives—none confide in her, yet all value her more than in her treasured days—to suggest that Lena could have worked at her maternal role in a satisfying way had it not been for her dependency on her American lover, who also supported her drinking. Once he has extricated himself from a family he did not want despite his fondness for them, a new husband—not Alex's social equal, but well off financially—appears, and Lena once more becomes the wife bound up in a husband's needs. Nonetheless, the couple plan a home for the children until "the flying bombs upset all plans."[8] Then the parceling out of children to relatives begins again. This time the daughter Laurel is too old for such moves. She accepts pearls from an uncle, alienates his wife for good, and stands at the end of the novel as a figure whose displacement is threatening to the future of the country. Unlike the young daughter in Christina Stead's *The Man Who Loved Children* (1940), Laurel is not a potential artist; she is an "ordinary" young woman whose vital family has failed her in the sweep of war over England and who will not easily recoup that loss.

Evaluating *Saplings* in 1978 in the context of fiction about women and children written during the two world wars, Mary Cadogan and Patricia Craig offer firm praise: "It contains no trite conclusions and no evasions."[9] Much about Streatfeild's adult war novels seems resonant in terms of current theories about gender and the maternal. Focused on women's precarious position within economic and social systems that allow scant room to their sensuality, *Saplings* insists on men's importance in negotiating livable patterns for families. Since it shows losses of children in wartime, and the varieties of family life in peacetime, this narrative seems written from the perspective of one whom Sara Ruddick would call a peacemaker. Even Lena, with her pleasure in the body, adds to the critique of war because her eroticism devalues sacrifice and transcendance, implicit to the mystique of war. In a peacemaking culture drawn from maternal thinking, "bodies are at least as important as the causes that use them."[10] Alex's care for the children—Ruddick would say that he was their mother—suggests the congruence of Streatfield's insights with those of Julia Kristeva, who urges that the relativity of symbolic and biological existence become the basis of a new ethic.[11]

Susan Scarlett Novels

Although she published work under her own name that depicted sexuality as intrinsic to human behavior, and she criticized her mother and sister in autobiographical writing such as *A Vicarage Family,* Streatfeild used a pseuodonym for 12 romance novels published by Hodder & Stoughton from 1939 to 1951. Initially she devalued such books and thought of the adult fiction as her important work. But as a writer of children's books she learned to resist literary snobbery. Nonetheless, the romance novels—nine produced during the war and three shortly after—were "secret progeny" (Bull, 176). According to Angela Bull, the romances demonstrate Streatfeild's clumsiness in writing about romantic love (176). While Streatfeild's sexual practice was open to speculation, her diaries imply a passion for women, beginning with Daphne Ionides (Bull, 102). To the extent that her personal history shifted her interest away from a consuming focus on male-female relationships and helped her to tell other stories and open new narrative space where various relationships could be deemed important, Streatfeild's life gave a particular vivacity to her writing. The bonds between women in a household, sibling relationships, and parent-child relationships have emotional intensity in her adult novels and children's books.

In the romances a stock plot generally prevails: two women, one scheming and the other innocent, are attracted to the same man, who sometimes seems unwilling or unable to choose between them. Written to keep her household going during a period when paper shortages and other wartime measures threatened her income, these novels are of limited historical interest. Unlike the adult novels, they do not offer a chronicle of the period, nor do they critique class or gender boundaries. Children are of little importance. The typical household is lower middle class, with a "mum" who smoothes out problems, as in *Clothes-Pegs* (1939); who is a problem herself, as in *Pirouette* (1948); or who has a problem, as in *Love in a Mist* (1948). In most of the novels the central problem is, of course, whether the right young woman marries the man, often a more worldly urbanite from a higher class.

Streatfeild's pulp fiction offers two main opportunities for analysis—one to view popular values of a particular audience (presumably female) of the war era, and another to identify how Streatfeild drew on life experiences and used them differently in various genres. A third opportunity is a lesson in Streatfeild's skill at the microlinguistic level; in such adult novels as *Saplings* dialogue and narration convey witty and ironic tones valued by modern literary critics, while the romance novels use clichés and predictable plot structures. As a romance writer Streatfeild shows little individual flair, even though many such writers will, besides offering conventional structures, bring new elements to the formula or incorporate their personal visions into it (Cawelti, 12). Some critics believe this to be Charlotte Brontë's accomplishment in *Jane Eyre*. Streatfeild's family formula in adult fiction and children's literature is inspired, whereas she used little of her innovative and visionary energy for her romances. Yet such an assessment is necessarily tentative.

Janice Radway's study of one group of romance readers argues that empirical data from a community of readers is necessary to study such works; without such data, a critic can easily oversimplify the issue of why readers demand certain kinds of characters, plots, and situations in their pleasure reading.[12] Such criticism tends to devalue the female audience of the romance, assuming that readers are either unreflective or naive. Similar problems are involved in assessing children's books or any works for which one is not the intended audience. In the case of the romance, class assumptions as well as gender play a major role in evaluation.

Specific data from Susan Scarlett's readers is not available, but it is important to note Radway's conclusion that the readers she studied required a reversal of the emotional abandonment and other oppression they suffered in real life (Radway, 558), providing ways to deal with such problems within a framework supporting the continuity of their daily lives. These narratives did not ask readers to alter basic life patterns; rather, they confirmed them in values they wanted to believe in the face of great frustration. As short-term therapy, the preferred novels displaced needs temporarily onto fictional characters and provided readers with the role of observer/participant.

Streatfeild's romances do not offer the specific requirements of Radway's group of readers, but then that is Radway's point: audiences have needs induced by cultural circumstances, although as other critics point out, gender dichotomy continues to be reinforced in British as well as in American readers.[13] For wartime readers, the emphasis on clothes, furnishings and gifts (one lover sends a tablespoon in each bouquet, signifying "sugar") may serve to temporarily assuage these items' absence, as well as an opportunity to moralize about the virtue certain to win the love of the young man. For example, the recipient of the tablespoons, in *Pirouette*, is firmly committed to being a dancer despite the allure of love, until the rival proves to be the superior performer. Only then will she join another ex-ballerina, on a ship to Rhodesia with their respective husbands.

Whereas the first romance, *Clothes-Pegs,* includes new curtains for the heroine's mother as a condition for marrying a member of the peerage, the bride insists on choosing a humbler diamond in order to charge the curtains against the value of her ring. In *Summer Pudding* (1943) an aptly named plot involves a mix of romances and an economic intrigue casting a shadow on the heroine's integrity; the resolution demands she be cleared of suspicion of trying to cheat the landlord of a summer house offering respite from a war-torn London. So we might hypothesize the pleasures afforded to a wartime audience by the shower of creature comforts imagined within a framework of need and sacrifice closer to their daily experience than material goods.

In some cases Streatfeild's use of historical detail is exceedingly superficial, as in *Murder While You Work* (1944). Beyond worries about using American lipstick and having a run in her hose, the heroine seems more a production of crime novels than of anything Streatfeild or her readers might have experienced as munitions workers. Published shortly after two children's books using conventions of the melodrama—*The House in Cornwall* (1940) and *The Children in Primrose Lane* (1941)—this romance suggests Streatfeild's awareness of intertextuality. No longer would she be able to trace each book to an experience of her own, as she did in her 1939 Carnegie Award acceptance speech. Like *Murder While You Work*, most of the romances make only surface use of details of Streatfeild's life, while they show her facile and prolific power to imitate conventional stories, especially that of Cinderella. Quickly evoked settings, such as the vicarage in *Under the Rainbow* (1942) and a theater company in *Poppies for England* (1948), were drawn from her experience.

The last of the romances, *Love in a Mist,* crosses the genre boundaries more than the earlier ones do, using a married heroine who wants her five-year-old boy to be a film star. An American married to a British grocer, the housewife Ruth is the only "sensible" daughter-in-law, but she discovers for herself the need for submission to her husband, as in

Streatfeild's adult novels of the period, when her child's spoiled behavior becomes apparent. Thus, while characters in Streatfeild's children's books are validated when they sing, dance, or act, and marriages in the adult novels endure worse ills than disagreeing about a screen test, the happy ending of the romance nonetheless indicates the Streatfeild heroine is indeed "sensible" (virtuous) in knowing her place, and she will be rewarded for it.

Dialect, in both the children's and adult novels, serves to alter the worldview of the text and resist the monoglossia, or unitary voice, generally offered to female readers (Reynolds, 108). In the romances, however, dialect is an unambivalent sign of bad taste or villainy. Moreover, Streatfeild deliberately offers clichéd language, such as a hero's feeling "a new glory in the night when she nodded" (*Summer Pudding*), or his calling the red-headed heroine "my little lioness" (*Murder While You Work*). By contrast, the dialect speech of the gardener who speaks the last line in *Saplings* heightens the irony of the text by demonstrating how the appearance of wealth hides the damage to Laurel and the other children of Lena and Alex. Likewise, the attraction between lovers in Streatfeild's other books is presented in indirect or ironic ways.

Novelist of the Postwar Period

In the 10 years following the publication of *Luke* (1938) Streatfeild's impressive range of writings included a few short stories and some radio scripts, newspaper articles, plays, and book reviews. She wrote a substantial amount of nonfiction as well, producing a newsletter for the Women's Voluntary Service. The roles of critic and nonfiction writer would become increasingly important in her career as, building on her heroic work during the war, she became more and more a public figure representing national traditions and values. But for a number of years after the war she would continue her work with adult fiction.

A novel depicting postwar London, *Grass in Piccadilly* (1947) uses Streatfeild's familiar "family house" as a basic plot device but interweaves with that the condition of postwar London and its intermingling classes. Though marred by bizarre touches and by stereotyping of Jews, the novel represents Streatfeild's growth into a contemporary historian. A complex set of characters and relationships dramatize the difficulties of creating homes again. Both the physical barriers to that process and the psychological scars of the war are set against the sociological realities of London.

Nancy Armstrong's 1987 study of domestic fiction argues that the creation of the novel is crucially related to the concept and practice of power in society. Drawn from a central tradition of female power in the private sphere as represented in novels, individualistic notions of what is normal have pervaded ordinary life and political choices since the eighteenth century. Placed against such an analysis, Streatfeild's best novels for adults suggest at least an interesting variation of this dominant cultural understanding. Gender intertwined with class forms a political process that makes resistance a personal action, linked to private property. This process (liberal humanism) is the basis of subjectivity, including psychosexual identity (26). Who, what, and how we desire, in short, are cultural phenomena: "By occupying a place in the mind, the household made it possible for masses of diverse individuals to coexist within modern culture" (258). Armstrong's concept of the domestic woman as reproducer of the notion of household (and thus of modern culture itself) describes Streatfeild's final novel of the war era. A penchant for displaying the interdependence of various classes under one roof, drawn from her vicarage upbringing and applied to her own relations with a secretary and a housekeeper, informs her vision of postwar London. Close to the ethos of her best-known children's books, *Grass in Piccadilly* offers the notion of household as a multivocal economic unit whose purpose of socializing children is set in a framework extending pastoral myth to urban utopia.

The owners of a large London house, "five stories with a basement, no lift, and no central heating,"[14] take their only option to profit from their investment by moving from the country to the city. The house cannot be sold in the postwar economy, but tax benefits will accrue to the owners who provide housing for a number of families. Living in the city under these circumstances is preferable to seeing Sir John Nettel's country estate divided, as it inevitably must be. Charlotte, his wife, explains to her stepdaughter, Penny, that the grass covering the destroyed houses in the neighborhood is akin to their own move to London as "country hay seeds transplanted" (*GP*, 6). Solid, wholesome Charlotte sees an opportunity to heal a breach in the family when she asks Penny to look at the house as it is being divided into flats. Penny, like the sophisticate Claire of *I Ordered a Table for Six*, represents the central focus of Streatfeild's concern. How will such a woman, scarred by her husband's death in the war, make sense of life (and reproduce the norms of domestic happiness)?

Having endured her son's trial and imprisonment for murder, Charlotte nonetheless seeks to bring Penny back to health. Penny pro-

vides a doubting commentary about a class system that allots the basement to a Cockney couple and two upper stories to businessmen and
their families, the Willises and the Bettelheims. But she has a question:
"Who's going to live on the nursery floor?" (*GP*, 7). When this floor is
offered to her, she agrees to live in another part of the house, but she
negotiates a housing arrangement for a writer, his wife, and their child of
four, Jane.

Penny conceals her closeness to Jane, but tenants in the building—
the Jewish housewife and the Cockney custodian—notice the emotion
behind her mask of ennui. The story proceeds through dialogic methods,
with tenants on various floors and the Nettels' servants from the country, Hannah and Mabel, sharing their observations about one another
and about the couple on the top floor. Little Jane is cared for by her
father, Jeremy, but her mother, Freda, is cold and neglectful. Gradually
Jane's care is shared among Jeremy, Penny, and the housewife, Paula
Bettelheim.

As a sign of the promise of this arrangement, Jane is initiated into
ballet by her play with the Bettelheim daughter. Streatfeild uses multiple points of view, revealing Paula's ability to soften her husband's sta-
tus-seeking and selfish behavior and Jeremy's sacrifice of his plans to
marry another when Freda announced her wartime pregnancy. The
Cockney couple in the basement is linked to Jane and the others by their
shrewd observation of relationships and by their giving a home to a cat
Jane loves but is not permitted to keep. The cat in turn connects the
park outside, and its homeless old man, with the residents of the house,
especially Jane.

Jane is a child of war at many levels. Penny had given birth to her by
an American, concealed the birth from her husband and family (he was
later killed in the war), and arranged to have Freda trap Jeremy into
marriage to give the child a home where Penny could remain in touch
with her. Admitting this "story of irredeemable blackness" to her
father—the "sort of thing that happened in fields and haystacks in the
village at home," he notes (*GP*, 205)—provides for Jane's safety but
alters the history of the family and its image of itself. A Jeremy-Penny
romance, following his divorce, is hoped for by Charlotte and hinted at
in Jeremy's reflections. The nursery space, which he had made safe for
another man's child, may yet offer him—because of his generous love
and duty—all of the comforts of home with Penny, who will inherit the
property.

Melodramatic in its outline, the plot is executed skillfully because of Streatfeild's keen ear for dialect and class mannerisms. Moreover, the sacrifice of Jeremy within the domestic offers a contrast to the many governesses and nannies of Streatfeild's fiction who dedicate themselves to children; in the war-torn landscape the deception and sexual repression of Jeremy so that Penny can watch over Jane becomes one more wartime sacrifice. Though not justified by its outcome, Penny's manipulation of both Jeremy and Freda is revealed as a desperate measure to shelter Jane and retain connection to her. Penny becomes an ironic image of the domestic woman reproducing the notion of household because it continues a civilization. The presence of refugees, and of persons from different classes occupying what becomes essentially one household, removes the possibility of pretense and forces the upper-class family to "settle in" to its new biological makeup and also to an economic and moral history forever changed. Unlike modernist classics like E. M. Forster's *Howards End* (1921), however, the merging of social classes is less a biological than a domestic process. In her children's books of the era, Streatfeild's interest in the domestic found subtle and clever expression.

Chapter Five

War and Its Aftermath: Children's Books, 1939–1951

The children's books Streatfeild produced during the 1940s varied from conventional thrillers like *The Secret of the Lodge* (1940) to the superb *Party Shoes* (1945), with its voicing of English traditions in an apparently simple story of a new dress and shoes. By working her interest in the war, in America, and in the arts of various kinds into her children's books, Streatfeild avoided convention and repetition. She continued to grow in her knowledge of children's literature, avoiding the traps of topicality and faddishness. The difficulty and satisfaction of craft and art combined as her subject with the intricacies of relationships of all kinds. Males, in the wake of war, assume more importance in the family formula, subject, like women and children, to economic dangers and often as dependent as women and children on the combined strategies of the group for survival. For instance, the depressed father in *Movie Shoes* (1949) refuses to go to California to recover without his family and accepts a loan from the governess. While *Ballet Shoes* depended on the archetype of the absent father, *Skating Shoes* (1951) includes generous and selfish brothers, good and bad uncles, and present and absent fathers. At the center of family novels such as *Theater Shoes* (1944) and other "Shoe" books is the competence of children.

Besides continuing her original flair with family novels in which children have careers, giving a new respectability to the way theater was depicted in children's books (Cadogan and Craig 1986, 286), Streatfeild surpassed other children's writers of the war era in her depiction of people of the working class (Bull, 180). Using multiple perspectives and social history as her strong suit, Streatfeild wrote novels for adults and children that offer insight and pleasures of various kinds to readers then and now.

The Secret of the Lodge and The Stranger in Primrose Lane

The same decade that saw Streatfeild writing books between bombing raids and canteen trips witnessed her continued use of children's literature as one of several strategies for economic survival. But given the times, this literary mode presented an outlet for her sense of humor, delight in story and pageantry, and her motif of children's competence. Though two children's novels written early in the war strike Angela Bull as a betrayal of Streatfeild's analysis of child-adult relationships and factual observations (Bull, 177), both of these books show admirable use of suspense and the conventions of thrillers. Streatfeild attributed her creation of the novels to wartime circumstances that precluded travel and research. The imaginary heroics of the books may be read as a parallel to Streatfeild's own heroics once she obtained her mobile canteen in October 1940 and began her steady rounds bringing hot drinks and food to people huddled in the uncomfortable underground shelters during bombing raids.

The Secret of the Lodge (published in England as *The House in Cornwall*) was written during the same period as *The Winter Is Past*, with its rescue of Tommy Vidler by Sara and his mother. In the children's novel four siblings visit a mysterious uncle in the country because they have nowhere else to go. The two boys and two girls, in the familiar age range of 10 through 14, quickly encounter the forbidding Dr. Manoff. With his arms hanging to his knees, tongue moving often over his lips, bulbous mouth and bullet head, Manoff is one of Streatfeild's rare villains—a former dictator from a shadowy kingdom, Livia.

Clues the children pick up, including listening to the crackling stays of the housekeeper on her errands and observing that the chauffeur has no tongue, share the macabre, even humorous story line that clearly participates in a children's thriller tradition. Through teamwork and personal sacrifice, the siblings discover the hidden secret in this not-so-pastoral country mansion: the crying child they hear from time to time is Rudi, the boy king of Livia. Part of their rescue operation includes giving Rudi coffee as an antidote to poison, but it also encompasses the necessary airplane at just the right time. Like the ending of *Ballet Shoes*, with its promise of reuniting the Fossils, the final chapter promises a reunion with Rudi in Livia.

The Stranger in Primrose Lane (1941) reveals in its English title, *The Children in Primrose Lane*, closer ties to her other novels. Although the children are from working-class families, few authentic details of working class life are included. Instead, the Smith, Brown, and Evans families are given specific characteristics: the Smiths excel in school, the Browns make better workers, and Millie Evans is "a mixture of Flossie Elk and Nicky Heath" (Bull, 179) because she manages to be center stage even though she does no more than the other children to solve the mystery about the "stranger."

This man has intruded into the empty house where the children have set up their ideal play space. He hears them talking about Mr. Smith's regiment and its secret move and also has access to the extensive map collection David Brown left in the house. Eager to overcome the effects of their casual revelations, the eldest girl, Sally, helps the group to devise an elaborate plan to trap the man whose accent suggests he is a German spy. Marge, the character most representative of Streatfeild's own childhood, is taken as a hostage. The other children move to the rescue, engaging in a few quarrels as they make plans but are calmed by precocious Millie. Together, the girls wrap the spy in a gypsy's rug, and fat Marge sits on him until help comes.

The Primrose Lane story emphasizes the children's competence in noting details and reasoning about clues. It includes a layer of domestic details missing in the previous book and important to catching the spy. Some of the complexities of family life are present—children overhear parents talking (about privileged information), older siblings protect younger ones (to a degree), and Millie's family keeps the secret about the spy (even though they spoil her). The neighborhood is changed by war, with fathers preoccupied and the empty house available for play and intrigue. Despite Streatfeild's awkward plot structure, the book has many traces of her skilled dialogue.

Dennis the Dragon and Harlequinade

At the start of the war Noel Streatfeild's growing distinction as a writer for children was less important to her than recording the full story of her times in historical novels or helping in the effort to keep the population safe. Yet the two novels of this period indicate a wise gesture on Streatfeild's part—the practice of telling a story for its suspense and the presentation of oppositional categories common to narratives related to childhood play and entertainment media. Prior to these attempts under wartime duress to use conventions of children's popular novels,

Streatfeild had enjoyed producing a short fantasy, *Dennis the Dragon* (1939), illustrated, like *Ballet Shoes*, by her sister Ruth Gervis. This book, though a moral fable commenting on social conventions and the need to resist conformity to snobbish values, was an amusing example of a theme of conjuring Streatfeild had used in her first attempts to write for children's magazines. Its wartime publication precluded wide circulation and reviewing. It points to Streatfeild's early awareness of genres within children's literature and her willingness to use them, as she did romance conventions, as part of her life as a writer.

Harlequinade (1943) uses the realities of war, with its disruption of institutions and relocation of urban children to the countryside, in a metaphoric framework of the circus world Streatfeild had developed in her acclaimed *The Circus Is Coming*. The opening of the book uses clear prose to establish a winter mood congruent with the disruption of five children's lives: "Like flotsam and jetsam left as the tide goes out, so the receding circus had left behind nothing but the children."[1] Unable to practice their skills in an open field, as they had in other seasons, they discover the house of an old actor. He provides a practice place, and costumes, for playing circus and practicing skills and, more significantly, tells stories of Harlequin, linking the children's remembered arts with a past much older than they and vital to the present.

Streatfeild writes, "The old man's words fell like rain into a pond, every drop making its own circle on the water. Each of his words made a circle in their imaginations. Nearly four hundred years ago, or a thousand if it came to that, meant nothing; a stage at a fair had no time" (*H*, 22). Harlequin, "a creature born of the laughter of the crowd" (*H*, 22), enters the children's concept of the circus and of their play, healing them and delighting their old storyteller. The psychological change runs parallel to a change in the winter wind, charmed by the "laughter of nearly four hundred years" (*H*, 45). The voice of the narrator merges with the old man's commentary at the end of the children's performance when he urges the children, "Bring it back."

Streatfeild's use of the Harlequin figure as a central device for social and moral values indicates a flowering of her interest in children's literature as an artistic expression and prepares for a later commitment to her role as storyteller and guide for the young. The brief tale, beautifully illustrated by Clarke Hutton with a collage of carnivalesque figures, emphasizes the competence the children gain through rigorous practice. It also suggests mythic reasons for pragmatic action in the lives of artists and others coming to grips with loss and change.

Theater Shoes and *Party Shoes*

Between 1945 and 1951 Streatfeild produced four children's novels that established fully the pattern she had begun with *Ballet Shoes* and *Tennis Shoes*. Though she seemed to see the books as individual works, their use of such key elements as house, multigenerational or multiclass family, and children's competence at serious work in the arts gave them a certain commonality despite the varied titles of the English editions. American publishers tended to exploit the repetition of the key elements by imposing the "Shoe" title again and again, capitalizing on readers' desire to repeat satisfactory experiences while enjoying variations in a formula.

Commenting on the complex design of *Theater Shoes* (published in England as *Curtain Up* in 1945), Angela Bull describes a "bran tub of a book" (183) in which Streatfeild is not quite in control. Bull particularly dislikes the fact that Sorrel, the eldest of the three Forbes siblings sent to live with their Grandmother Warren, an actress, when their father is missing in action, seems less forceful and likable than her egocentric cousin Miranda. True, Sorrel is a "good" girl, as much like Alcott's Meg March as Susan Heath of *Tennis Shoes*, but she is not necessarily unappealing in her concern to act maternally toward her brother, Mark, and sister, Holly. Furthermore, she is not immune to feelings of jealousy and competitiveness toward them and toward Miranda, as each child is trained at Madame Fidolia's "Children's Academy for Dance and Stage Training."

The family dynamics the novel describes—which is part of Streatfeild's own experience—and her bold move to explore several aspects of her past—vicarage life, learning to act, and the war's impact on families and other institutions—mark the novel as an important step for the writer. Streatfeild decided to forego a simpler plot in exchange for memorable sibling relationships, the idea of home as the reward of, and means to, significant work, and the satisfaction of seeing several children succeed even in time of war. The novel presents an array of different personalities and age levels in the three siblings and their two cousins. Thus, while offering many of the pleasures of Streatfeild's other children's novels, *Theater Shoes* uniquely deemphasizes linear structure in favor of new connections and conflicts.

In fact, readers had to some degree elicited one strand of the book: because children wrote frequently to Streatfeild asking for more stories about the Fossils of *Ballet Shoes* and worried about Posy, Manoff, and Nana's fate in a now war-torn Czechoslovakia, Streatfeild wrote them into the structure of the novel in a move that acknowledged an important convention of writing for children. Like Heidi, the Borrowers, and Ramona, the Fossils' life continues beyond one book. Pauline, Petrova, and Posy each offers a scholarship at Madame Fidolia's. Madame bestows one of these on each of the three Forbes children, and the Fossils write letters to the child they support, maintaining their individual traits. Petrova sends various tools to Mark as surprises, and Posy decides to endow another scholarship when it becomes clear that Holly is no dancer. Pauline, who most resembles Sorrel in being the eldest, in chafing at shabby clothes, and in being less eccentric than Petrova and Posy, emphasizes her connection to Garnie in her letter.

While introducing the Fossils complicates the various chapters in which their letters appear, their contact with the Forbes children, fostered by Madame Fidolia, advances a central concern of the novel—the notion of care for children extending beyond a particular household and reflecting the recent evacuation of children from London.

Madame Fidolia, too, takes on a fostering role toward the children, sitting Holly on her knee at a crisis point to get the child's account of her theft of Miranda's briefcase (Holly wanted to look like the other children in professional garb). Madame tells the children at the academy—whose mothers plan their clothes and send them treats—to extend to Sorrel, Mark, and Holly the kind of concern their mothers have shown for them. More than once Madame demonstrates firmness, too, and this justifies the firmness Sorrel exerts with her siblings when she must. The mysterious, dramatic Fidolia—keeping alive the myth of excellence and family solidarity of the Fossils—manages to sound credible, not preachy, in urging her pupils to care for one another.

Being mothered is central to the book. Streatfeild uses a unifying thread spun from the pubescent girl's search for her dead mother and for personal identity. Telling the story of Sorrel rather than that of her well-mothered cousins Miranda, the daughter of Shakespearean actors, and Miriam, the daughter of a comedian and an actress (both mothers are Warrens, as was Sorrel's dead mother, Addie), can be said to contribute significantly to narratives of female ambition. Sorrel and her siblings discover a heritage previously kept from them when they are sent to live with their mother's mother, herself an actress and the widow of one actor and daughter-in-law of his famous father, Sir Joshua Warren. So immersed in acting is this family (its son is in Hollywood) that Addie had to cut her ties with them in marrying Bill Forbes, a naval officer and son of a clergyman.

Streatfeild opens the novel with a vicarage as the Forbes family's temporary home, for the first time exploring her vicarage roots in a children's book. Sorrel, Mark, and Holly stay with their Grandfather Forbes during school holidays since their father has gone to the war. Their grandfather is busy with his reference book on animals of the Bible—with whom he seems to confuse the children at times—so his death matters mostly in its economic impact. Streatfeild depicts the vicarage servant, Hannah, as a hymn-singing Puritan with great concern for the children. Like Nana of *Ballet Shoes*, she cuts and patches clothing and shields the orphans when she can. She calls in the bishop to explain to them, over tea, why they must move to their Grandmother Warren's house in London and give up their respective schools. In a mode consistent with child-adult relationships throughout the novel, Sorrel reads a subtext in the bishop's remarks and moves him toward more honesty. Like it or not, the Warren house on Ponsonby Square must be their home now. The estranged grandmother's break with her daughter must be understood as part of the Warrens' love for their theater tradition. As in other instances, Streatfeild assigns to a bishop a tolerant worldview accommodating of difference.

While the vicarage serves only as a way station for the children, Hannah is the means by which Streatfeild continues the Forbes family's influence. She knows what is appropriate for "Mr. Bill's children," down to the issue of whether Mark must wear white stockings (he does not want to, and Hannah sees that he will not have to). Hannah's hymn singing, and Puritanical views of the theater, contrast with the habits and opinions of Mrs. Warren's Cockney housekeeper, Alice, and her traditional slang rhymes—the "head" is a loaf of bread, the "stairs" are apples and pears. She is embedded in the culture of the household, where theater is life and where household routines rotate around performance schedules.

Both servants are humorous figures, yet both are recognized as essential mothering figures—unable, because of their numerous duties (mainly economic in nature, keeping the household running by patching and making do), to supply all of the care needed. Like Annie, the cook of *Tennis Shoes*, in their articulateness, both women supply a dialogic framework to the children's assessment of their situation. What is to be their future, if they cannot be educated as planned by their father? In particular, Sorrel worries about Mark's preparation for the navy, in his father's footsteps.

In this novel Streatfeild demonstrates her love for the life and art of the theater, which offered her her first independence. Though Sir Joshua is the dead patriarch, the Warrens' pride and panache are the children's maternal heritage. Mark surprises himself with his talent at the academy. His adventures are humorous incidents in which he pretends to be a bear rather than a prince, and much time is devoted to the teachers' cultivating his imagination. At the end of the story, however, he clearly will have the appropriate education for the navy. For Sorrel, and by implication for Holly, discovering that "our mother liked reading Shakespeare"[2] is a beginning of identification with Addie's talent. Maternal aunts, and the eccentric, dramatic grandmother, watch over the development of Sorrel's talent with the dedication of fairy godmothers.

Although Sorrel embraces willingly the surrogate mother role she has tried to play, reminding Mark and Holly that "all I am is just an old mother" (*TS*, 62) in the pantomime they devise for their audition with Madame Fidolia, her notion of herself and her powers are considerably enhanced by finding herself pronounced "your mother's daughter" (*TS*, 247) when she plays Ariel in her uncle's production of *The Tempest*. Her feeling for the role and her ability to get behind the words are movingly described by Streatfeild as she demonstrates the girl's growth. At an audition for the BBC, 12-year-old Sorrel is able to bring to life another Shakespearean character, Titania, the role Streatfeild had played in her twenties: "The lines came out of her mouth, just nicely rehearsed words, but meaning nothing. Then suddenly the studio was not there . . . and she was speaking in a proud way to Oberon, who looked, in her imagination, rather like Uncle Henry looked when she saw him in the films" (*TS*, 225).

Motivation is economic as well as familial; as usual, these issues are interrelated to advantage. The house at Ponsonby Square has no "bees and honey," Alice tells the children; "art is life" becomes a believable paradigm. Their profession and their family life are inseparable for the Warrens. While a humorous aspect of the novel, their rituals and rivalries explain both the loss suffered when Addie left the theater/family and the importance of family in engaging a child with the larger world. A troubling aspect of families—the ways they promote the class system by furthering their own members[3]—is not critiqued by Streatfeild, but she does offer a wider view of the system of fostering children than found in many novels. Moreover, to reproduce the household of their grandmother would be to repudiate the counter-tradition offered by Hannah and their own mother, who left the theater/family.

Theater Shoes successfully addresses serious issues such as family imposition of vocational choices by depicting the Warrens as a repertory theater. Within this setting belonging to a family has ritual but inventive
possibilities; the family is "unreal," a product of the social imagination,
and capable of redesign. For example, Grandmother mysteriously assigns
Sorrel her mother's old room, luxuriously furnished and filled with
things she had used. But Mark is given a small, dark room nearby, and
Holly is assigned to the old nursery with Hannah. Later Sorrel—who
shares their mother's pajama cat pillow with Holly but cannot console
Mark for the unwelcoming quarters—realizes that Mrs. Warren wants
all of the children placed near Addie's room. She had blocked out a stage
for them to interact with Sorrel's authority and unwittingly deempha-
sized the centrality of the son and heir of his father's military career.
Perhaps she succeeds in her designs on Addie's son, since Mark glories in
his stage training even though he pursues his goal of returning to his old
school in due time.

One of the most successful scenes in Streatfeild's work is her depiction
of Christmas at the Warren household. The pageantry of Christmas at
the vicarage, where Hannah sang "The First Noel" as a solo, "with the
children managing the Noel bits" (*TS*, 154) and band instruments
appearing in the stockings, is replicated with Alice as audience and
paper instruments for the chorus before they go off to Hannah's church,
"just what we might have had at home" (*TS*, 158), as she says. But the
evening brings a new sense of Christmas when Miranda and Miriam
arrive with their respective parents, the Brains and the Cohens. For several months their grandmother had been feuding with her daughters.
Yet the family dinner, completely secular, evokes the ongoing fun and
security of being a Warren and marks the Forbes children's acceptance
when the grandmother toasts their missing father and wishes them his
safe return.

The transition marked by this toast is initiated when the cousins
arrive. Each family makes an "entrance," enacting roles of surprise or
parody and signifying the movement through the various possible emo-
tions in a family. Uncle Mose Cohen, a successful comedian, punctuates
the rituals with exclamations of "Vell! Vell! Vell!" from his stage act (*TS*,
161); he also exhibits warmth and a freeing generosity toward the children, who take "a great fancy to Uncle Mose" (*TS*, 161). His running
commentary on how he had led the Christmas turkey on a gold ribbon
to the house heightens the children's sense that the festivities are not
"true" but meant to evoke laughter, joy, and community. Uncle Mose

offsets earlier anti-Semitism in Streatfeild's adult novels (e.g., *The Whicharts*), although his overwhelmingly positive representation suggests the vestiges of stereotype.

Grandmother is the "star" of Christmas, however. She makes her entrance after the cousins arrive. She "stood in the open doorway. She was wearing a dress of trailing black chiffon, and fox furs, and her hair was held up on the top of her head with a diamond comb. . . . She stretched out both arms" (*TS*, 163). On cue, the daughters and sons-in-law greet her, the men kissing her hand; then Miranda and Miriam "danced across the room," crying "Granny, Granny!" (*TS*, 163). Uncle Mose gives a wink and a nod to Sorrel, whose theater impulses surface; she catches hold of Mark and Holly, moves them toward the grandmother for a kiss, and then decides to lead her to her chair. Enthroned there, Mrs. Warren examines her daughters' gifts to her, turning one into a joking exchange with Uncle Mose and another to a memory of a stage role when she had to look dowdy. She responds to Uncle Francis Brain, Miranda's father, when he pompously reminds her that umbrellas are scarce, answering him "in a very good imitation of his own voice" to give her thanks (*TS*, 165).

After dinner the theatrical mode continues for the toasts, with Grandmother toasting a picture of her son Henry and giving speeches about the Cohens and the Brains. The children, sipping their small glasses of port slowly to make them last, wonder how many healths will be drunk; then Mrs. Warren alters the mood by holding up her hand for silence to toast their father. Sorrel, Mark, and Holly almost cry, but Uncle Mose "had got off his chair and was walking round the table on his hands" (*TS*, 167).

Following the toasts, charades—using Shakespearean characters— evoke laughter from all but Uncle Francis Brain, whose performances on stage and household use of a "caramel voice" are parodied by Grandmother and Mose. But Streatfeild makes a place for him in the ritual when Mark's singing moves the family to an awed silence; Brain pontificates, "Beautiful, beautiful," and moves Grandmother to the evening's closing line, "God bless you all," circling back to the opening of the chapter. There the narrator had emphasized the ways traditions are established and maintained because they are "amusing and gay and Christmassy" and so a part of all future Christmases (*TS*, 154).

Each chapter of *Theater Shoes* has a careful, albeit highly textured, structure like the Christmas chapter. For example, chapter 14, "First Night," incorporates Holly's yearning for a leather briefcase so she can

feel part of the academy; Sorrel's mothering of her by giving up the pajama cat; the children's incorrect assumptions about Hannah when she
does not sing while preparing them for the grandmother's opening night
(Hannah is both certain of her own Puritan views of the stage and very
proud of the children and their talents); a new dress for Sorrel, to replace
an outworn velvet she would have had to wear without the Cohens' sensitivity; Sorrel's curbing of Mark so he cannot disgrace the family at the
opening by stealing attention from the stage players, Grandmother and
Miranda; and a play enacting Miranda's clever, obnoxious, and ultimately corrected behavior. Miranda exults in her role, acting afterward like
Grandmother on Christmas, kissing each of the cousins she usually
ridicules. The triumph of Miranda highlights the sadness of Holly in the
next chapter, when Posy's dance scholarship is taken away and bestowed
on Miriam. But Holly's chapter closes with a classmate bestowing the
remainder of a Mars bar, "a dusty, bitten little end of chocolate" the girl's
mother had bought out of her monthly ration (*TS*, 215); the girl is acting the way Madame Fidolia has directed.

In another chapter Uncle Mose notices Holly's comedic talent when
she is playing with Miriam, and announces that he will visit Madame to
carry out Miriam's wish that she be educated for dance alone, and also to
arrange for Holly's training in comedy. The same chapter, "Plans,"
merges the Fossil narrative with Mark's dilemma. There is a place for
him in both family traditions, because Petrova Fossil understands his
need to prepare for life on the sea. She arranges for him to be adopted
and mentored by Gum, who now runs a nursery for war babies. Like
Madame Fidolia, Gum fosters magically the lives he accidentally
encounters; these two mysterious figures from *Ballet Shoes* deepen their
engagement with children's daily lives under the constraints of war.

A second Christmas at Grandmother's brings the children's father
home but does not put an end to the stories Streatfeild would now build
as a tradition within a tradition: "Shoe" stories as part fairy tale, part historical and social account, part sheer passion for the encompassing pleasure of the family novel. Continuing to examine the rather quiet older
girl in many of her children's novels, associating the girl's attaining voice
with her growth in the arts, Streatfeild touches on an important theme
of current developmental psychology—the self-doubt Carol Gilligan
finds in the narratives of 11-year-old girls. Gilligan's samples, drawn
mainly from middle-class and white settings in the United States during
the 1980s, do not represent all versions of gender roles girls learn. Yet
her work strikes a resonant chord. Streatfeild's use of such a girl as a cen-

tral character of *Party Shoes* (1947) is especially interesting for its linking of the enjoyment signified by new clothes with the deeper issues surrounding the rituals of clothing and female experience.

Party Shoes (the English title is *Party Frock*) strikes Angela Bull as equal to anything Streatfeild wrote and a sign that she had recovered powers exhausted by the war. According to the kind of formalist criteria Bull employs—emphasizing unity of plot, character, and setting and fast-paced dialogue revealing the suspense and worth of the content—Streatfeild shows her talents to great advantage in this novel of the postwar period. It deserves to be read and studied as a classic of children's literature not only for its craft but as a brilliant examination of group process, personal maturation, and connection of present to past from an English perspective. Streatfeild's knowledge of the theater, experience with parish pageants, and delight in the foibles of all classes shape this story of how ritual theater furthers the life of individuals, families, and nations.

Between her discussion of pageantry in *The Children's Matinee* of 1934 and *Party Shoes* in 1949, Streatfeild and her compatriots had lived through a devastating assault on their homes and lives. Before Virginia Woolf's suicide in the wake of the bombing, Woolf had used the pageant as a focus for *Between the Acts* (1941), an examination of class, community, and history attuned to the sadness as well as the humor and irony of living. In Woolf's novel an eccentric woman, Miss LaTrobe, writes the play and keeps the action moving from behind the scenes, coping with the various social and personal needs of her actors—including a clergyman named Streatfield. Miss LaTrobe has been examined as an example of women's power and importance, as well as a manifestation of gender role shifts that interested Woolf.

Noel Streatfeild's children's novel accomplishes some of the same cultural commentary. *Party Shoes* also depicts the yearning for community of the postwar era. Within the constraints she accepted for the children's novel, such as a suppression of references to sexual desire, Streatfeild exploited her ability to present multiple points of view and the relativity of time and space. She extended the scope and depth of the family novel by drawing children and adults into a rich common task with ultimate social affect.

The formal design of *Party Shoes* is that of group process, a giving and taking according to interwoven criteria of individual needs, tradition, and art. At the center of group process is performance, the work of giving meaning to the past, present, and future. Framing the story is a

party dress and shoes sent to Selina Cole, a cousin of the large family of
Dr. and Mrs. Andrews, by her American godmother. "In an English village at the end of a long war,"[4] as Mrs. Andrews puts it, there is no occasion for a 12-year-old to wear organdie and satin. Having a party is
impossible in the face of transportation, clothing, and food shortages.

Streatfeild introduces the book with a preface to her readers telling of
her niece's similar worry—that she would outgrow a beautiful dress
before being able to wear it. By the end of the novel when quiet Selina—
whose parents are absent because of the war—has worn the dress to
enact the role of Dreamer in the splendid pageant occasioned by the
American gift, the worries about transportation, clothing, and food dis-
appear in a spirit of sharing inspired by the production. And Phoebe, the
humorous younger cousin, inherits the outgrown dress, an ending as
important as having American troops intervene in the fate of the abbey-
turned-manor house where the pageant takes place, by recycling it as a
youth hostel.

Unlike the characters in *Theater Shoes*, gaining a place in a family is
not a concern for Selina, even though she is typically more reticent and
reflective than the Andrews cousins. The observer stance is her strength,
even at the beginning of the novel when she hopes for a parcel of candies
to share because the six cousins have no godmother in America. But
Selina's ability to wait, to hold her tongue at the right moment, to con-
sider the effects of an action on others and on a desired result, become
increasingly powerful personal tools as the idea of putting on a pageant
thrusts her into the work of talking to the more difficult people and
finally of being stage manager for a huge panorama of English life—a
figure something like Woolf's Miss LaTrobe in her understanding of her
authority and how to use it.

Thoughout the practice months Selina had efficiently run errands and
anticipated difficulties, yet she had not practiced for her role. Philip Day,
the wounded war veteran and nephew of the local squire who had
become producer when the children's original idea needed bolstering,
ignores her requests to practice and claims ignorance of the party dress
as catalyst for the pageant. Her angry confrontation with Philip evokes
his "having-an-idea look" (*PS*, 279) and inspires the eventual use of
Selina as Dreamer of the pageant, an Alice in Wonderland device origi-
nally thought of by her cousin, the ballet-loving Sally. Selina's well-
timed explosion at Philip is one dramatic example of the dialogic nature
of the novel, one character influencing through her or his speech the
ongoing subjective experience of others and of plot events. Selina's con-

nections with her cousins are also essential, however, as are their connections with one another.

The girls of the family, Sally and Phoebe, share importance with Selina in the novel's structure. In each case personal talents are already known to be theatrical, unlike Selina's less flamboyant attributes, which prove to be as intrinsic to art as the girls' respective abilities in ballet and poetry. Sally originates the pageant through having the best idea at a "committee meeting" the children hold to think up an occasion for Selina to wear her dress. Though her brother, John, refines the idea of a ballet with Selina as Dreamer to that of a pageant, Sally's interest in ballet and ability to empathize with others remains a strong part of the novel's process. When her delight in dance is temporarily overshadowed by the trained ballet dancers recruited from the next town, she is so moved by their art that jealousy is not an issue. Streatfeild uses her technical knowledge of ballet to render Sally's cooperation believable and admirable, rewarding the character with a scholarship to the academy at the end of the novel.

Phoebe's poetry, laughed at within the group of siblings, is defended before others, and even Philip has to be "kept in order" by Selina, who tells him that "she wrote the scene and she must do it the way she likes" (*PS*, 214). Philip and Phoebe then have "a proper meeting between equals," with nine-year-old Phoebe eventually won over to being a May Queen rather than the young Anne Boleyn she had imagined. Though Phoebe's ahistorical verse is written out of the pageant, her dignity is preserved. One by one, each scene written by the children is revised and changed as the pageant takes on the majesty of Philip's insights from his stage experience; only Phoebe's writing, however, is incorporated into Streatfeild's text.

The older boys of the family, John and Christopher, and preschoolers Augustus and Benjamin participate in the pageant and its inception, but their futures are not bound up in the arts as Selina's, Sally's, and Phoebe's might be. The older boys run the "committee meetings," with John as eldest including even the babies in the deliberations. Away at school while the pageant grows, he readily gives over authority to Philip—perhaps because his scene, on horseback jousting with his father, meets his expectations better than his original idea. Christopher, Sally's twin, offers the comic relief, inviting seven boys to tea the week there is little food and designing a scene in which the single woman who works in Dr. Andrews's office enacts the role of a witch, though one based on history rather than Halloween.

Like the boys, their father changes little because of the pageant. He is the lawgiver—directive and decisive at the outset, getting the children to plan their time and insisting that they maintain their grades. But the children's mother, weary from her household cares, comes to life once she becomes part of the process of the pageant. Her forebodings about costume needs as the ideas alter come true, yet the costumes she produces with the help of the Days' housekeeper, Mrs. Mawser, become the focus of the novel when the last fire of its history threatens the huge abbey. The community saves the house and the costumes in a thrilling scene where Selina pumps some of the water, her young female strength supplementing the efforts of the fragile old butler Mr. Partridge. The fact that the community rescues its past prior to the Americans' fortunate purchase of the abbey is intrinsic to the vision Streatfeild drew from her love of the theater, especially Shakespeare and the classic ballet.

Streatfeild's family formula is extended in *Party Shoes* to all of England, embracing the Allies, especially Americans, as well. The threatened house of the "Shoe" books is in this one a repository of England's story, deeded to the Day family by Henry VIII and suffering from repeated fires because of "the curse of the monks" who will be satisfied by having the abbey a hostel once more. The abbey is shown to be the property of the common people, through a number of strategies, including the country dialects of the squire and his wife. While mothering at the familial level becomes overt only on the day of the pageant, when Mrs. Andrews knows how to keep the children and their father calm, mothering at the national level emerges as a key to novel when Mrs. Day is transformed by her costume and makeup to Elizabeth I and the happy ending of the Days being able to stay in the area to run the hostel confirms the traditional and mythic role of authority redefined by the common people, Americans included.

As embedded in the fast-moving story as its elaborated historical and psychological aspects are the numerous instances of humor in every chapter. Exploiting her readers' ability to laugh at those perceived as "other," Streatfeild uses local children's refusal to take off their shoes to dance (their Mums had cautioned them against removing any clothing lest the "creative" life corrupt them), a Cockney evacuee's hinted ribaldry in singing "Knees Up, Mother Brown," and an absentminded vicar to display human foibles. Because of the shifting point of view, however, each character is at some time "other," even Selina, who finds herself on a path hedged by cauliflowers and cabbages during her confrontation with Philip. The humor of *Party Shoes* is remarkably depicted as whole cloth to the action, not relief from its suspense or import. In her vision of cooperation, especially of shared economic power, Streatfeild achieved a formal control over her materials that writes a triumphant ending to the difficulties she had endured as a writer during wartime.

Movie Shoes and *Skating Shoes*

Movie Shoes (1949) was published in England as a serial in *Collins Magazine for Boys and Girls* and as a book titled *The Painted Garden*. It moves to a new locale, Hollywood, as Streatfeild attempted to gain distance from the war and its aftermath by researching a new subject matter—film. The text resembles such earlier books as *Tennis Shoes* in its focus on a troublesome girl, Jane Winter, whose father is still referring to her, lovingly, as "you little horror"[5] at the end of the novel. Unlike her siblings—Rachel, 12, who excels at ballet and Tim, younger than Jane, who is gifted in music—Jane is ordinary. She does, though, enjoy her dog, and this turns out to be more important than one might think in the story of how Jane becomes Mary in a film of *The Secret Garden*.

The Winter family is in trouble at the outset, because their father is depressed and cannot earn a living as a writer. The children have a mother and a governess-nurse, Peaseblossom, who had stepped into the family because the mother could not cope with her first infant and housekeeping responsibilities. The solution for the emergency is to move to California for the winter, to stay with the father's sister, Aunt Cora. The governess's convenient legacy, however, provides the living expenses. The sunshine works for the father, and the Hollywood–Santa Monica atmosphere proves lucky for the children's "careers" when Rachel is mentored by Posy Fossil, and Tim by a Liberace-type radio performer. Jane's brief acting career occurs because she makes friends with a director whose dog she wants to walk for pocket money. Her plain, contrary aspect is her entree to the screen.

Poor behavior on the set, caused in part by the teasing of an unpleasant child star, Maurice Tuesday, almost causes Jane to ruin the film. But the boy who plays Dickon, David Doe, has "magic" with animals, and his mother supplies the needed strategy for Jane to keep the role: she imagines Maurice as a chipmunk and thus is impervious to his taunts. Her second chance also hinges on the director's getting advice from his dog, who wags his tail to have Jane kept on. A spray of orchids from the directors, as Jane returns to London with her family, becomes her one moment of surpassing her siblings.

Several elements from Streatfeild's repertoire are repeated in this novel. Jane is somewhat like Nicky Heath, although nothing in the book parallels the humor with which Nicky is presented. Unlike novels in which children earn money to keep the family together, this one gives them the more individual purpose of furthering their own development or, in Jane's case, finding a way to compete with her siblings. The governess never becomes the humorous, acceptable figure that Miss Lipscomb, the doctor's spinsterish assistant, is in the pageantry of *Party Shoes*; her repetitive advice to "win for our side" seems irrelevant, since the children exhibit little of the bonding common to Streatfeild's families. The unloving aunt supplies a context for the action, as Aunt Claudia would in *Skating Shoes*, but her whiny voice and social conformity offer nothing so valuable as Claudia's attention to Lalla's techniques.

A few kind adults in servant roles help the children; notable is Bella, the black cook whose connections help Tim get jobs with his music and whose religious faith predicts that if the Lord wants him to have a piano, he will have it, and she will smooth the way with Aunt Cora. In the 1949 edition Bella speaks in dialect, but some of her expressions— "trashy, no account"—are adopted by the children. Another helper is Mr. Phelps at Jane's studio, who somewhat parallels the gardener in *The Secret Garden*, understanding children rather than gardens. The father is the rescuer of Jane when her behavior nearly ends the filming, taking her on an outing by herself where she encounters Mrs. Doe and the advice about imagining her way out of her difficulty.

On the whole, the repetitive elements seem the least successful aspect of the book. The family is not much fun, the governess unconvincing, the mother too nice. The book is relatively short for this stage of Streatfeild's career, approximately 100 pages fewer than *Party Shoes* but a little longer than *Skating Shoes*. Writing for serialization, and intrigued by the California trip on which she observed Margaret O'Brien being filmed in *The Secret Garden*, Streatfeild seems to have tried for a simple structure like that of *Skating Shoes*, with its doubling of Harriet and Lalla rather than the rich multivocality of *Party Shoes*. But the task of comparing the family's California experience with the healing potential of *The Secret Garden* was only partially embraced; though the Winter family is in an emergency at the opening of the novel, Streatfeild could not attribute to her central household the life-threatening despair necessary for the parallel. Direct narration, rather than dialogic action, offers less humor and warmth at key scenes, such as the argument over whether to accept

Peaseblossom's money, perhaps because of limited space in which to move the family abroad and construct a meta-narrative about Burnett's book.

In terms of social history, Streatfeild retains her sharp observational powers, noting details about the ship, the household work, and the scenery in California. The plot reflects the need for a car, the emphasis on material goods at Christmastime, and the commercial aspects of acting or writing for Hollywood. Perhaps reflecting Streatfeild's growing interest in radio scripts, some of the best moments come not from the use of historical detail or from dialogue, as in previous books, but from suspenseful turns of the plot, usually based on mistaken interpretation. For example, Jane thinks she is being considered as a dog walker, not as an actress; Rachel thinks a call about a film part is for her, when it is the director interested in Jane; and—unforgivably—Aunt Cora tells Posy Fossil she cannot possibly get Rachel to dance lessons, relaying news of a call from a "Miss Mossal or something." Posy mimics everyone by doing little dances, and her presence enlivens the book sporadically as she transforms Rachel into a professional dancer. Pauline, wiser for the wear, advises against film roles for Rachel, who does not get selected for *Pirouette*, an ephemeral work (bearing the title of Streatfeild's first Susan Scarlett book).

The attempt to describe the filming of a children's classic represents the most interesting aspect of the novel—its original title's reference to a "painted garden" conveying some of the difficulty and complexity of Streatfeild's task. She needed to deal with the artificiality of the movie set, the unsequenced filming, and the rigors of a child star's routine while offering a good reason for the reader to learn all of this. In contrast to Rachel's love of dance and Tim's absurd musical pranks, Jane's temperament and inability to act give little hope for the film as a valuable medium. Though Jane argues about the interpretation of the book, resisting the presence of Mrs. Craven's ghost in the garden because it is not in the book, her argument is a manifestation of her contrary disposition rather than a sign of her aesthetic judgment. Streatfeild conveys details of the work, such as the hot lights and sweating brows of the actors, but none of its meaning as an art form. Only in the Maurice-as-chipmunk strategy does she explore the nature of acting without the structure of the stage drama. When Jane returns to England with a reed pipe made for her by Dickon-David, her motivations range from training her dog to showing up her siblings by becoming famous for attracting animals.

Despite the shallowness of the family story, the crassness of California as well as its glory come through in the novel. The two levels of the narrative are linked by the song "California, Here I Come!" that the children hear of on the boat and improvise to the melody of "Good King Wenceslas" until learning the actual song provides occasions for various lyrics. These oral aspects, as well as the action-based plot and conventional child character, have made the book popular enough for new editions and for an audiocassette recording. And for some of Streatfeild's readers, *Movie Shoes*, with its insufferable but likable child protagonist, "provided a standard which could not easily be maintained" (Cadogan and Craig 1986, 295) as Streatfeild moved toward more lightweight books. Her next children's novel, however, strikes Angela Bull as outstanding in its characterization of a child reared to be an ice-skating star.

Skating Shoes (*White Boots*, 1951), written while Streatfeild had already discovered a new medium, radio, and was producing scripts for the highly successful series on a vicarage family called the Bells, reflects the writer's ability to draw productively on her personal repertoire as well as her readers' interests. Always alert for new story ideas, Steatfeild noticed references to ice ballet in readers' letters; her idea of doing a skating book was seized upon enthusiastically by her American editor, Bennett Cerf, and she found herself researching a sport she knew nothing about (Bull, 205).

Streatfeild prevailed on her secretary to take skating lessons, observed skaters, and asked a famous skating judge to review the manuscript. Besides using her research resources, Streatfeild may have drawn on her new friendship with Margot Grey, the hotelkeeper with whom she merged households and enjoyed a shared dog, Pierre. As much as *Skating Shoes* is technically accurate about the culture of skating rinks, it is even more compellingly a drama of friendship with accurate sociological and psychological recognitions by two 10-year-olds, Harriet and Lalla, of what it means to be involved in another's play, work, and financial and emotional contexts. The crisis of the book—when each girl has collapsed physically from the strain of impending loss of a shared life threatened by professional jealousy—shows how deeply the two lives are entwined when Olivia, Harriet's mother, brings Lalla out of her virtual breakdown by listening to her, and when David, Lalla's uncle by marriage, reveals that Harriet, not Lalla, has the makings of a champion skater but that Lalla's future lies in professional skating as a "comic Queen of the Ice." More than a one-on-one exchange, friendship is a wider circle of intimacy and stability; to destroy it would tear apart a carefully constructed world, even a newly formed family.

In later children's books—*Thursday's Child* (1970) and *Far to Go* (1971)—Streatfeild drew overtly on tales Margot told of her own childhood, but *Skating Shoes*, coming at the beginning of a deep relationship between the two women and after Streatfeild had lost Daphne Ionides and another friend, Theodora Newbold, to their possessive involvement with each other (Bull, 197), draws a great deal of its strength from a vision of merging lives and the threat of betrayal by unwanted emotion.

As the story of two friends rather than the struggle of a family to maintain a household, *Skating Shoes* seems removed from many of Streatfeild's books, especially *Ballet Shoes*. Moreover, it differs from the wartime books, including *Party Shoes*, in seeming to be without specific historical context. The subtlety of the novel in both aspects—as commentary on family and as chronicle of an age—makes it a rich text for discussion. In the immediate postwar period and well into the 1950s British families lived through continued scarcity of food (until 1947, bread and potatoes were rationed); an acute housing shortage, with decisions being made about rebuilding bombed areas of cities; a serious shift from an agricultural to an urban society; and great need for new roads and vehicles. The same period saw the beginning of national health care and a lowered infant mortality.

Perhaps most important about this period was that the new generation was born to parents whose habits of socializing within the community were quickly altered by the advent of television. Other factors were the difficulty for the landholders in maintaining large houses and domestic help and the inability of educational institutions to address the stratified class system—even though people of all classes had more frequently mixed during the war era.[6] Within this context—not the highly charged wartime emergency but a slow struggle and transition in economics—Streatfeild's story of two little girls who meet at a skating rink uses all of these material conditions as its basis.

Skating Shoes opens with an emphasis on health care. Harriet Johnson looks, her brothers say, like a daddy longlegs—her face has all but disappeared and her legs are too thin and weak after a long illness. The opening chapter sketches in the Johnsons' situation: they once lived in the country and were rich; now their father ineptly runs a shop selling produce and game that Uncle William (called the Guzzler in school, for good reason) sends from the manor. William sends only what he does not want, making the shop unreliable and unspecialized. The towns-people are not used to buying fish and fruit, odds and ends, at one store, especially since the rabbit or trout were things William had rejected. The family (parents George and Olivia, brothers Alec, Toby, and Edward, and Harriet) eats whatever is not sold, making cooking difficult. But the cheerful Olivia—who wears worn, tasteful clothing under her large apron—makes meals out of "enough rabbit for two . . . a very small pike . . . grouse . . . very old, as if it had been dead for a long time . . . and . . . sauerkraut," the latter an imperative because Uncle William had sent seven hundred cabbages "and it's only Wednesday."[7]

There is no money, in the Johnsons' apartment over the shop, to send Harriet to the seaside, or to give her ballet lessons to strengthen her legs. Nonetheless, a family doctor, though overworked, has a resource to offer: a patient who owns a skating rink will let Harriet skate for free. And the family has its own resources in Alec, who will deliver newspapers to pay for skate rental, and Toby, a math whiz, who computes the potential worth of the two shillings Alec will have left over each week as a basis for getting into the grocery business "on the growing end"—procuring and producing better vegetables for the shop. In one brief chapter Streatfeild conveys the warmth of the family even in its reduced circumstances, the tenderness of the father even though he is one of the more obtuse fathers in her fiction, the spunk of Harriet in voicing her needs to the doctor, and the sideline humor of the small brother, Edward, whom Toby and Alec call "a born cad" because of his me-first attitude.

Though the Johnsons seem an odd family with their struggling busi-ness and shrewd sons, the parceling out of the manor house, difficulty in transporting food, and arrival of a new generation reared in small quar-ters with new stimuli capture something accurate about the postwar period. Even the attentive doctor seems consonant with the improved medical system all could use. The unselfish older brother overcomes the financial pressure on the family more profoundly than his two shillings a week might portend; his employer—an old man cherishing models of horses his father and grandfather had ridden but unable to own any of his own—supports his dream to buy a pony and cart for hauling produce and thus ensures that the family can educate Toby at Oxford. Toby, a source of humor in the text because his conversations are phrased as arithmetic problems about selling vegetables in imitation of his befud-dled father, is no fusty Don-in-the-making. Toby is a pragmatic engineer who measures the garden space Harriet's friend Lalla shares with them and devises a way to get strawberries to market without seeming like a thief to Lalla's Aunt Claudia.

Aunt Claudia is the villain of the book until finally she understands that she cannot treat Lalla like a "champion race horse" and reincarnate Lalla's father, a prize-winning skater whose skates dangle above Lalla's bed with the mixed message to do as he did (presumably to skate, but possibly also to fall through thin ice and drown, as he and Lalla's mother had). Some significant gaps in the text occur around the cardboard Aunt Claudia. She is the stuff of melodrama; no explanation is offered about her coldness, snobbishness, or determination to make Lalla a champion. Had she, for example, been deprived of skating lessons or attention in favor of the dead brother? Why does her husband, David, a lawyer, stay married to her when he is so obviously a pleasant fellow with empathy for Lalla and the Johnsons?

Interrogating the text this way leads almost nowhere; Streatfeild used a free hand in constructing her plots, crossing the genres of family novel/domestic fiction with fairy tale/romance as she chose in a children's book. But a few important traits, and a great deal of the plot structure, are rooted in Aunt Claudia's inexplicable coldness. Perhaps the most important plot device related to her singleminded drive to make Lalla a skater is Uncle David's ability as mediator between the two households. Because he and Harriet's father attended the same school, the old-boy camaraderie legitimizes the Johnsons in their reduced economic circumstances, strengthening the idea of a family's rootedness in other social networks at the same time that it emphasizes the class base of Streatfeild's novel.

Aunt Claudia's love for ostentation and social status (the Johnsons barely pass muster only because their old furniture is "good") makes her, ironically, her niece's best audience. She watches attentively as Lalla figure skates and free skates; unlike Lalla's Nana and her governess with their separate inner lives (Nana knitting contentedly as long as the child is safe, Miss Goldthorpe repeating Shakespeare in her head), Claudia knows and enjoys the spectacle of ice skating. Once Harriet's mother and Lalla's uncle—with the crucial help of the Johnsons' doctor—have rescued the girls from their estrangement and warmed Lalla's heart again after a metaphoric plunge through the thin ice represented by her aunt's false dream for her, even Claudia becomes acceptable and useful. At last her money will buy the right dream—Harriet's continued training to be a champion.

The home Aunt Claudia has constructed for Lalla is ruled by her despotic wishes for the girl's discipline as a skater. Everything is regulated so that Lalla must diet, must be tutored at home, must spend most of her time at the rink. But with money comes its comforts in a Streatfeild novel, not the least of which is Nana, promised a handsome sum in the will of Lalla's dead mother if she stays until Lalla is grown. Nana has the usual kindly aspect, knitting fine wool underwear for Lalla and Harriet to wear when skating. Though she tries most of the time to avoid insubordination, Nana will not have certain things in her nursery: her child will not go hungry, and she will not be deprived of a friend. Thus, Lalla can make dripping toast at teatime, and Harriet can be camouflaged—whisked out of the patched jersey or rusty velvet from home and temporarily clothed in Lalla's things when she visits and may be seen by the aunt.

Fortunate in her nurse, Lalla is even luckier in her governess, as most children in the Streatfeild "Shoe" books are. In this case "Goldy" chooses her job so that she will not have to become a headmistress at a school. When she sees Lalla's playtime eliminated by Claudia in order to visit shops and be fitted for exhibitions, Goldy gives up her Saturdays to offer "lessons" about London, taking Lalla to plays or on excursions with her own funds. One of these excursions is the opportunity for Olivia to have time with Lalla and clear the way to having Lalla recover from her fear of failure. Having said she wanted to be in a family when she met the Johnsons, Lalla is cured by the same doctor who sent Harriet to the skating rink.

The network of kind adults paid to care for Lalla includes a skating trainer who shepherds Harriet from beginner to potential champion in just two years and who advises against Lalla's being pushed too fast through her tests for medals. He asks to teach Harriet as well as Lalla, once Lalla herself has taught the "daddy longlegs" to move on the ice, for the sheer pleasure of developing a talent he sees and also because he believes Lalla will do better at her figure skating if she has some competition. Thus Harriet is given lessons with Lalla all day—ballet and fencing as well as skating. Streatfeild's depiction of her growth as a skater thus combines a story of childhood play with sound psychology, and a recognition of how a latent talent would be lost without "knowing the right people."

Angela Bull sees Lalla as the heart of the book. True, she is a spirited girl, something like Miranda of *Theater Shoes*, and having a talent for mimicry Nana has encouraged. Yet Harriet, too, has spunk: her initial conversation with the doctor about her daily trips to the river make her "colder and colder and bored-er and bored-er" (*SS*, 7), initiating the chain of events. Moreover, she voices a concern of the conservative author about bureaucracy, describing how at her convalescent home the beach designated for exercise was at the bottom of a cliff that she could not climb back up. The doctor mutters "Idiots!" and makes his private arrangement to give an extra visit to the skating rink owner.

Individual actions and distinctive character are not all that Streatfeild presents here, however. With a fabric of family life and the varied kinds of mothering offered by Olivia, Nana, and Goldy, and the essential interventions of the uncle, brothers, and instructor, the individual flair of Lalla and the quiet power of Harriet can offer them the prize of successful careers. In this novel the overriding issue of friendship and its high stakes takes precedence over even the usual Streatfeild emphasis on training and the satisfaction of performing. Still, while Harriet embraces her talent for figure skating, Lalla flies across the ice reveling in freedom.

Although the United States fascinated Streatfeild, her growing interest in the children's book world and its literary standards, and in English history and her own childhood memories, proved more powerful inspirations for her later years. The preservation of art forms and local community, and the changes necessitated or made possible in English families, seem a logical outgrowth of Streatfeild's war experience. Her journeys from home after the war (she had visited Holland on a government program as well as gone to California) seem to have made her content with her household as well as her vocation as children's writer. Streatfeild's brief 1950 toy book, *Osbert*, featured children's concern for their dog, a bedraggled-looking part-poodle. Their savings, pooled in a committee meeting, provide him with a permanent and bowtie. Spiffed up, the pet is "the most beautiful dog in the world."[8] Jane's dog, Chewing Gum; Fortesque of *Myra Carroll*; and Streatfeild's own dog, Pierre, participated along with Osbert in her stories of domesticity as an adventure worth preserving, even in the context of bombs, ration books, and the relativity of time, place, and personal identity. A final book of the period, *The Theater Cat* (1951), a toy picturebook in which a cast adopts a cat who likes the theater, indicates Streatfeild's willingness to be playful with her central concerns of domesticity and drama.

Chapter Six

Fiction and Drama: A Transition, 1952–1961

Streatfeild's last four novels for adults—three of them stories of conventional women or families and one, *Aunt Clara* (1952), more playful with the notion of family and household—mark her gradual abandonment of a form she had used to explore childhood, family, and economic themes. Still convincing in their descriptions of domestic life but resisted by some reviewers because of their wordiness and melodrama, the novels relied more on third-person narration and less on revelation through dialogue than works such as *The Whicharts* and *Saplings*. Streatfeild's talent with dialogue, however, found an outlet in a play, *Many Happy Returns* (1953), and in radio scripts begun as a new venture in the 1950s.

Many Happy Returns

Early in the period of her last adult novels Streatfeild collaborated with her friend Roland Pertwee, who had helped in the publication of *The Whicharts* by sending the manuscript to his agent. Together the two old friends wrote a funny play reminiscent of Oscar Wilde. This comedy of manners and money satirizes greed among family members as they try to prove worthy of inheriting an old woman's money and pokes fun likewise at youthful idealists, romance, and innocent "church ladies" like those in numerous stories of vicarage life Streatfeild told during the latter part of her life. Though the innocent Aunt Ada has unwittingly signed a legal note to pay for church repairs, she is rescued by an old man with a cynical view and a keen knowledge of the law. First, however, some hilarity is generated by Ada's would-be suicide; family members substitute port for poison, and teetotaling Ada does not know the difference until she wakes up, befuddled.

Despite the fast-moving plot and comic repartee, the play was presented only on single occasions, and Streatfeild and Pertwee did no further joint writing. As an indication of Streatfeild's interest in older characters' perspectives, and as an example of the clash of worldliness and innocence her vicarage life had demonstrated, the play stands as an interesting variance in a prolific writer's history. Using the same sense of timing needed for theater comedy, Streatfeild enjoyed more success with her radio scripts and children's novels of the decade.

Mothering Sunday

Without the historical context of war and without the unambiguous alliance with children's experience typical of Streatfeild's best novels, *Mothering Sunday* (1950) depends on a problem-solving format unlike the philosophic or experimental approaches of contemporaries like Elizabeth Bowen, Ivy Compton-Burnett, and William Golding, yet also unlike the romantic plots of domestic novels by Rumer Godden and other popular women writers. Streatfeild's story of an older woman draws on some of her tried and true methods—various points of view within a family converging in a constellation of mother-love or emotional warmth, class differences used to underscore diverse family situations, and the interweaving of plot strands through a dramatic conflict. Yet one reviewer[1] claimed to be reminded of Virginia Woolf's *The Waves* (1931) because of a tonal quality Streatfeild conveyed through the perspectives of Anna Caldwell and her five grown children. The moral issues at the heart of the book—how to trust one's history and practice as a parent and how to accept the complexities of family systems—are treated with compassion and optimism rather than with the irony of Streatfeild's earlier family novels.

Anna, the protagonist of *Mothering Sunday*, observed first in her garden and a bedroom cluttered with family pictures, is believed by her part-time housekeeper to "have her little ways" typical of failing old people. These include a distancing style when the names of her children—Henry, Jane, Margaret, and Felicity—are brought up. The name of a fifth, Tony, cannot be mentioned in polite company. Anna is preoccupied, refuses to have her beloved granddaughter, Virginia, to visit—even though she has nearly raised the girl—and goes on mysterious drives in her old car. Warned by the housekeeper, Anna's family prepares to converge on her to check on her health and safety.

The reader learns midway, the family at the end, that Anna is hiding Tony in her house. He is an army deserter in trouble with the law. Besides his desertion, his crimes include carrying a gun and breaking and entering. Not insignificantly, he carried the gun in order to express solidarity with another outlaw who wanted to lend it to protect Tony, and he broke into a house thinking it was his sister Margaret's and believing she would condone the act. Tony's marginality is thus linked to his tendencies to form questionable affiliations. Anna proceeds to compare the bond she and Tony have maintained—a bond different from the reserved behavior she exhibits toward her older son, Henry. The tradition of the "stiff upper lip," often advocated for boys in Streatfeild's children's books but shown to be alienating in her adult fiction, is scrutinized by Anna and her daughter-in-law Carol, whose American insistence on the centrality of mothering the novel both critiques and endorses.

Although Anna wants to consult her daughters' husbands for legal help, she remains silent because Jane has lost a son in the war and Felicity's marriage seems loveless. So she attempts to persuade her much-loved youngest son to turn himself in to the police. Only when the family converges, however, bringing the grandchildren because Felicity and Carol (Henry's American wife) resist Jane's rigid plans, does Tony finally take the mature step of protecting his mother by surrendering. Tony attains "manhood" by an action predicated on a ceremonial falsehood. The resolution is effected through a staged conversation planned by the sons-in-law after a grandchild's dog reveals Tony's presence. Henry also resolves his childhood pain and sense of lack by engaging in the artful conspiracy planned by the other men, thus becoming at last a protector of Anna (rather than, in Oedipal terms, her rejected suitor). The men's awareness of the children's discovery results from the two sons-in-law having a major importance in childrearing.

In the course of the story Anna's mothering of each child is remembered as they prepare to visit her. Henry, reserved and seemingly cold to his mother, recalls his inability to hold her love through his dutiful achievements. Jane remembers being shunted to boarding school when her father died, while Margaret—a single physician who lives with another woman—remembers thriving. Felicity—always unpredictable and "vague"—has a quarrel with her mother because she thinks Anna supported Felicity's adultery and expects traditional standards from her. Tony, shown only in conversation with Anna, offers her the devotion she thinks has ruined him; she regrets not sending him away to school and having used Felicity and Tony to assuage her loneliness when her husband died.

Margaret's views, filtered through her woman friend's mind, offer a middle child's reconciliation for everyone. Margaret alone understands Jane's bitterness at losing her son in the war and subsequent neglect of her other children for immersion in social causes; she remembers a childhood when their brother Henry understood brilliant Jane, and when Jane was bonded through that relationship with all of the family. Now

Jane's inability to accept the death of her son places her in rebellion against public authority. She laments Tony's surrender as if it were a sign of weakness, and the novel ends with Anna's "pity for her blindness."

The old woman, Streatfeild suggests, now accepts the inevitability of what Lacanian critics call the law of the Father. Her reconciliation with Felicity, however, shows this law as benevolent: rather than supporting adultery, her sharing of news that Felicity's lover was dead resulted from the care and concern extended by Felicity's husband, who has regarded the bond with the lover as one of friendship. Relationships are fluid, interdependent, and ongoing in this novel. The "rescue by men," abetted by children and a dog, works in the family's best interest. Nonetheless, the novel resists a complete endorsement of such a reality.

Jane's bitterness is left to be worked out, although solutions to pain do not come from the dead but the living. War may have precluded a resolution for her. Tony's presence in Anna's house, moreover, is invasive and depicted with some of Streatfeild's best irony, including Anna's crawling on her knees to discover cigarette ash he persists in dropping. And Carol's yearning for her boarding-school children is validated. *Mothering Sunday* thus points out some things women lose by conforming to the Law of the Father; Margaret and her woman companion are able to maintain suitable private and public lives, which the married women cannot. In fact, the "best" mothering is Margaret's mediation, rooted in her secure professional and domestic arrangements.

Aunt Clara

The last of Streatfeild's adult novels involving an unconventional household is one of her most amusing. *Aunt Clara*, an effective spoof of middle-class mores, uses Streatfeild's own experience more directly than do her other novels of the 1950s. An elderly, frumpy, and pious woman inherits her uncle Sydney's dubious wealth: a leased flat in London; a Cockney bookie-turned-valet, Henry; a saloon; five racing horses; 14 greyhounds; stock in gambling operations; two "putative" children who are circus performers; a former madame and four of her "girls."

Having startled her family by co-owning greyhounds and attending races with Margot—while gaining a good deal of weight—Streatfeild uses their mild consternation about her unconventionality as the occasion of a prank by the fictional Uncle Sydney. The old man, alone in his bomb-damaged flat when Henry arrives as a night safety warden, creates a partnership with the homeless Cockney. Sydney's eightieth birthday party is a calculated affront to the relatives, including the vicar Maurice and his wife, Doris. It takes place, however, only after Clara's kind and unobtrusive help in cleaning up the garbage dump the war and Henry had made of Sydney's drawing room. Combining the realities of postwar life—the difficulty of disposing of garbage, for example—with gentle fun about Clara's life as a kind of lay nun, Streatfeild depicts Clara's innocent path through the selfishness of her siblings and the questionable morality of Sydney's legacy.

As Aunt Clara—viewed with stout support by the nieces and nephews who remember her being summoned to nurse them in childhood illnesses—traces the nature of Sydney's property, she ponders the rights and wrongs of her actions, bursting into hymns when she needs to pray but always proceeding with confidence once she has discovered the "right" in a situation. Her decisions result in special attention to the horses and dogs, as Sydney directed, but also care for the dogs' elderly trainers (the woman a mirror image of Clara, albeit a Cockney) and punishment for the cruel abuser of the horses.

The two circus "children"—teenage trapeze artists named Andrew and Julie who are quite obviously not descended from Sydney—become virtual wards of Clara and the valet Henry, who form what Clara regards as a family in the leased flat in London. There Andrew is initiated into city pleasures by Henry, while Julie is tutored (at her request) in received pronunciation so that her courtship by Clara's solicitor will proceed appropriately. Clara continues to investigate "her" saloon and what is, in effect, "her" house of prostitution. Meanwhile, she manages to fend off, kindly, the moves of her family—Maurice's to have her house his daughters in the flat and a niece's to have her take responsibility as a godmother for a new baby. Clara's quiet death occurs after she writes a will giving Henry the saloon, Julie the long-term inheritance (Andrew is on his way to stardom), and lifetime security to the old dog trainers, the madame, and the prostitutes Sydney bequeathed her.

While not as subtle, compact, or touching as a Barbara Pym story, *Aunt Clara* does show Streatfeild's commonality with this now famous author of the same era. The "dotty" old woman has the same steady values as Pym's aging Anglicans. But the interest in animals, formation of a class-diverse household, and tolerance for the foibles of family members are part of Streatfeild's usual repetoire. Humorously depicting how a "saint" views ordinary life, the novel suggests Streatfeild's retrospective enjoyment of her father's sometimes incomprehensible goodness.

Judith

Judith (1956), written after Streatfeild had branched into nonfiction for children that emphasized the value of an English heritage, uses an exile framework to tell a girl's coming-of-age story. Judith is reared by her divorced mother, a writer living abroad, and by a devoted governess, Miss Simpson. She spends much of her time daydreaming that Miss Simpson's unconditional love is actually the way her cold mother feels about her. When her remarried father returns to England from the United States and asks that she attend his sister's wedding, Judith is introduced to her father's mother and a number of aunts on both sides. Streatfeild ably describes the division within Judith as she enjoys her father but defends her mother. Later she parodies her mother's snobbish family, disgracing herself in front of the wedding guests, including her cousins the Carlyles. Returning to Europe, Judith reflects on the instability of love and the need to conform to others' expectations.

In the second half of the novel teenage Judith is abandoned by her mother, who summarily sends her to her father's siblings when she learns of her lover's death. Here the story draws on familiar Streatfeild territory: an extended family, aunts on both sides, with various viewpoints about what should be done with Judith; a stage school, where she encounters "Lance D'Espoir," a boy who subsequently involves her in his fencing of stolen jewelry; and sibling relationships among the Carlyles that exclude Judith rather cruelly. When Judith tries to borrow money for Lance from her former governess, the latter is alerted to the girl's desperate need for love. In a new plot twist for Streatfeild, the retired governess has the means to fly to New York and ask Judith's father and stepmother to send for the girl at once. Given stability and the steady love of the stepmother, Judith finally achieves emotional balance in marriage and motherhood.

Streatfeild disliked divorce and its effects on children, capturing this attitude in the novel. The various aunts who would help Judith if they could, and the hardened aunt, former war worker, and mother of the Carlyles who must, reluctantly, give her a home, offer realistic portraits of people immersed in their own affairs unable to connect with the homeless child and yet not entirely unsympathetic characters. The kindest people, except for Miss Simpson, are most ineffectual in helping Judith. Many comments by the narrator emphasize the vulnerability of a lone child, while depicting the Carlyles' bonds with one another.

The melodrama of Lance harkens back to the tawdry aspects of *The Whicharts* and other stage novels but seems poorly integrated into the family story. Judith's grandmother, however, does "see through" his self-characterization; like Anna Caldwell, she is an interesting depiction of an older woman who is a loving maternal figure but one unwilling to share her home entirely with a child. The "rescue by governess" occurs through the support a kind, wealthy aunt—a member of the peerage—has given Miss Simpson as manager of an old-age home founded by the aunt. As is true for many of the characters in Streatfeild's children's fiction where servants and foster mothers like the Fossils' Garnie form protective alliances, Judith's class position enables her safe passage. But Miss Simpson's enjoyment of her life is genuine—a theme Streatfeild continued to develop in her nonfiction about satisfying work.

The Silent Speaker

Busy with her many children's novels and nonfiction and with a new editing role, Streatfeild did not publish another novel for adults until 1961. *The Silent Speaker* uses a mystery plot to explore an aspect of female identity. Helen Blair, a beautiful woman, gives a selective dinner party. As the guests are driving home and her husband is driving his foster sister, Selina, to her hotel, Helen kills herself by placing her head in the oven. Guests from the party, including a journalist and a four-times-married woman, discuss their views of the afterlife while seeking an explanation for the suicide. They trace clues based on Helen's having read the daily paper after the party.

Meanwhile, Helen's husband, Tom, and a distraught Selina believe the Blairs' daughter, Verity, had read a letter from Tom to Selina and told Helen about it. The letter indicates that Tom and Selina have been lovers. Tom wants to tell the coroner about the past adultery, precluding a future marriage to Selina because of the scandal to the children of Tom and Helen. Through the efforts of the journalist and others, however, the plot suspense ends when a witness from Helen's wartime experience comes forward. He reveals that a soldier lost his life saving a cowardly Helen. The soldier's widow, though supported by an allowance from Helen, eventually died a suicide. That news prompted Helen's despair, not the awareness of Tom and Selina's attachment.

Like Streatfeild's other stories of unhappy women, such as *Myra Carroll* and *Judith*, her last adult novel traces unhappiness to early years marred by loss, usually of parents. But Helen Blair fails at war, not love, in her youth; this failure of courage explains her restlessness as well as her children's preference for the warm, settled Selina. Selina lives in Ireland, keeping the children every summer and representing Streatfeild's enjoyment of pastoral settings. Helen had deprived Tom of the chance to buy Tallboys, the manor once the home of Selina and Tom; Streatfeild links her to urban sophistication that is brittle at the core. The novel includes interesting dialogue "below stairs," as housekeeper and butler warily discuss the woman's death.

In presenting the dinner guests, however, Streatfeild uses direct narration in a confusing sequence. Besides the technical weakness, Streatfeild's last novel uses clichéd language to refer to guilt about sex, never resolving the conflict she set up between the institution of marriage and Selina's "natural" instincts. Ultimately more interested in family householding than family disintegration, Streatfeild felt no further compulsion to be a novelist for the adult market. In suggesting courage during wartime as a mark of a successful female life, she explored a theme that proved resonant in children's literature as well. In some ways the notion of patriotism she had developed during her war service became the grounding for a new identity—not as popular author but as critic and standard-bearer for children's literature and as advice-giver to children.

Chapter Seven

Children's Literature as Vocation, 1958–1978

Streatfeild's late adulthood can best be viewed in terms of her simultaneous production of nonfiction and fiction. Her interest in the past and in social mores characteristic of her nonfiction helped to uncover new areas for fiction writing. The fusion of fiction and nonfiction in her autobiographical books gave her a new outlet for her narrative skills at a time when she had given up writing novels for adults yet was exploring her vicarage roots through the humorous Bell family radio programs and novels. The story of William Streatfeild's aging nanny, a beloved figure from childhood, indicates how well Streatfeild understood the sources of her creative energy.

Nonfiction grounded this period but was inspired by the novelist's family, class, and nation. Nonfiction earned her money to maintain her household and life-style; more than that, however, it made her certain of her narrative voice when old age might have diminished the children's author as changing literature fashions ended her writing of novels for adults.

From 1950 until 1977 Streatfeild wrote nonfiction and edited anthologies, more than 30 books in all. At the start of the 1960s she abandoned adult fiction, and her children's novels changed so much that *Apple Bough* (1962) became the last book perceived as a "Shoe" book (*Traveling Shoes*). Her radio scripts about the Bells offer a humorous view of the conditions that caused her pain in childhood (a too-saintly father, hand-me-downs, and lack of distinction at school). She created in Cathy a particularly effective mother figure. Simultaneous with these creations were the first autobiographies, generated by an invitation from her American publisher, Helen Hoke Watts, after Streatfeild spent several hours entertaining her with vicarage memories. As Streatfeild wrote the autobiographical works she produced children's novels such as *The Magic Summer*, reflecting a deepening understanding of the past as her source of inspiration.

Even the Gemma Bow books of the late 1960s, for all of their
description of popular music, culminate in the successful rendering of
historical stage roles by Gemma, whose personal journey as an adolescent mirrors the one described in the autobiographies. *Gran-Nannie* supplies the same kind of biographical footnote for Streatfeild's career as a
writer that the autobiographies do, pointing to the aged Emily
Huckwell as an explanation for the writer's values and voice.

The Bell Family: Radio and the "Shoe" Formula

If Streatfeild's first children's novel about a vicarage family had
tapped into a new vein of memory by depicting parish pageantry as
national community, her novels about the Bell family narrow the focus
to the skirmishes with scarcity Streatfeild remembered from a childhood
spent in inappropriate clothing or in savoring of annual vacations for a
relatively large family. *The Bell Family* (1954) and *New Town* (1960)
(renamed, respectively, *Family Shoes* [1956] and *New Shoes* [1960]) concern the four children of Alex and Cathy Bell, who live in working-class
neighborhoods of London where the vicar's family stretches modest
resources to include the good schools, dancing lessons, and genteel furnishings experienced as necessities of the educated middle class. In addition to embracing the subject of a vicarage childhood for her children's
novels, these two books originated as radio scripts.

From 1949 to 1951 Streatfeild had written successful programs produced by Josephine Plummer, surpassing the popularity of previous children's programming in Britain (Bull, 203). While the novels based on
these scripts use familiar elements of Streatfeild's fiction, they do so in a
manner reminiscent of the radio medium. More episodic in structure
than a novel like *Party Shoes*, with its wartime healing and change, and
more dependent on the antics of a mischievous child (Ginnie, who calls
herself "Miss Virginia Bell") than on a serious crisis like that in *Skating
Shoes* (even though the latter was written at the same time Streatfeild
wrote the Bell scripts), the Bell novels highlight variations in voice and
tone, quick punch lines, and melodrama. They demonstrate Streatfeild's
gifts as a humorist and offer a rather new perspective on older traditions.

The audience of the Bell family radio programs was beginning to
recover from wartime scarcity and rationing. In fact, Britain was experiencing a transition to affluence featuring full employment and increased
mass consumption without paying attention to the needs of the elderly

or other groups outside the main economy.[1] Streatfeild's series dealt with the struggle to maintain social ideals in a consumer society. Without complaint (except in occasional frank chats with her mother), cheerful Cathy Bell cuts up hand-me-downs from callous nouveau riche relatives, fashioning a chair cover from a velvet skirt too dreary in color for her daughters, the ballet-gifted Jane and the broad-beamed, not-so-gifted, and yet central Ginnie (there are two sons, Paul and Angus). Living on his modest salary, which his wealthy industrialist father has refused to supplement with hard-earned "brass" because of his opposition to his son's decision to be a clergyman, Alex Bell and his family uphold values of absolute family solidarity, tasteful appreciation of fine but shabby furnishings, and intellectual and artistic accomplishment. The constant emphasis on clothes, food, shelter, education, and desirable leisure plunges the saintly but somewhat underplayed vicar into the stream of consumption despite his wish for a more spiritual existence.

Both sets of grandparents complicate the Bells' contentment, dangling more affluence in exchange for compromise, as in the case of Alex's father, or setting standards without being able, any longer, to contribute financially to the Bells, as in the case of Cathy's retired father, a physician. Alex's brother and family parade their wealth, spending money on programs for a ballet that might buy a dancing costume for Jane. But having affluent relatives affects the Bells in other ways; humor derives from the strange hand-me-downs of ball dresses from Aunt Rose, or from the ballet performances or zoo visits the grandparents provide. Ordinary circumstances of children's lives—the threat of quarantine for mumps that Ginnie may have contracted through her "satiable curiousity" (as she puts it in an appropriate allusion to "The Elephant's Child") or earnest efforts to help the family by earning money through piecework—turn the special occasions and the need for other holidays into heightened drama.

The family formula shifts from valuing a house as the site for ongoing reproduction and production, as it functions in *Ballet Shoes*, to the drawbacks and makeshift qualities of living in vicarages designed for another era and without the feelings associated with ownership. The six family members, not their property, become resources. Thus, Streatfeild endows both parents with warmth, charm, and immediacy. Frequent "togetherness" scenes appear; for example, after Ginnie scolds her paternal grandparents, uncle, aunt, and cousin for their absurd hoarding and pretentiousness, the Bells ride home together in the uncle's chauffered car, comforting Jane because all chance of the grandfather's paying for ballet lessons seems gone.

"Miss Virginia Bell" has made her father "very angry indeed," but his punishment for her—early bedtime for a week to correct the overtired condition he blames for the spirited articulation of the family's rage— evokes her "grand" response: "As a matter of fact . . . she gets bored hearing people talk, talk, talk, all the time."[2] Though familiar situations and characters appear—the dream of good dancing lessons for one child; the singing, loyal housekeeper who volunteers her time for some projects; the acute need for clothes; the loved dog who brings good fortune by winning a contest—the first Bell novel departs from Streatfeild's literary precedents other than the house-as-stability groundwork.

Just as the parents have greater visibility and effectiveness in the novel's episodes, the relationships among the four siblings diminishes in intensity. Even though Jane and Paul share a secret and mutually empower each other to keep their dreams of training to be a dancer and a doctor, respectively, the dramatic focus resides in extreme actions each child takes rather than in their loyalty or dialogue. For example, Jane faints because she is working too hard to save for a vacation; Paul almost mails a letter to the grandfather agreeing to enter his business and give up preparing to be a doctor. Solutions to the older children's pain come through the antics of the younger children. Ginnie unwittingly lets the grandfather know of the need for a holiday (he is her kindred spirit, successful at drawing out her imagination as well as her wrath). Angus demands dancing lessons as his birthday wish, winning the grandfather's support and ultimately leading to Jane's being given a scholarship by her school.

Though intertwined in these plot events, the siblings' actions are essentially separate. In part, this development heightens humor and suspense needed for the original medium, but it also suggests a shift in Streatfeild's understanding of her difficult childhood. Ginnie is the center of the family; her parents spend much of their time dealing with the situations she creates. "Miss Virginia Bell" is more complex than other mischievous children in Streatfeild's books, such as Nicky Heath of *Tennis Shoes*. Sewing flowers onto her mother's only dress, Ginnie is a loving and imaginative nuisance-to-be-nurtured; Alex will not permit Cathy and Jane to reveal their horror at the transformed dress. In the more idyllic family scene Streatfeild offers, Ginnie Bell shines as its center. She is not the foil to the idyll but rather its best product. In some

ways Ginnie seems more autobiographical than Nicky Heath, because
Ginnie's willful imagination and conscious self-creation seems a "portrait
of the artist" in the making.

Streatfeild's work lent itself to radio because her multiple perspectives
and varied episodes worked as oral drama. The habit of using servants as
important characters, for example, meant that a variety of inflections
would be used. In addition, the device of having Mrs. Gage sing hymns
as she worked provided a humorous but vicarage-appropriate sound
effect as an episode began. Placing the vicarage in the city, Streatfeild
capitalized on street noise; in the neighborhood of London row houses
"people shout a lot, and bang a lot, and laugh a lot," and in the High
Street "there is an almost continuous street market of a very shouting
sort" (FS, 13), with Cockney peddlers contrasting with radios blaring
from stores. Scenes with the children returning one by one from school,
or of "discussions carried on in a shout" from various parts of the vicarage as the family gets ready to attend the ballet—Jane shouting to her
mother about bath salts, her mother answering from the kitchen but
also calling up to Angus about his shirt for the occasion—work well
with Streatfeild's emphasis on daily domestic realities and personality
differences. The medium brought out a propensity for one-liners, especially as spoken by "Miss Virginia Bell."

Streatfeild had earlier identified basic materials for the children's novel
in the notion of family economics and children's competence to sustain a
household through diligent work and prospective fame. Most of the
households were socially questionable environments. Now Streatfeild
moved toward offering the vicarage family as a besieged economic system
sustained mainly by its virtue and cleverness in drawing from other relatives. The Bells are socially questionable in their poverty, caused by Alex's
idealism in entering the church despite his father's disapproval. A long
journey from the Whichart-Fossil model, the Bells are amusing and likable, narrow and ordinary, but as much an idyll in their way as was
Garnie's family.

The second Bell novel, New Shoes, supplies the second half of the
story Streatfeild mentioned on a dedication page of the first. Relating a
familiar issue of childhood—the move to a new home in a place offering
both advantages and disadvantages—and drawing on her memories of
such a move in childhood, Streatfeild combined with these common and
personal perspectives the immediate context of a changing culture. The
book describes the Bells' move to Crestal New Town, a suburb of
London where a traditional village is now surrounded by forbidding

concrete apartment blocks for the burgeoning population displaced by the bombing and rebuilding of London. Just as the children of *Party Shoes* had spurred a community to a vision of the past that would heal the present, the Bells transform the alienated, uprooted parishioners into a vibrant community with room for all classes, ages, and regional or ethnic identities. As an example of how Streatfeild could rework central experiences and materials into a stunningly new story, the second novel starring "Miss Virginia Bell" is outstanding.

The success of *New Shoes* lies in part with its sound-based techniques. The narrative overview in the first chapter introduces the specific voices, inflections and themes of the six Bells, their dog, Esau, and Mrs. Gage, the mysteriously full-time housekeeper it would seem the Bells cannot afford. This time Mr. Gage's voice is introduced as well, his greengrocer's chant of "Cel'ry luverly cel'ry"[3] amplifying the combined urban-rural context soon to perplex the Bells and, in good measure, to be mightily assisted by Mr. Gage's shrewd understanding of both business and people. With the first event an unexpected call on Alex and Cathy by the bishop, the story moves into both humor and suspense by a rich depiction of Mrs. Gage's relationship with Cathy. Shifts in tone and mood offer lively dimensions to the plot as Cathy takes Mrs. Gage into partial confidence about the move, mollifying her by acknowledging that there is a secret.

The children's reaction when they hear the news of the move evokes predictable dilemmas about schools. Paul and Jane will be better situated for their schools, but the younger children will have to transfer. Ginnie surprises everyone by doing an about-face in her attitude toward her "school for poor clergymen's daughters," Saint Winifred's. She insists on staying, even though there will be no transportation. Here, of course, the plot thickens. But it is a superb characteristic of this novel that the seemingly unrelated episodes—Ginnie's startling welcome of her whiny, rich cousin Veronica for a weekend, Angus's attachment to his array of goldfish, Cathy's decision to sell some of Aunt Rose's hand-me-downs to buy Jane a dress and thus align herself with her daughters rather than her husband—turn into thematic devices essential to the touching story embedded in the often hilarious doings of Ginnie.

Ginnie finagles a chauffered ride to Saint Winifred's by persuading Veronica to attend; by the end of the novel, once the context of a New Town community festival changes the dynamics of place and personalities, Ginnie's extravagant promise that spoiled Veronica will become an outstanding student has come true; the pet club started by Angus has become an inspiration for all kinds of other groups; and Cathy's desire for a garden causes the whole family to unite in resisting the crass but well-meaning offer of Alex's father to pave and decorate a cement rock garden.

As in *Party Shoes*, a manor house and its remaining residents contribute significantly to the success of New Town Days, the flea market/fair/circus Ginnie and the old admiral think of together. Unlike the war novel, however, this story faces the newness of the community. Land to be purchased for a community center is the site of the almost-miraculous pulling together of the parish. The ancient village, with its vicarage garden and manorial grounds, becomes a basis not of the New Town center but of Mr. Gage's start as a farmer, fulfilling his long-held dream of growing what he sells. Streatfeild deftly manages to satirize industry—Uncle Alfred thinks of bishops as mill owners deploying workers, not calling vicars to new ministries—yet emphasizes productivity, industriousness, talent, and training in the family and townfolk.

One example of how she focuses on group projects and community identity through individuals' contributions is the way Mrs. Taylor, an embittered woman grieving for a family troubled by the move to New Town, is instantly revived by the prospect of sewing 200 dance costumes for Jane. Her children return home to boot, now that New Town is interesting. Different from earlier treatments of the pageantry or community theme, this novel skillfully employs humor as the medium for very profound truths well known to its audience but in danger of obliteration. "Fat Ginnie in her pink dress, and her ridiculous poem" (*NT*, 147) at her father's farewell party, Alex calling on New Town residents in a refurbished old car and using a loudspeaker to explain his wish to meet the members of his new parish, and the family talking nearly at once when they realize the contributions each can make to bringing people together are among the funny but powerful moments in which the plot becomes another example of Streatfeild's versatile reordering of the memories of youth and the contingicies of the present. No longer earning a living but making a life, the Bell children represent Streatfeild's growing perception that the narrowness of a parish was a valuable artistic source.

Other "Shoe" Novels

Between *Family Shoes* and *New Shoes* came another formulaic family story of the late 1950s, *Dancing Shoes* (1957), which plays on themes of artistry and vocation more reminiscent of *Ballet Shoes* than *Party Shoes*. Published in England as *Wintle's Wonders* and drawing on the image of "Lila Field's Little Wonders," the children's dance troupe that fascinated Streatfeild as a child, the novel portrays the tension between high art and its popular forms. It examines with some irony the intent of Cora Wintle, owner of a stage school producing popular shows, to turn two orphaned sisters, Rachel and Hilary, into "Wonders."

Rachel, the niece of Mrs. Wintle's husband, Tom, is plain, sallow, and intent on carrying out her dying mother's wish that she help her adopted sister—the daughter of a dancer—to continue learning ballet. Hilary—attractive, trained, and ultimately without ambition—displays comic flair rather than artistic genius. Under the guidance of another of Streatfeild's important governess types, Mrs. Storm, Rachel turns out to be a "wonder" of the sort Streatfeild most approves: she loves Shakespeare and becomes an accomplished stage actress. With strategic guidance from a nanny type, Miss Purser, Hilary is a contented member of the troupe, and Rachel becomes a wiser, more sensitive and refined girl by the end of the story.

Always dreading her destiny as a "Wonder," Rachel cringes at the thought of wearing garish costumes and moving in step with the other girls. Different in coloring and body structure—a difference her artist uncle Tom recognizes and values—she needs only a new cut to her dress and a color like those her mother had chosen for her to catch the eye of a casting director for a play about a child orphan accepted for her own value.

Angela Bull cites *Dancing Shoes* as a stumbling block for Streatfeild (213), agreeing with the *Times* reviewer who saw the writer now imitating her own work. Yet the orphaned, special child and the girl resistant to authority are more the subject of Streatfeild's future work than of her past. The three Fossils, for example, form a triad of talent from the first, and "Miss Virginia Bell" operates forcefully within a loving nuclear family. Rachel's outbursts about Hilary's being molded into a "Wonder" are in danger of melodramatic misinterpretation such as the Fossils and Bells never impose on family members. Rachel seems jealous of Hilary, at least in Mrs. Wintle's eyes. Miss Purser (who owns the building where Wintle operates her school) and Mrs. Storm (who will not teach Hilary or the Wintles' spoiled daughter Dulcie unless she can continue to teach Rachel) oppose Mrs. Wintle successfully without upsetting the system in which everyone finds a place.

The girls of the troupe assist the orphaned sisters, and Streatfeild elaborates—as she had in *Circus Shoes* and *The Whicharts*—on the behind-the-scenes socialization of performing children. Though many of the elements of Streatfeild's literary repertoire appear in the novel, including what might be called the semiotics of clothing (Rachel's love for a marigold dress her mother bought her and ultimate regaining of the ability to wear orange well when her color returns) and an examination of heredity (Hilary is American by birth), the focus on what sisters are worth enriches the glitzy (albeit enjoyable) melodrama of the plot.

A crucial question raised by the novel is whether to value the training provided by the Madame Fidolias of the world (Hilary's original teacher is called Madame Raine) over the showy entertainment offered by Wintle-trained performers. While the depiction of Rachel as ugly-duckling-in-barnyard conveys class distinctions inherent in the idea of "genius," it is unfair to describe this preference as Streatfeild's unqualified view of the arts. Rather, Streatfeild conveys the multiple needs for entertainment rightfully claimed by a diverse public. The troupe members' enjoyment of television, for example, is presented as normal rather than debased, as one might expect in a novel valorizing a set of class-based aesthetic assumptions.

Streatfeild certainly participates in a discourse rooted in class stratification, and she writes from a privileged position. Yet her vicarage childhood imbued her with a theory of community more than merely tolerant of difference and quite strong in its vision of a social fabric dependent on all strands. In Rachel and Hilary's difference and sameness as sisters, in their diverse contrasts to Dulcie Wintle's overvalued yet nonetheless real talents, in Streatfeild's hearty appreciation of economic necessity as well its dangers of exploitation, *Dancing Shoes* stands with the rest of her novels about performing children as a clever, often profound, look at childhood. Rachel, Hilary, and Dulcie are "wonders" in their differences.

Traveling Shoes (1962) is the last of Streatfeild's family stories renamed by U.S. publishers to capitalize on the classic *Ballet Shoes*. Its English title, *Apple Bough*, accurately represents the quest for home this novel depicts; this title, however, conceals the topic of performing children also central to the work—a topic that sustained Streatfeild through the end of the 1960s despite her constant shifting from fiction to nonfiction. As she would in the later (1968) Gemma books, Streatfeild develops the theme that classical music, ballet, and popular music and dance are interrelated. In the Forum family of *Traveling Shoes*, each child is named for a great musician: Myra for Dame Myra Hess, Sebastian for Bach, Wolfgang for Mozart, and Ethyl (or Ettie) for Dame Ethyl Smith. But Sebastian's prodigious gift means the entire family—including parents

David and Polly and the indispensable Miss Popple—will travel with the child from one concert city to another over a period of four years. Wolf's desire to compose popular songs, Ettie's to dance (for Ninette de Valois, replacing Madame Fidolia as a reference point now that Streatfeild had become a historian of sorts), and Myra's gradually recognized talent for running a home all are subordinated in favor of Sebastian's talent with the violin until Miss Popple, or Poppy, intervenes by asserting her independence. Poppy's removal from the family, done deliberately as a helping gesture, requires new arrangements for all.

A summer in Devonshire with her grandparents and reacquaintance with the dog, Wag, she had reluctantly left at the start of Sebastian's tour brings to the foreground Myra's latent gifts for relationships and domesticity. As in many other Streatfeild books, including the autobiographical trilogy, the figure of a grandfather alters the outline of a family. Representing wisdom and care for the future of all of the children, the grandfather inspires Myra to orchestrate new possibilities for Wolf and Ettie, to announce that their training in music and dance must continue in London. Besides guiding these two siblings, Myra discerns the cause of Sebastian's high fever after surgery; she alone realizes he is mourning a lost chance to own a rare violin. She visits Sebastian's manager at the Savoy, who makes clear his good intentions and immediately sends the violin to the sick child.

With each family member, except Myra, occupied with training and other professional work, Streatfeild draws together the early cues that Apple Bough is the family's true home. Sebastian buys the house for his sister; she, like Poppy before her, will create a centered household for the siblings as they come and go, and even for the parents, who will take a London flat in order to continue supervising the young children.

The descriptions of various cities and the unique characterization of each of the siblings lend interest to this novel. In the delineation of homemaking as a valued occupation, however, Streatfeild struck a new and prescient note. Unlike earlier books like *The Whicharts* and *Ballet Shoes* in which Rose and Garnie conducted households by default and as instrumental to children's careers, the focus throughout *Traveling Shoes* remains on the oldest child's skills at managing daily life. Polly, the mother, prefers being a painter to being a housewife, even though she enjoys playing with and socializing her children. Before Poppy came to work for the family, the Forums had led a chaotic domestic life, with the children in shabby clothes and the meals from tins. Without implying Polly deficient—she has the same vagueness all of the artistic family members exhibit, with only Myra and Poppy "clear"—Streatfeild demonstrates the tensions and choices that would become common for middle-class families after the 1960s. Polly's initial insistence on the whole family traveling with Sebastian was contingent on Poppy's accompanying them; though the class implications of the plot are clear, the gender-role implications enrich the picture.

Poppy is a most admirable figure, a worthy model for the daughter of the family who excels at the same things Poppy is good at. Streatfeild's emphasis is on choice and on individual variation. Like Charlotte Perkins Gilman in the beginning of the twentieth century, Streatfeild seemed to advocate specialization of functions. Her benign view of the class system—like earlier families she created, this one acquires the services of a Cockney couple willing to move to the country with Myra—cannot be overlooked. Yet Streatfeild's keen insight about the "management" aspects of domestic life gives this novel a refreshing wit and an up-to-date tone during an era when feminist theorists in the United States stress the importance of domestic work, whether done in private households or in public service positions. Contingent on choice and specialization as it is, Myra's vocation takes its place beside that of other family members.

The issue of homemaking—a personal mystery to Streatfeild, who was clumsy and disorganized in all endeavors related to it—surfaced again in her later novels, where children learned daily survival out of necessity or democratized families shared in household tasks. Myra, at the center of a family plan they call "Operation Home," enables the family to survive fame, distance, and the loss of tradition threatened by having its decisions made by agents and publicists. Streatfeild thus elaborates on a major Western postindustrialist pattern: the quiet domestic daughter is a vital link in civilization even during childhood.

Other Children's Novels

Although the 1950s and 1960s included Streatfeild's branching into nonfiction and radio scripts, followed by her abandonment of fiction for adults in the early 1960s, her disciplined writing habits and increasing interest in children's books as a cultural field enabled her to produce a number of novels other than those labeled "Shoe" books. Many were notable for Streatfeild's ability to take current topics and explore them humorously yet with a degree of seriousness as well. Likewise, her fiction for children allowed her to turn her own experiences into marketable works, even when that experience was unpleasant or extravagant.

Between 1963 and 1979 Streatfeild wrote eight such books, at least two of which—*The Magic Summer* (1967) and *When the Siren Wailed* (1977)—are arguably among her best works. In addition, she wrote two clusters of books drawing more on literary convention than on personal experience: the Victorian melodramas based on Margot's mythic orphanhood, *Thursday's Child* (1970) and *Far to Go* (1976), and the series of Gemma Bow novels begun in the 1960s. Some critics see this period as a general falling off in the quality of Streatfeild's writing for children, but even those of her books thought shallow offer some important sociohistorical representations.

Several of the novels give insights into Streatfeild's political and cultural views. For example, *Lisa Goes to Russia* (1963), the aftermath of an uncomfortable trip Streatfeild took in 1960, examines the tension between individualism as the English practice it and group values as the main character's Russian cousins articulate them. Though nine-year-old Lisa initially resists the austere living conditions and shared property she finds in the Soviet Union, Streatfeild allows her to take on the culture of her cousins, wearing an apron and baboushka when they go to a dacha and admiring the ballet and circus training of her older cousins. On the whole, however, the book is decidedly Anglocentric. Descriptions of crowded apartments, "ugly" lamps, and slow travel reflect some of Streatfeild's disagreeable experiences in the country.

The many humorous touches based on Russian domestic life—the children flood a hotel room when a faucet will not turn off, and shopping amounts to a "Mad Hatter's Tea Party" Lisa enjoys—and the interesting descriptions of ballet history make the book an example of Streatfeild's ability still to turn difficult circumstances into a narrative valuing art and culture. The book has a relatively simple structure, since neither Lisa's siblings nor the adult figures are developed. In fact, distance from adult figures, especially parents, is characteristic of this group of novels—a sign that Streatfeild was responding to a children's literature market defined by the Enid Blyton books and by an older tradition in children's fiction in which substantial action occurs in the absence of grownups. The absence of figures like Garnie, Nana, and Poppy who previously played such important roles demonstrates a versatility unusual in such a prolific and relatively popular author. Sales of Streatfeild's books remained steady throughout her lifetime, rivaling those of C. S. Lewis's books while rarely equaling the popularity of Enid Blyton's (Bull, 238).

Skill with story lines and humorous depictions of changing social conditions often kept Streatfeild afloat when her abilty to travel or encounter new people limited her access to story material. A 1964 novel, *The Children on the Top Floor*, satirizes both her own expanding girth and the ways that television creates reality. Surrounded by "women shaped liked cottage loaves with a head on top," television star Malcolm Master (referred to as "Mistermaster") is comfortable at home with his mother and his old nanny. But his television character announces a desire to be a daddy. Through this metafictional device, Streatfeild re-creates Gum, the Fossil father. Four babies are left on his doorstep. Initially referred to by their wrapping or conveyance, they are called Bathinette, Rug, Carryall, and Basket until a TV producer suggests nursery rhyme names: Tom (Thumb), Lucy (Locket), Margery (Daw), and William (Wee Willy Winkie).

Continual references to the artificial and superficial enliven the story of these children, who—like the Dionne quintuplets—grow up in an orchestrated, commercial environment under contract just as Mistermaster is. To the rescue comes not a landed grandfather, as in many Streatfeild books, but the other familiar intelligence—a governess who resists Nanny's passive acceptance of her controlled environment in favor of teaching the children about ordinary reality through hands-on experiences. A trip through the city to a pet shop, for example, engages their attention. It also introduces their first delayed gratification—a desire for a puppy. Coinciding with the governess's plan to offer a life free of television and enriched by Shakespeare and other cultural knowledge, the children's desire for a puppy precipitates a gradual disintegration in the artificial domestic space. Illness, work, and the abdication of Mistermaster bring out talent in the children and alter their interpersonal relations to include ordinary tensions. Mistermaster returns to a changed top floor, with the implication that—despite the comforting steadiness of Nanny through it all—the world of television fantasy will never loom as large again as the world of work, play, and human relatedness.

Throughout the 1960s Streatfeild published copiously. Two novels in 1967 suggested the resonance of the family novel in her hands, with its depiction of children immersed in economics and in shaping material culture. In *Caldicott Place* (published in 1968 as *The Family at Caldicott Place* in the United States) Streatfeild used a spare style and highly structured plot devoid of the eccentricity of many of her enduring works. Yet her sure touches—a dog that brings back to life an amnesiac father, a house that offers redefinition of a family and its livelihood, and the interrelatedness of village workers and manor residents—make this story of suburbanites-turned-country-dwellers work.

Using both coincidence and predictability to advantage, Streatfeild depicts a somewhat errant youngest child, Tim, as the family's source of renewal. Tim disobeys instructions, trying to visit his father, who is in the hospital after a car accident. Clutching flowers grown by his father, Tim wanders into the room of the woman whose chauffeur caused the accident and leaves the gladioli with her. Her will names the nine-year-old heir to a mansion in the country; instead of life in a cramped flat because of the father's illness, the family finds transformation in the pastoral setting. Between Christmas and Easter, cutting their own wood and keeping their own rooms heated, the three Johnstone children and the three wards of their solicitor who help to pay the bills become a "clan instead of a family," as the ballet-trained daughter tells her recovered father.

Though not funny as the Bell family are, the Johnstones have Tim's fortunate naïveté and the melodramatic character of one of the wards to both lighten the story and make it move toward an ending in which a gardening father and a housekeeping mother will ground their livelihood in rearing children other than their own at Caldicott Place. In contrast to stories where children earn money to keep a house, here a house enables parents to earn money to keep children.

One of many books in which Streatfeild explored her childhood memories of her grandparents' house, *Caldicott Place* reiterates a theme of stability through place, contrasting with adventure formats common to many family novels. No rescue from an island, no threat from marauders shapes the plot; the suspense revolves around the father's recovery through Tim's unerring sense of what to do, and around the character conflicts within an expanding family in need of their father. Convenient guidance from retainers—the housekeeper and the solicitor—and close cooperation from the housekeeper's married daughter enhance the plot's predictability while maintaining a variety of perspectives. With a few pages at the beginning of the novel describing the skills of the children's father—he gardens, fixes things, organizes parties and outings— Streatfeild makes plausible his willingness, after recovery, to become a sort of innkeeper-father at Caldicott Place, giving up his factory job and suburban life.

Making the household a place of production, Streatfeild critiques the excesses of individualism and private property inherent to the suburban life of the Johnstones and to the failures of modern life behind the homelessness of the three wealthy wards. Like *The Magic Summer*, written during the same period, *The Family at Caldicott Place* demonstrates the power of Streatfeild's personal past as a source of storytelling.

Angela Bull notes that *The Magic Summer* (published in England as *The Growing Summer*) is both one of Streatfeild's best children's novels and the last to receive critical acclaim (Bull, 233). As Bull adds, however, Streatfeild continued to write prolifically even after a stroke in 1968, and her books held their own with the reading public; occasionally, in fact, her nonfiction broke new ground. Looked at as a partial self-portrait as well as a second critique of suburban "ticky-tacky" (Bull, 233), Streatfeild's sole novel about Ireland adds powerfully to the work of her later decades.

In *The Magic Summer* Streatfeild draws on a friendship with Rachel Leigh-White begun during the air raids. Streatfeild visited her friend's seaside house in western Ireland annually, and the house was featured in the television film made from the book in 1968. Many details of the text are autobiographical, including an account of catching a lobster and the contrast between magnificent scenery and simple, even primitive, domestic life.

The Magic Summer stands out among Streatfeild's children's novels in part because of the whimsy and eccentricity of poetry-quoting Great-aunt Dymphna, who must take in the four Gareth children when their father is ill. Witchlike and yet ultimately vindicated by the growth of the children at her Ireland seaside home, Dymphna at one level seems a fantasy creature, rare in Streatfeild's work. At another level she represents Streatfeild herself—inept and impossible at ordinary domestic tasks yet transcendent in her knowledge of how to live: "Help yourselves, children, help yourselves."[4] Another facet of this character is her communion with nature; the sea gulls "tell" her things before cables do. Dymphna's fantasy, values, and groundedness in nature are imparted to the children, who leave Ireland with no offer of another visit by their privacy-loving aunt but knowing poetry, the vital significance of housework and each person's responsibility for it, and the magnificence of nature as source of food and habitat.

As Bull points out, Streatfeild uses shifting viewpoints skillfully; Dymphna cannot be replicated as a nanny or a governess can be. The children must make what they can of the challenges and questions she poses for them; she represents not the stable world in which various classes live under a common roof but the mad (not insane, as the children are told) view of those who know enough to question convention. Perhaps, like their father, they will never be completely at home in suburbia again but will share his hunger to be free and alone with objects of consuming interest unvalued by others. Dymphna collects odds and ends from household sales; her nephew collects germs from rare places. Poet and scientist, they see beyond the ordinary.

At Reenmore, Dymphna's huge and dilapidated house, the ordinary is unavailable. Plumbing does not work. Food must be gathered and cooked, water hauled, order made within ultimate chaos. Much of the book depicts Penny, the eldest girl, trying to cook, clean, and wash; at the end of the story it has become clear that her efforts cannot—even should not—succeed, because "Penny is a fool. The more you do the more you may" (*MS*, 189). Dymphna sandwiches this remark between an admonition to Alex, the eldest boy, that sailors do their own laundry, and a quick recitation about the Jumblies going to sea in a sieve. Sudden twists like this one between moral guidance and nonsense are common to the book, which juxtaposes small struggles to boil eggs and wash dishes with cobwebbed corners of the house and midnight adventures on the beach. In commenting on the artistry of the novel, Bull dismisses a subplot as irrelevant, but—while certainly reminiscent of conventional children's books—the story of the hidden boy, Stephan, serves to highlight the value of helping oneself, of making one's own living in a most basic sense.

Stephan is a film star who hides in Reenmore, coercing Alex and Penny to shelter him by claiming to be fleeing from Communists. Keeping the younger children out of the secret, the older ones complicate the situation; it seems that Naomi and Robin might have detected the boy's identity. Like a worm lodged in an apple, Stephan is a spoiler. He demands food, then complains when it does not suit him. In part an obstacle to be dealt with and successfully integrated into their routines, Stephan also represents the children's failure to understand what Dymphna's house means to her. His querulousness and usurpation of space, his incompetence, parodies theirs. A neighbor explains about Dymphna's love for her home and space, but this didactic intervention is less convincing than the very incongruity of selfish, commercial, and exploitive life existing within the sanctuary Dymphna has struggled to create. The hidden boy is also like Dymphna, however, in needing a refuge and being relatively undeserving of the glories of Ireland. Consigned by Streatfeild to life with a tutor back in England, Stephan is smuggled out of Reenmore; just as abruptly the children return to Medway, their suburban house near London, when their father recovers. The ending recognizes Ireland's difference in time as well as in place.

Domesticity, during the magic or growing summer, becomes a sustenance one helps to produce and that in turn produces the self. In Medway the domestic is arranged by the children's mother. In Reenmore, Dymphna supplies basic ingredients—dried herbs, fishing gear to be unearthed, a neighbor to bring eggs, borrowed sheets—but the tempos of the household are unexpected, spontaneous, extreme, and almost never easily explained. Not a Robinsonade because Dymphna undercuts the conventional and yet supplies civilization in its most vital sense, the book is more a coming-of-age tale. Dymphna resembles Katherine Paterson's earth-mother Trotter of *The Great Gilly Hopkins* (1978) because, in the terms of the novel, her ways are unassailable even if not replicable.

Viewed in part as an autobiographical vignette—Streatfeild's ineptness at cooking or even doing her own hair were documented by Leigh-White, and she herself was a kind of refugee from contemporary life—the novel should also be recognized as Streatfeild's acknowledgment that she owed something to other writers. If the seacoast setting and plot about domesticity were from her store of memories, something about an interdependent set of siblings fending for themselves and acquiring a new sibling resembles quintessential children's literature. The book bears a dedication to Elizabeth Enright, "because I so greatly admire her books." Enright's Melendy children, left on their own at a country house, have a series of adventures culminating in their father's adopting the brother they have acquired (*Then There Were Five*, 1944).

Enright's early novel, *Thimble Summer* (1938), ranges over time and place through the effective technique of story-within-story; the book balances the orphan narrative with the domestic, suggesting through the thimble as talisman the magic of summer play at home. A hardiness of perspective presents flawed adults' impact on children's lives, despite the basically happy endings. Having assumed, through her nonfiction and editing projects of the 1950s and 1960s, a grande dame presence in the world of British children's literature, Streatfeild's gesture in old age toward an American writer of family novels seems to point to the complexity and richness of children's books. Like her own fictional youths, Enright's characters aspired to be dancers, composers, and the like, and their childhoods were spent in acquiring the culture that would make such lives possible.

In 1974, as she worked on autobiographical books, Streatfeild used her vivid memories of the London bombings and her work with Cockney families in Deptford to produce one of the few novels in which she focused on working-class children. *When the Siren Wailed* uses a tight narrative style and fast-paced, detailed dialogue to describe how three children from a poor family experience the war. Taking care to explain class differences, mainly between the Cockneys and lower-middle-class families in a Dorset village where the London evacuees are sent, Streatfeild offers brief narrative comments to explain the children's manners and clothing. For example, when nine-year-old Laura shows her fascination with a sewing box, Streatfeild contrasts how Laura's mother had kept a needle and thread out of reach of the children; she mentions here and elsewhere in the novel the effects of long-term unemployment on families like Laura's.

Despite their poverty, the Clarks are loving parents, and the book is structured around the children's escapade of returning home to London during the bombing. Their street is nothing but rubble, their mother found only through the help of civilian defense workers, and their needs met by canteen workers like Streatfeild herself. In what seems at first an artificial twist, the Clarks are billeted again in Dorset with a ballet-practicing girl, Dulsey, whose family takes advantage of the space they are assigned. As the plot unfolds, however, Dulsey's family becomes part of Streatfeild's theme of how different groups lived in one another's homes and found ways to survive and even enjoy their time together.

Among Streatfeild's novels for children, *Siren* is notable for its historical setting and accurate detail. Attitudes toward Neville Chamberlain and Winston Churchill, the rescue of troops at Dunkirk, and the devastation of London are integral to the family narrative. In a link to adult novels such as *Saplings*, with its grandfather-rescuer, Laura and her two brothers instead lose their Dorset squire-protector to death. They are reunited with their parents through their own efforts and the help of many war workers, some of them other Cockneys. The epistolary segments and the network of information add to the book's historical authenticity.

Thursday's Child and *Far to Go*

Other Streatfeild works of the 1970s that reach back in time but are associated more with storytelling finesse than with historical memory are the two she spun from the combined power of her friend Margot's alleged birth to an unwed daughter of a gentleman and the imaginative

appeal of her grandparents' manor. *Thursday's Child* tells of Margaret
Thursday, an orphan supported by a mysterious bequest and supplied
with "three of everything," including Sunday underwear. Determined to
evade a cruel matron, she and three other children collude. One girl,
Lavinia, works as a maid while Margaret protects the girl's two little
brothers. With a furious energy drawn from a feeling that "the mother
she had never known was encouraging her to assert herself,"[5] Margaret
escapes by the light of the moon, disguising herself as a boy and hiding
among canal people. Though Lavinia and her little brothers prove to be
gentry related to the owners of the manor where Lavinia works,
Margaret resists domestication by the same family, insisting that "I'm
Margaret Thursday and I only need me" (*TC*, 216) and that she had her
own mother. Fast-paced and suspenseful, filled with amusing allusions to
Little Lord Fauntleroy and to *Bleak House*, the whimsical tale was made
into a television film.

In the sequel, *Far to Go*, Margaret is staying with a family of actors.
Her success as an actress, however brings trouble: the cruel Matron of
the previous novel attends one of the plays and recognizes the runaway.
Escaping as she had before, through a window, Margaret manages to
vanquish the cruel woman. Once again, her victory comes on the heels of
powerful anger. Somewhat like Pippi Longstocking, Margaret refuses to
end her orphan status by staying with a willing family; she has "far to
go." Perhaps the two Margaret Thursday books were an outlet for
Streatfeild as she produced several books depicting children's growth
within families. Just as Margot represented an unusual alliance for a
vicar's daughter, Margaret is a feisty sibling to the family-seeking Fossils
and other Streatfeild characters. The book's humor and the vividness of
the images associated with Margaret and her "Sunday underwear"
allowed Streatfeild to maintain her popularity with the public, if not
with the critics.

The Gemma Bow Series

The 1960s were Streatfeild's most prolific decade. Angela Bull suggests that her 1968 illness might have resulted from overwork, from
what Bull views as an obsession to produce more books (Bull, 238). Yet
as a chronicler of her times, Streatfeild found that the 1960s presented a
number of challenges. Perhaps the rapid authorship of four novels about
a child star's need for a family as well as for affirmation of her difference
was an attempt to record the shifts in musical taste of the 1960s and to

document that family life and national tradition could interact in valuable ways with modernity.

Dismissed as tasteless because of Streatfeild's apparent bowing to kitsch in describing plastic costumes (Cadogan and Craig 1986, 295) and viewed as mainly ephemeral and uninspired by other critics (Bull, 237), the Gemma books also constitute a new genre for Streatfeild: a series about a set of characters who move from childhood to adulthood, in the manner of L. M. Montgomery's Green Gables novels and the Betsy-Tacy books by Maud Hart Lovelace. Reissued in the late 1980s and still in print in the early 1990s, the Gemma stories merge the orphan tale with the family story and at the same time depict the struggle for vocation as both adults and children experience it. Parallel to Streatfeild's autobiographies depicting the integration and individuation of a difficult daughter, the saga of Gemma's development offers another forum for Streatfeild's vision of the family as primary educator but not isolated from social contexts shaping its choices.

In form the four Gemma Bow books—*Gemma* (1968), *Gemma and Sisters* (1968), *Gemma Alone* (1969), and *Good-Bye, Gemma!* (1969)—differ from such contemporaneous novels as *The Magic Summer*. Direct exposition is more prominent than distinctive dialogue, Streatfeild's usual technique. While this method deemphasizes originality of character, it does allow Streatfeild to spin a textured yarn, replete with the intrigues of show business and social mores. And while the child characters often speak in clichés, they also comment on one another's style in speech and behavior. For example, Gemma brings pseudo-sophistication from her life as a former child star, yet she knows little about music—an expertise of her aunt and uncle's family that she acquires during her time with them. One cousin, Ann, is the proper girl, like Meg March; another, Lyddie, is a copy of the Fossils of *Ballet Shoes*.

The Gemma books describe each child's independence and growth in a special talent: Ann sings, Lyddie dances, and their brother, Robin, composes or "swirls" tunes. Gemma shows herself multitalented as producer, singer, and banjo player before she is able to grow into a strong stage actress. The expository method allows this plot to carry a major theme of interdependence: the children lead separate lives, yet their simultaneous careers intersect in the act they form for a charity benefit, "Gemma and Sisters." The success of this act guarantees both financial security and the personal and professional growth of the children.

Adults play a major part in the series. Alice and Philip Robinson, parents of three, represent the "ideal" ordinary yet cultured English people.

Philip's career as a violinist is cut short by arthritis. Alice—the first of Streatfeild's mothers to function entirely without household help—takes a part-time job but continues to prepare three meals a day, with Ann doing tea. Low key and supportive, Alice contrasts with her movie-star sister, Rowena, whom she reared. At the outset she wonders if Rowena will ever need her again. When Rowena goes to Hollywood, she boards 11-year-old Gemma with the Robinsons. Gemma's gradual recovery from the pain of separation and rejection is the focus of the books. Philip understands Gemma's recognition of herself as "a very backward washed-up film star" and initiates her growth as a musician.

Only gradually does Gemma—by the third book—see herself as another Alice, a person who brings others together and is multitalented. Alice's daughter Lyddie retains empathy for Rowena, even when Gemma, hearing her movie-star mother lie to get a part, decides she does not respect Rowena any more. Like Paterson's Gilly Hopkins even in mailing a letter that precipitates a crisis—Gemma complains about school in order to find something to tell Rowena, and the latter insists on a change of school, threatening Gemma's growth as an actress—Gemma acquires the virtues of the Robinsons as well as sharing in their music.

The family stage act provides a new career for Philip, who is its agent. Lyddie, forbidden by her ballet teacher to participate, pursues a self-destructive course, nearly ruining her career when she breaks a hip bike riding to develop muscles allowing her to tap dance in the act. Surgery restores her chances as a ballerina, but the tension between family life and pursuing one's own ambition is clear. In her Posy-like behavior, however, Lyddie successfully upholds what Carolyn Heilbrun calls a "narrative of ambition" (Heilbrun, 24). Through Lyddie's taking on Rowena's flair while Gemma takes on Alice's steadiness, each girl survives the tests to her self-worth and talent.

In the context of Streatfeild's turn to autobiography during the 1960s, the Gemma books may be seen as the writer's breaking of a silence about her experience on the stage. Unlike the more fanciful Whicharts, the Robinsons supply a context for the actress daughter somewhat like an updated vicarage milieu. The interventional and firm father and the initially remote and gradually central mother are reminiscent of Streatfeild's own parents, and overall the books explore what it "really" means to be a gifted actress—the needed opportunities, the connections, the competition, the interpretive strategies, the relative nature of evaluation. The books end with Ann the most notable sensation, but each career in process looks promising, and Gemma recognizes herself as both one of the Robinsons and the daughter of a mother with whom she alternates as a star, like the figures in a Swiss clock. The notion of temporality and change built into this metaphor give Gemma implicit permission to vary her career and draw on multiple talents developed in the family.

The last of Streatfeild's children's novels—*Meet the Maitlands* (1978) and *The Maitlands: All Change at Cuckly Place* (1979)—show a lessening of her powers but indicate that she imagined herself combining several of her old plots and subjects into a family saga for children like the ones she had written for adults, such as *Caroline England*. Still interested in the process of mothering, she described the rearing of a family who lost their mother temporarily to tuberculosis and had multiple female caretakers. One critic described the Maitlands as "preposterous and antiquated, but mysteriously readable and affecting,"[6] which is relatively strong praise for Streatfeild's final books. Linking her disparagingly to "Nesbitshire," this critic underscored how well Streatfeild had learned her accidental craft as a children's writer of impressive stature.

Chapter Eight

Nonfiction and Life Writing

Historian and Conservator

The serious triumph embedded in the postwar *Party Shoes*—its celebration of England's past and future—shaped Streatfeild's nonfiction, which became increasingly significant to the author, culminating in autobiographical and biographical books that linked her to a new era in the late twentieth century. Three subjects were central to Streatfeild's numerous nonfiction works: England's history, the arts (especially ballet), and advice for young people. Two of her books inviting special note—*Magic and the Magician: E. Nesbit and Her Children's Books* (1958) and *The Boy Pharaoh, Tutankhamen* (1972)—move into the areas of literary and world history. For the most part, though, Streatfeild made England and its culture her main preoccupation. Both observant and playful as a nonfiction writer, she found ample outlets for her talents and interests in this task.

Six books written between 1951 and 1964 comprise Streatfeild's foray into telling the history of England for a young audience. Using the same crisp wording and internalized dramatic structure characteristic of her fiction, these books display Streatfeild's gifts and how historical writing can be applied to children's literature. The first of these works, *The Picture Story of Britain* (1951), addresses an American audience, using the rubric "I should like to tell you" to explain in rich detail what it means to live in the British Isles. Replete with descriptions of work, rituals, weather, and even the temperament of the population—they are "philosophical," a word that means "you must not *count* on getting what you want," and "fonder of gardens" than of all else—the picturebook demonstrates how Streatfeild warmed to her task of explaining Britain to Americans. Broad categories, such as "traditions," are used to structure the book with minimal integrating narrative but many interesting examples.

In 1952, still working from time to time on adult novels and an experienced script writer for the patriotic Bell family series, Streatfeild agreed to the request of her publisher, Michael Joseph, for a book describing the social history of England. Though she disliked the study of history, Streatfeild found a way into the task when she recalled her father talking about a flint arrowhead he had found in terms of the civilization it represented. Published during the Coronation year of Elizabeth II, *The Fearless Treasure* certainly carries the nationalistic tone of the era. But it also displays Streatfeild's cleverness at constructing child characters and their interactions. Like another prolific writer in an earlier age, Charlotte Yonge, Streatfeild drew on contemporary pedagogical and fictional methods. Yonge, directly influenced by Sir Walter Scott (Cadogan and Craig 1986, 16), emphasized heroic moments in what she termed a "cameo" technique designed to appeal to young readers of her account of English history, *Cameos from English History from Rollo to Edward II* (1868). Streatfeild's personalized method nearly a century later also used selected, representative scenes, but fictional child characters of her own time were given roles in the past, experiencing the moral and physical dimensions that Yonge's interventional narrator explained directly.

The didactic frame of the narrative involves a mysterious summons to six children from various regions and social classes. Each will be going on a journey with a Mr. Fosse; each is told at school of being selected. In the course of the story, as the group visits progressive stages of English history, the children's genetic and social heritage is uncovered. William Beaumont, son of a parson, finds his roots in Norman culture; Grace Thwaite, a miner's daughter, recognizes herself as a Viking or Saxon; Robert Ackroyd, son of a baron, is descended from a mill owner who prospered during the industrial revolution. John Fish, son of a shop keeper, comes from Flemish stock. And Elizabeth Hamblett, daughter of a poor Cockney clerk, finds an ancestor who was a Lord, while Selina Edgecomb of the landed gentry finds an ancestor on a Devonshire manor. Entering the fun of the story through descriptions of food and clothing, and using the developmental theme of problem-solving and discovery of talent in each child's manner of questioning and acting in the historical stages, Streatfeild manages to give an ideologically freighted yet entertaining account of the social history of her country.

Streatfeild shows the son of industrialists leading in creative, speculative thinking, the daughter of the gentry in need of humbling, the miner's daughter stoical and practical, and so on. In a final contest about creating a better future for England, the Cockney noblewoman Elizabeth has the best idea—to cultivate a spirit of freedom, the "fearless treasure," in the hearts of children. Spunky and even difficult on the journey, Elizabeth has dreaded discovering her own origins.

The book offers a richly textured view of England's history: invasions, agriculture, politics, religion, and ritual. Though driven by an optimistic vision in which the "pattern" of English society means that everyone has a place and oppression can be overcome by remembering Saxon freedom and the courage of past peoples, the narrative also suggests the "rise" of commoners who become educated and the "fall" of upper class people who (like Elizabeth's ancestors) encounter bad luck or are caught in social changes beyond their control, such as those of the industrial revolution. Each family has its own character, demonstrated in the personality of the child from the twentieth century. The cleverness of the story, and its detailed patterns, promised to keep Streatfeild in the public eye as a historian for children.

The interest in the contributions of various social groups shapes a 1956 collection of workers' stories, *The Day before Yesterday: Firsthand Stories of Fifty Years Ago*. One worker, a nanny named Sarah Sedgwick, describes a life tending "other people's children." The book explores the lives of many child workers, showing how children once labored in coal mines or were sent away as servants in their early teens. Streatfeild freely offers her notions of a just world: laws are inconsistent, requiring children to be licensed for the stage, yet allowing a system of tutoring tennis players and skaters favoring the children of the well-to-do. Introducing the story of Helen Atkinson, an activist who knew the Pankhursts, Streatfeild comments that the community should avoid becoming polarized over issues like suffrage.

A 1958 book, *The First Book of England*, emphasizes England's identity as an island valuing privacy above all, but with rituals and traditions, such as the monarchy, best explained by the notion of the British as a large, extended family system. In contrast to the devaluation of suffrage in the 1956 book, this one mentions the omission of women from government and describes the contributions of several women, beginning with Boadicea and including Streatfeild's ancestor Elizabeth Fry. Describing most Britons as living "between the extremes of a cottage and a castle," Streatfeild's version of English history fails to describe the economic effect of colonial expansion.

Other books for American publishers include a 1958 biography of Queen Victoria in the popular Landmark series, giving rather extensive descriptions of the political context surrounding Victoria's birth, childhood, education, and monarchy. Crediting Victoria's governess, Louise Lehzen, with the queen's successful integration of strong will and discipline, Streatfeild draws on Victoria's diary as well as other primary sources. A mother-daughter conflict, Streatfeild argues, helped to make Victoria regal (a projection, perhaps, of Streatfeild's own history). Challenging formulaic patterns of children's biography as a genre, Streatfeild gives a detailed account of a person framed by a web of social relationships and political pressures while emphasizing that person's personal history and accomplishments.

Streatfeild's primary picturebook of 1964, *The Thames: London's Royal River*, includes maps, photos, allusions to such literature as *The Wind in the Willows*, descriptions of neighborhoods like Chelsea, and a theme of change and continuity exemplified in swans swimming on the river. Unlike Victoria, whom Streatfeild acknowledged to be unaware of the lives of working people, the vicar's daughter brings in descriptions of various trades plied on the water over the centuries. Nonfiction gave Streatfeild a unique opportunity to explore the idea of work in ways different from her family novels. *The First Book of Shoes* (1967)—playing off her reputation in the United States as the author of "Shoe" novels—gave Streatfeild another opportunity to demonstrate how a narrow focus (here shoes worn by people from various groups over time) allows a glimpse of multilayered society.

A number of books Streatfeild wrote in the 1950s and 1960s allowed her to promote ballet as a suitable ground for endorsement by London's cosmopolitan population. They also allowed her to argue that ballet is a suitable art for the United States, through a method demonstrating the importance of crossing national boundaries in constructing meaning. In *The First Book of the Ballet* (1953) Streatfeild depicts an American girl, Anne, learning ballet in exacting stages, with the help of her father and his idea of using chalk and paper to overcome "rolling" feet. Anne practices diligently, inspired by interwoven stories about the history of ballet.

Beginning with the patronage of Catherine de Medici and culminating with the careers of Anna Pavlova, Ninette de Valois, Agnes de Mille, and Lucia Chase, Streatfeild traces the evolution of ballet and its incorporation into various national cultures and new media, including film. She outlines the career of great dancers through their time as choreographers, when their bodies remember and pass on the creative and meticulous joys of ballet. The "Madame Fidolia" muse of children's fiction is incorporated into nonfiction, as the book ends with "Madame Natalie" noting her own secret joy in Anne's dancing.

A longer book, *The Royal Ballet School* (1959) is an engrossing history and advocacy of ballet, stressing the writer's favorite themes: the value of teachers in bringing out talents, the richness of tradition and innovation in ballet, and the inadequacy of laws limiting children's access to training in the arts. Explaining the need for and effectiveness of White Lodge, the preparatory school for the Royal Ballet, Streatfeild dismisses concerns about children's well-being there by stating, "I believe if the value of getting used to an audience and the feel of the stage were put in the scales, against the chance of the child's becoming too theatrical or burned out, the first would prove to have the most weight."[1] She also deflects fears about male homosexuality in ballet by describing the "thoroughly male existence" led by boys in their quarters, where the neatness and display of teddy bears and other toys in the girls' house is contrasted with the boys' basement club room and messier environment. Acknowledging that some male dancers are "effeminate," Streatfeild points to the forgotten pattern of many marrying and having children, and she urges parents to encourage boys in dancing, where their futures would be more economically secure than those of girls, who nonetheless are urged to be dancers.

The book's strength lies in Streatfeild's style throughout, as she incorporates a detailed history into a narrative argument. Strong contrasts, oral qualifiers, appropriate similes and metaphors, and anecdotes allowing both shift and continuity are characteristic. Clearly writing as an insider, Streatfeild allows herself to criticize British conformity and reticence in the face of children's education for the arts. For her, a national priority should be a "dynasty of great directors" made possible by support of the Royal Ballet School.

Cultivating children as audience for the arts was another milieu for Streatfeild's enthusiasms. A 1966 book for British and North American audiences, *Enjoying Opera* (published in the United States by Franklin Watts as *The First Book of the Opera*), emphasizes learning how to enjoy the human voice as the most "emotion-rousing sound the world knows."[2] Contrasting national preferences as part of the story of opera, Streatfeild urges child readers to recognize shifting interpretations of politics and history, suggesting they listen to Wagner for a "thrilling experience" (*FBO*, 26) and value the role the arts can play in drawing people together.

For Streatfeild, the arts are in process; the past is not better but better known. As in the Gemma Bow books, Streatfeild suggests that creativity with clothing and music are key to growing up. She lists several ways children can put on or take part in operas. *A Young Person's Guide to the Ballet* (1975) reflects the writer's willingness to draw directly on her own life as a model for another generation; allusions to "Lila Field's Little Wonders" and a "lifetime of matinees and evenings of rapture" ground the introduction of "ordinary children" to the lifelong pleasures of ballet.[3] Using a boy and girl in ways comparable to the narrative line of *The Fearless Treasure*, Streatfeild demonstrates the greater ease by which the boy is accepted and the vulnerability of the girl to economic limitations. Nonetheless, Anna Pavlova, illegitimate and poor, and Beatrix Potter, latecomer to fame, are shown as part of the girl's resources for persistence. So is a teacher able to find other teachers and supportive of various kinds of dance and media.

While the boy has access to the classical tradition in this narrative, the girl is challenged to use her knowledge of the tradition and the barriers to her success in it by widening the scope of dance itself. Meanwhile, however, the boy's main obstacle to success in the Royal Ballet is his father's ambivalence about dance as a career for a son. Like other books of the late 1970s, this final text about ballet moves Streatfeild into a future in which feminist critics of the arts and recognitions of homophobia in culture would require new accounts of cultural processes in the construction of gender.

Motivated in part by economic gain and in part by her increasing delight in being a resource for the young and for an ideal of citizenship rooted in her family's social position, Streatfeild took on several editing projects. In 1950 she produced *The Years of Grace*, vignettes of career advice for youth "to avoid your being a misfit like I was."[4] Its postwar theme is gaining information and taking action to avoid a difficult passage to adulthood. In a 1955 book on manners, *Growing up Gracefully*, Streatfeild's introductions to chapters on various topics deconstructs each concept presented and then places the concept as worthwhile in a system of manners geared to respect for the rights of others. For example, advice about smoking stresses the inappropriateness of smoking in public rather than simply forbidding smoking. Jokes at the expense of others should be avoided, but avoiding such jokes (e.g., racist ones) can develop internal standards of fairness.

Confirmation and After (1963) stresses the process of learning "a colossal heritage" with implications for creativity and global social change—a process offering lifelong challenges. All of these edited collections directed British youths, especially girls, to adopt positions compatible with their own heritage but aware of world issues. Another popular edited collection is *By Special Request*, a group of short stories. Streatfeild's prolific pen also produced a spate of calendar booklets and a holiday book exploring British Christmas rituals. *The Noel Streatfeild Christmas Holiday Book* includes such autobiographical references as the time her report card was "so bad it actually made my mother laugh"[5] because Streatfeild could not explain why two positive points had been assigned out of a total of 100.

Streatfeild did not always succeed in practicing the virtues she advocated, however. A 1958 book, *Magic and the Magician: E. Nesbit and her Children's Books*, offended the first biographer of Nesbit. Doris Langley Moore resented Streatfeild's use of material released by Nesbit's daughter for a revision of Moore's book; Streatfeild used this information in her own book before the revised biography appeared. Streatfeild thanks both Nesbit's daughter and Moore herself for "generous help and encouragement" in preparing the book, probably assuming that she had the right, in her quickly assembled book, to include Moore's discoveries if she credited the biographer. Not always accurate about Nesbit—stating, for example, that she bore eight children—Streatfeild used the opportunity of literary biography to stress ideas about writing important to her own development.

In a children's book, she claims, a gifted writer draws on childhood memories but does not offer much information about her or his adult life. A somewhat unconventional and even deprived childhood can be the basis of brilliant children's literature that is not mimetic but reactive and constructive. "Solid home life," mothers linked to a certain fear, one character speaking for the author, and varied uses of successful formulas are aspects of Nesbit's writing that Streatfeild admired. Although most of these characteristics pervade Streatfeild's writing, she does not generally construct single characters who represent her values, employing interactive and dialogic methods to depict families as a whole. Only in the vicarage autobiographies does she allow one "I" to be the center of consciousness in her writing, achieving in these final books a variation important to a long and prolific career.

A triumph of Streatfeild's nonfiction was the 1972 historical work coinciding with a British Museum exhibit. *The Boy Pharaoh, Tutankhamen* highlights, as the much earlier Nesbit book does, the ways that Streatfeild's embeddedness in London social networks offered her opportunities for new writing challenges. Replete with bibliographic and scholarly references and handsome photographs and maps, the books offers a colloquaial tone and a clear, organized, dramatic marshaling of detail. Opening with a discussion of class in ancient and modern contexts, Streatfeild describes the role of "heredity, luck and environment"[6] in Tutankhamen's life and that of the archaeologist who discovered the cache, Howard Carter. The role of the workers who built the pyramids and that of the men who decided, for their own reasons, to leave the boy pharaoh's remains intact are included as part of the story's excitement. The glories of an exacting and dedicated profession—archaeology—are exhibited along with the artifacts of the boy pharaoh. Themes of interconnected times, places, and social groupings give the book vibrancy and make it readable.

Three Autobiographies and a Memoir

Angela Bull analyzes the vicarage books as novels rather than autobiographies, stating that they lack the "unvarnished truth" common to the form (Bull, 220). She compares Streatfeild's account of her life with the historical record in letters and family descriptions, noting how the books use more than the thin veneer of name changes—cited by Streatfeild in her introduction to *A Vicarage Family*—to falsify the narratives. The first book offers "grains of truth puffed up into lurid horror stories" (Bull, 220) and "highly dramatized misadventures" to tell about Victoria Strangeway (Streatfeild's invented name) as a misunderstood adolescent. The work is structured like a romance, with an invented passion for a male cousin ending in his wartime death.

The second book, *Away from the Vicarage* (or *On Tour*), minimizes Vicky's extensive theater experience in favor of describing her yearning for her family and questioning of the way she, a bishop's daughter, was spending her life. Her father's sudden death offers not the vision of home she had been conjuring up during her repertory tours but an uncertain future as a writer. The third autobiography, *Beyond the Vicarage*, seems shapeless and emotionally empty to Bull (229), offering a diminished version of the self and failing to trace the development of Streatfeild's career as a children's author. Unlike the earlier volumes, which caught at least some of the truth about her father as a saintly but imperfect parent, the last seldom refers to his memory and depicts her widowed mother as pathetic—a change from first volume's indictment of Janet Streatfeild (Sylvia Strangeway).

The biographer's discussion of the vicarage books is of particular interest at a time when much feminist literary theory addresses the issue of life writing by and about women. Bull uses a method of comparison between the novels and the historical record to support her notion of autobiography as unvarnished truth. But using another method—of noting what is placed in the foreground and speculating on the purposes served by particular narrative structures—we can draw from the

complicated definition of self-construction in autobiography sketched
by Heilbrun and others. *A Vicarage Family* stresses the idea of Streatfeild
as difficult daughter with a father who meant to guide and nurture her
but was flawed in his very saintliness. While numerous scenes in the
book show the father's care for the difficult daughter, his prayers for
guidance often result in worsening the situation. For example, when he
decides that Vicky will be confirmed early in order to subdue her rebellious spirit, she tries to ruin the event by throwing an inkwell at the
governess.

While Vicky's "thirteen copies of 'The Imitation of Christ' and seven
of 'Thoughts Before Holy Communion'" (*VF*, 219) do not turn her into
a temperate person, the silence surrounding her tantrum incorporates
her into an extended kinfolk structure where she is accepted and given
more appropriate direction. Usually this direction centers in her mother's
minimal gestures: recognizing her as a potential writer, allowing choice
of fabric and style for the confirmation dress, acknowledging the boredom of vicarage routines and the need to circumvent them by alternative
rituals like flower collecting. Commenting openly on the mother's
insuffiency as stemming from her childhood with a cold stepmother,
while depicting the class assumptions behind the father's role as vicar—
he himself never recognizes these—Streatfeild constructs a narrative in
which descriptions of material life, including the solidity and comfort of
her father's childhood under the supervision of the much-loved Gran-
Nannie, subvert notions of duty and spiritual earnestness represented by
the vicar.

Much like the families in *Parson's Nine* and *Party Frock*, the Strangeways'
strength comes from the imaginative possibilities offered by a restrictive
yet ritualized and extended social position. Reading the autobiographies is
a way of discovering implicit sources for Streatfeild's novels, even though
these books are themselves fictionalized; narrative and its powers become
the central fact in the life of the vicar's famous daughter, who depicts
Vicky discovering the pleasure of inventing families during a flower-gath-
ering expedition with her mother on a family holiday (*VF*, 191).

In explaining the creative process whereby writers are both con-
strained by discourse and yet inventive, some theorists note that the people who make "gender trouble" or challenge conventions of socialization
as daughters seize on the "interplay between originality and acceptance
of tradition as the basis for inventiveness."[7] The emotional distance
between mother and daughter in Streatfeild's memory called forth com-

pensatory connections, including partially invented families, siblings, grandparents, servants, and schoolmistresses.

Yet the flashes of insight into Vicky-Noel's future are most historically accurate and resonant at moments of disjuncture with Mrs. Strangeway-Streatfeild, who herself only partially accepts the rituals of the High Church parish. While her father's ability to listen to Vicky and to care about his wife's coldness toward her offered emotional support, her mother's less intent but more socially accurate attention enabled Streatfeild to resist the formalities and confinement of piety. Bull is correct in noting the melodrama of the first volume, but the trilogy reveals some truths behind the writer's self-fashioning as an autonomous woman with a problematic position in a family she turned into stories earning her the respect of a nation.

On Tour was billed as "an autobiographical novel of the twenties," highlighting Streatfeild's historical descriptiveness in the same way the earlier volume's focus on Victorian mores made it a product of a certain era. In the foreground of this volume are the discovery of acting and writing potential (when Vicky acts in a Mother Goose pantomime and encounters child actors to write home about) and the gap between the vicar's attitudes toward sexuality and the daughter's observation that she could never talk to her father about her true self—"the sort of person men nudge other men for knowing."[8] With a new sister in the nursery, the grown daughter observes changes in childrearing fashions; the mother gives up having a nanny in order to provide money for Vicky's schooling, although she had earlier remarked, "It's as though I was never meant to get quite free" (*OT*, 55) on discovering her late pregnancy.

The family narrative, the never quite getting free, subsumes the theater narrative; no experience on tour seems as rich as the remembered vicarage. Bull's reading of this centers on Streatfeild's avoiding the subject of her acting career and devaluing sexuality. But recent studies of female development have placed value, at least among middle-class women, on the prepubescent period of "voice"—the period, in Streatfeild's case, of inventive play and thrown inkwell. In shaping her early adulthood as sexually tawdry, in identifying child actors as an inspiration, the writer reaches back to a female self who transgresses but has a safe community. Calling this the "girl within," Emily Hancock has argued that the middle years are a space where nature and society allow a girl to flourish even as she develops critical skills.[9]

Boundless ambitions are possible, untested by the constraints of female subordination in marriage and vocation.

Allied with her father during this period yet left to her own devices in playing and learning, "the girl" in other works of children's fiction has generated such imaginative images as Harriet the Spy, Mary Lennox, and Garnet, the latter the creation of Streatfeild's admired Elizabeth Enright. Vicky's yearning for "a solid background" or home (*OT*, 167) conflicts with her yearning to "make somebody of *me*" (*OT*, 163). With the bishop's death, Vicky tells herself, "Get on with it. . . . You are on your own now" (*OT*, 168). The return home means there will be no vicarage; the implication is that Vicky will—safe from tensions with her loved, austere father—create a space for imaginative play and complex relationships centered on the memory of the childhood home.

Beyond the Vicarage begins with Vicky's character "knowing nothing and ridiculously full of self-confidence" (*BV*, 42), a kind of girl-self freed from constraints of class and social position when she lives in a boarding house typing her first book on her father's typewriter. Speaking aloud the dialogue as she wrote a second novel corresponding to *Parson's Nine*, Vicky received reviews she would characterize as nurturing: they "watered a slender plant into blossom" (*BV*, 54). Depicting her growing interest in Deptford relief work, surpassing the knowledge her father had of the area's unemployment, and guided into writing for children even as she searched in the United States for the germ of a new adult book, Vicky lights up "like a flame" at the idea of traveling with a circus to research a new children's book. Though fictional, this incident highlights the way Streatfeild constructs her adult self as an exhuberant learner. Moreover, she casts the bombing of London into a metaphor of community, where housewives prepare tea in the shelters and her own efforts were simply another level of food provision, like the children buying buns for rehearsals in *Party Shoes*. Cheered by a crowd as she bicycles into a parade area reserved for the king and queen, Vicky remembers her skirt blowing up, her glasses spattered with rain, and "still blushes" (*BV*, 175)—an image suited to Beverly Cleary's Ramona. Noting a kind of relief in achieving stolid middle age after the war, and free to travel after her mother's death, Vicky narrates her string of achievements as the product of a woman who had resisted the disciplines of childhood but acquired more depth during the war. In old age and certain that her dog understands his own death, Vicky sets down rules to live by, hoping to avoid interference in youth's pleasures and hopes, confident that "there is a world of interest still to come" (*BV*, 214).

Retaining the experimental aspect of "the girl" despite the settled if independent life she led, Vicky exemplifies an emergent feminist subject—the woman accomplished in the public sphere whose private attachments are primarily to women. Humorous and ungrandmotherly, Vicky seems self-deprecating; she is also endowed with strength and possibility by the open ending of this narrative account of a single woman at home in the world.

In a sense, Streatfeild's biography of a family servant, *Gran-Nannie*, is the final volume of the autobiography, as well as the writer's last engaging book. Boundaries between biography and autobiography are more fluid than commonly thought. More than one critic notes that biographers frequently "become" their subjects. Belle Gayle Chevigny, biographer of Margaret Fuller, calls this a reciprocal mirroring self; the subject "provides a sanctioning parent for the biographer, and . . . the biographer in turn validates the life under scrutiny,"[10] a common phenomenon when women write about other women. On three levels the old nurse of William Streatfeild had played the role of sanctioning parent for Noel Streatfeild. She had actually been a source of support and comfort when the rebellious daughter visited her grandparents in childhood. In the vicarage stories GranNannie provides food and a ready ear to the fictionalized Victoria, an all-accepting maternal embrace countering the advice of her grandmother about being her father's special daughter.

In many Streatfeild novels, especially those for children, the nanny was key to the configuration of the families; without the steady presence of Nana, for example, Garnie of *Ballet Shoes* could not have devised a plan to keep the Fossils together. As a source for her imagination, Gran-Nannie had been crucial to Streatfeild. In this final story of her family Streatfeild relates the origins and career of the servant, critiquing the class system while commending the sturdy character of Emily, who is not given the title and salary of a nanny until the mother of her employer insists her daughter treat the woman fairly. In clear, vivid language, the narrative relates the birth of the nanny during cherry blossom season at the start of the book; Emily's mother, hearing predictions for a "sweet life" for the child, might have smiled ironically at such predictions, knowing that "when her little girl was rising thirteen, up would go her hair and off she would be sent to work in one of the big houses,"[11] later to bring up a family in the same grinding poverty she would know all her life.

Streatfeild describes the close quarters—10 children in a tiny cottage—common on estates, and her acknowledgment of the inequities of the feudal system is forceful. Drawing on the coping power of ordinary people, however, she sketches Emily's mother as a woman determined to apply health and childrearing practices learned during her own servitude so that her children would not suffer from vermin and dangerous ignorance. When Emily does go off to work as a maid, her love for children, quick empathy, and energy enable her to earn a place higher than her destined one. As Streatfeild tells it, Emily notices William's mother's dismay when, a pregnant young wife, she tears a dress while visiting relatives in the house where Emily works. Speaking out of turn, Emily offers to mend the dress. Though the house employs numerous seamstresses, the young visitor is consoled by Emily's offer.

Eventually William's mother succeeds in having Emily come to her house to help in the nursery. The baby, John (William Streatfeild), has his own head nanny, from whom the young Emily learns the mysteries of how the gentry distance themselves from their children, and she pours her love into the growing family, even while compelled to work as a personal maid for the children's mother. Constant and wise beyond her years, she guides the children through their nanny's illness and death, protects them and herself during the tenure of an alcoholic woman, commits herself finally to her work when her husband of one year dies, and becomes the nanny to whom the grown John, a vicar, brings his little daughters when they are in need of affection and guidance. Streatfeild attributes therapeutic power to Emily in this book and in the vicarage stories.

The loving tone, suspenseful narrative, and clear values of this book support and pay tribute to the actual historical figure of Gran-Nannie, sanctioning her life as courageous and utterly worthy yet neither romanticizing Emily as a substitute mother or flinching from the realities of the class system. Caring for children, earning a living by this work, is condoned as a kind of nobility without the irony of novels like *A Shepherdess of Sheep*. This work of Streatfeild's old age does not view Emily's life as a humorous sacrifice: it offers a woman who finds a new home of her own, within a kinship structure and values system not utterly corrupt though demanding more from some than others. Managing not to lie or sentimentalize the gentry, Streatfeild extracts a "sweet life" for Emily even in the midst of contradictions, selfishness, and customs she does not approve of.

If the text offers a fourth level of sanction for Streatfeild herself— beyond its real, fictional, and metafictional elements—it would be in the acknowledgment that children's lives can be central to a professional without diminishing the worth of the calling or the genuineness of the love at its base. For a writer who had, since the day she was invited to write *Ballet Shoes*, become a "national monument" rather than a passing celebrity of theater and literature, the story of Gran-Nannie sanctioned a life of service, steadiness, and enjoyment of domestic dailiness.

In the final analysis Streatfeild lived such a life as well as creating versions of it. Having things be "Sir Garnet" was ultimately Streatfeild's literary accomplishment, as it was the nanny's personal vision. And, much as Virginia Woolf described a collective tradition of women writers, Streatfeild described a tradition of nannies from whom Emily learned. Unsurprisingly, Streatfeild affirms her own family, yet making a servant the subject of a final book about that family is, at very least, unusual; it is one of those things about Streatfeild's career that resembles Emily's.

Janet Streatfeild told Noel she would be the one to surprise them all. In telling the nanny's story and constructing her as muse, Streatfeild offered a final, important surprise, making her books as much a part of a future criticizing the class system as they were of a past validating those structures. Placing care for the children of others at the center of her vision, Streatfeild throughout her books depicted the competence and significance of childhood in her culture.

Chapter Nine

"National Monument," Enduring Voice

Noel Streatfeild's work endures for a number of reasons, ranging from her adept patterning of narratives to her representation of the economic and cultural basis of the family in specific historical contexts. Outstanding among Streatfeild's novels for children are *Ballet Shoes*, with its continuing popularity, meaningful roots in adult novels and folklore, and effect on later children's books; *Party Shoes*, with its use of pageantry as renewal in an era of devastation; and *The Magic Summer*, with its acknowledgment that eccentricity and isolation are costly yet powerful human strategies important to modern life. In addition, as a writer of nonfiction Streatfeild eludes the trap of universalizing all historical periods and places. She recognizes migration and invasion, rural-urban culture, and socioeconomic class as differentiating factors.

Among her nonfiction, *The Fearless Treasure*, *The Boy Pharaoh*, *Tutankhamen*, *A Vicarage Family*, and *Gran-Nannie* move well beyond the didactic model common to historical writing for young audiences. Many writers in this genre have worked from a simpler model, imposing contemporary perspectives on earlier times without acknowledging shifts in worldview and values from one epoch to another.[1] In nonfiction focused on her own time period, Streatfeild's didactic commentary in such anthologies as *Growing up Gracefully* contributes essential background for the study of childhood and children's literature. As Nancy Armstrong indicates, the advice manuals of an era are crucial to understanding such a collection (Armstrong, 257).

On these several counts, Streatfeild's prolific writing career and public life as cultural arbiter are demonstrably important for the study of literature. While children's writers are often assumed marginal to the determination of taste and ethnographic practices, Streatfeild played an important part in British self-definition after World War II. Her radio plays, numerous public appearances, and advocacy of the arts—combined with her advice-manual visibility—contributed to both residual class ideology and a definition of national values rooted in the changing contexts of twentieth-century English culture. Streatfeild's interest in the United States, for example, acknowledged a world in which writing is transnational. Without participating in Third World postcolonialism, she nonetheless acknowledged her family's history of sending its sons to India and probed at issues of property, status, and education related to empire.

Although Streatfeild's name is absent from the indexes of many standard texts on children's literature, her work is proving readable over time, and her influence on the field is becoming easier to recognize. New Puffin editions of *Ballet Shoes* and her other novels are adorned with the iconography of a new era. Not the round-cheeked Fossils of previous editions but a slender teenage dancer photographed in leotard appears on the *Ballet Shoes* cover. Photos on new editions of other "Shoe" books emphasize success in the performing arts. Like the new young audience looking for their own assumptions in their reading, critics influenced by methods other than formalism have also constructed Streatfeild's work in contemporary terms. Approaches that recognize the interlocking systems of class, gender, race, and other power hierarchies as significant to writers' and readers'consciousness explain most effectively the significance of Streatfeild's career.

Her formulaic patterns, immersion in historical context and material culture, and redefining of family in relation to economics are three major lenses for the study of this writer. Lois Kuznets's study of the "Shoe" formula is an example of how interesting features of Streatfeild's work can be highlighted by popular culture and other theoretical frameworks addressing reader interests. Feminist critics such as Mary Cadogan and Patricia Craig, looking at the historical contexts and common idioms of girls' books, have found her work of interest. The complex relationship between twentieth-century women writers and the international feminist context described by Karen Offen[2] brings to light the range of questions about mother/daughter relationships, sexuality, work and career, literary traditions, and the social construction of childhood implicit in Streatfeild's work and life. Likewise, feminist explorations of war and gender and feminist application of Bakhtin's notion of dialogics offer new ways to understand this prolific writer.

In a literary context where critics like Fred Inglis believe the best children's books are to be characterised by "boyishness"[3] and where an implicit moral tone values a "great tradition" removed from women's experience, Streatfeild—despite her love for the arts—has seemed dismissable. Perhaps because she so exuberantly told and retold stories of growing up as a difficult yet competent English daughter, Streatfeild's books participate in a shift in literary and social structures. Her most telling contribution is perhaps a redefinition of family as household—as an economic unit rather than a set of biological relationships.

As Myra Marx Ferree notes, "In a gender model, women as individual actors, agents with interests that are distinctive and meaningful, emerge out of history's shadows. Children as actors, negotiating identities, doing work (paid and unpaid), and contending for power, can be better conceptualized in this framework as well."[4] Ferree's analysis of the "new home economics" (Ferree, 252) is part of the discourse of women's studies, articulated from her position as a social scientist. Applied to novels where children are "actors" in the theater, the point is that Streatfeild moves into the sphere of appropriate and powerful metaphor in ways similar to other writers valued since the advent of feminist theory— Virginia Woolf, Rose Macaulay, and Margaret Drabble, to name a few. The reputation of other children's writers, including Frances Hodgson Burnett and Edith Nesbit, has also deepened as a result of interdisciplinary feminist analyses.

Moving the study of the family beyond the dichotomies of work/home, money/love, self-interest/altruism, and masculine/feminine is a key intellectual and social project of the late twentieth century. This context places Streatfeild in a powerful, discursive position. Resisting the common separations, including that of childhood from production, adult books like *The Whicharts* and the "Shoe" novels for children succeed in conveying the relationships between the family and other systems that shape and are shaped by it. Her child-artists are workers, producers as well as consumers, professionals rather than amateurs.

Streatfeild disliked protective legislation governing the earnings of children. Pauline Fossil and other child artists in her work are eager to spend their wages to maintain the households that make their survival possible. Rather than a regression to exploitive attitudes toward child labor, however, Streatfeild's attitude toward this issue is consistent with a notion of childhood emphasizing the child as social and moral agent. Rarely do her novels exhibit children exercising unwise judgments about money, because an inner dynamic among siblings, supported by a multivocal household such as that in *Ballet Shoes*, proves more judicious than actions proposed by isolated individuals. In her depiction of children as productive and talented, especially in the arts, Streatfeild offers a contrast to the use of the child-artist theme by Edith Nesbit several decades earlier. Nesbit spends time depicting the sensitive but partial vision of child-narrators who are writers in embryo.

Streatfeild's notion of artistic creativity, however, seems rooted in a complex web of relationships and actions as much outside of the artist's self as within it. Child-artists like Posy do seem to have innate, hereditary genius, while the quieter and more conventionally female Selina comes into her powers when she exercises responsibility for connecting and coordinating the talents of others. Yet Posy could not dance without Pauline, Petrova, Nana, and Rose, among others, and Selina exhibits sensitivity and individualism—stock qualities of the twentieth-century artist—before the pageant offers a context for her growth. Often the most humorous member of a family, such as Ginny Bell of *New Shoes* and *New Town*, is the most productive worker, thinker, artist, and citizen.

In a recitation of "important" children's literature titles, the names of what are usually thought of as "girls' books" are not heard, although literary critics, working from feminist perspectives, continue a lively discussion about *Little Women*. Increasingly, however, Louisa May Alcott's work seems less significant to contemporary child readers. In the United States, at least, Mark Twain, E. B. White, Dr. Seuss, and Maurice Sendak have wider popular recognition than writers like Maud Hart Lovelace or Louise Fitzhugh. Laura Ingalls Wilder's books may come the closest to being widely known books featuring a girl protagonist, yet the stories are thought to be historical and not simply playful.

Ballet Shoes, better known in British than in North American contexts, could arguably be considered a "girls' book" with the longevity and influence of a children's classic. Though Streatfeild incorporated male siblings into later family novels, her first children's book features a sisterhood. More so than *Harriet the Spy*, the Fossils dwell in a world defined largely by women, and they flourish there. While Petrova has interests in aeronautics, and a male mentor with a car and money, her talents and quest derive from her mother. Streatfeild enjoyed challenging conventions of gender within her securely traditional historical contexts.

Streatfeild may have avoided certain tendencies in the work of other children's writers to deemphasize the agency of girls, or of younger siblings of either sex, because of the particular childhood she experienced as a kind of excess daughter. But an equally important factor seems to have been Streatfeild's immersion in historical events. Wars, for example, upset monologic systems of authority (Reynolds, 108), and Streatfeild lived through two painful wars in ways that involved her directly in a changing society. It is at least arguable that Streatfeild's girl characters do not universally aim to please; nor is it they alone who provide a link with the past, or with other cultures, as Kimberley Reynolds (154–55) notes about girl characters in the work of a litany of British writers: Arthur Ransome, Enid Blyton, C. S. Lewis, Nina Bawden, Susan Cooper, Alan Garner, and Robert Westall.

The vicar's daughter articulated connections with the past as intrinsic to the lives of males as well as females. For example, Alex and Cathy, the Bell parents, are equally committed to the traditions their roles at the vicarage represent. But Cathy and her daughters, like Janet Streatfeild and hers, found ways to value the present and to resist the past's claim on all of their experience. The combined force of Streatfeild's personal life and her ability to observe a passing but lively parade of persons shaped by history moved her into astute portrayals of girls' experience.

A comprehensive study of Streatfeild's many books has precluded an extended discussion here of her relationship to other writers. That she was taught in childhood by Sheila Kaye-Smith, knew Storm Jameson and Rose Macaulay, was related to Kitty Barne, and displays occasional similarities to Virginia Woolf invites further study of writing communities. Streatfeild's links to theater, ballet, and a Church of England social world likewise make her career potentially productive for cultural readings. Recent work examining the mythologizing of war should include writers like Streatfeild, who lived through two major wars and drew on both to comment on the family and its ability to rear children. The papers of Streatfeild, including the unpublished diary examined by Angela Bull, remain in the private ownership of her family. Further study of these can help to focus on issues like the social construction of gender and sexuality and mother/daughter, father/daughter relationships as part of the study of children's literature. Another potential for study of Streatfeild and other prolific writers lies in the examination of iconography. The multiple editions of her books, with their shifting patterns of illustration, can demonstrate how children's literature is both a marketplace of ideas and a site of economic exchange.

American feminist scholarship typically emphasizes the expressive strength of women writers; in a British context class oppression, and in a French context psychic repression, would provide definitive vantage points. Streatfeild's writing offers material for all three kinds of commentary. Studying the work of women writers, especially writers for children, invites readers to develop relatively optimistic relational frameworks of interpretation. Such frameworks can acknowledge the oppression of women while noting the contextual features of dominance/difference. Indeed, Streatfeild's representation of childhood challenges conventional ideas about family, taste, work, and individualism.

The pink ballet slippers displayed in the bookstore window along with the first copies of *Ballet Shoes* offer a clear example of the paradox: class-defined, gender-based, redolent of imperialism, they appear to represent a way of defining elite status and keeping women alienated from their bodies. Yet Pauline and Posey Fossil strenuously resist this reading of the text of their lives. And Petrova Fossil points beyond the shop window, to the airplane circling, inviting, hinting of destruction, promising power. The political implications of being a "national monument," the disruptive powers of being an "enduring voice"—Streatfeild's Victoria-Circe pattern—remain.

Notes and References

Chapter One

1. Carolyn Heilbrun, *Writing a Woman's Life* (New York: W. W. Norton, 1988), 106; hereafter cited in text.
2. Joanne S. Frye, *Living Stories, Telling Lives* (Ann Arbor: University of Michigan Press, 1986), 3; hereafter cited in text.
3. Lois Kuznets, "Family as Formula: Cawelti's Formulaic Theory and Streatfeild's *Shoe* Books," *Children's Literature Association Quarterly* 9 (Winter 1984–85): 148; hereafter cited in text.
4. "Myself and My Books," *Junior Bookshelf* 3 (May 1939): 121–24.
5. Angela Bull, *Noel Streatfeild* (London: Collins, 1983), 141; hereafter cited in text.
6. *A Vicarage Family* (New York: Franklin Watts, 1963), 220; hereafter cited in text as *VF*.
7. Barbara Ker Wilson, *Noel Streatfeild* (London: Bodley Head, 1961), 19; hereafter cited in text.
8. *Beyond the Vicarage* (New York: Franklin Watts, 1972), 42; hereafter cited in text as *BV*.
9. Louise Maunsell Field, "An English Household," *New York Times Book Review*, 17 March 1935, 7.
10. Doris Langley Moore, *E. Nesbit: A Biography* (London: Ernest Benn, 1951).
11. *Magic and the Magician: E. Nesbit and Her Children's Books* (New York: Abelard Schuman, 1958); hereafter cited in text.
12. Mary Cadogan and Patricia Craig, *You're a Brick, Angela!* (London: Victor Gollancz, 1986); hereafter cited in text.
13. Nicholas Tucker, "Two English Worthies," *Children's Literature in Education* 17 (Summer 1986): 193; hereafter cited in text.

Chapter Two

1. *The Whicharts* (London: Heinemann, 1931), 8; hereafter cited in text as *W*.
2. Josephine Donovan, "Afterword: Critical Re-Vision," in *Feminist Literary Theory: Explorations in Theory*, ed. Josephine Donovan (Kentucky: University Press of Kentucky, 1975), 77; hereafter cited in text.
3. Janet Silverman VanBuren, *The Modernist Madonna: Semiotics of the Maternal Metaphor* (Bloomington: Indiana University Press, 1989), 182.

4. Terry Eagleton, *Literary Theory: An Introduction* (Minneapolis: University of Minnesota Press, 1983), 122.

5. *Parson's Nine* (New York: Doubleday, 1933), 313.

6. *Tops and Bottoms* (New York: Doubleday, 1933), 93; hereafter cited in text as *TB*.

7. David Cannadine, "The Context, Performance, and Meaning of Ritual: The British Monarchy and the 'Invention of Tradition,'" in *The Invention of Tradition*, ed. Eric Hobsbawm and Terence Ranger (Cambridge: Cambridge University Press,1983), 114.

Chapter Three

1. John G. Cawelti, *Adventure, Mystery, and Romance: Formula Stories as Art and Popular Culture* (Chicago: University of Chicago Press, 1976); hereafter cited in text.

2. M. M. Bakhtin, *The Dialogic Imagination*, ed. Michael Holquist (Austin: University of Texas Press, 1981); hereafter cited in text.

3. See Carol Gilligan, "Teaching Shakespeare's Sisters: Notes from the Underground of Female Adolescence," in *Making Connections*, ed. Carol Gilligan et al. (Cambridge: Harvard University Press, 1990).

4. *Ballet Shoes* (New York: Random House, 1941), preface; hereafter cited in text as *BS*.

5. Ellen Lewis Buell, "The New Books for Younger Readers: *Circus Shoes*," *New York Times Book Review*, 4 August 1940, 30.

6. *Tennis Shoes* (New York: Random House, 1938), 14; hereafter cited in text as *TS*.

7. *Circus Shoes* (New York: Random House, 1939), 8; hereafter cited in text as *CS*.

Chapter Four

1. *Luke* (London: Heinemann, 1939), 1; hereafter cited in text as *L*.

2. See Sandra Gilbert and Susan Gubar, *No Man's Land: The Place of the Woman Writer in the Twentieth Century*, vol. 1, *The War of the Words* (New Haven: Yale University Press, 1988).

3. Phyllis Lassner, "The Quiet Revolution: World War II and the English Domestic Novel," *Mosaic* 23, no. 3 (Summer 1990): 89.

4. *The Winter Is Past* (London: Collins, 1942), 316; hereafter cited in text as *WP*.

5. *I Ordered a Table for Six* (London: Collins, 1942), 105; hereafter cited in text as *OTS*.

6. Nancy Armstrong, *Desire and Domestic Fiction: A Political History of the Novel* (New York: Oxford University Press, 1987), 18; hereafter cited in text.

7. *Myra Carroll* (London: Collins, 1947), 148.

8. *Saplings* (London: Collins, 1945), 241; hereafter cited in text.
9. Mary Cadogan and Patricia Craig, *Women and Children First* (London: Victor Gollancz, 1978), 216; hereafter cited in text.
10. Sara Ruddick, *Maternal Thinking* (Boston: Beacon Press, 1989), 216.
11. Julia Kristeva, *The Kristeva Reader*, ed. Toril Moi (New York: Columbia University Press, 1986), 211.
12. Janice Radway, *Reading the Romance: Women, Patriarchy, and Popular Literature* (Chapel Hill: University of North Carolina Press, 1984); hereafter cited in text.
13. Kimberley Reynolds, *Girls Only? Gender and Popular Children's Fiction in Britain, 1880–1910* (Philadelphia: Temple University Press, 1990), 48; hereafter cited in text.
14. *Grass in Piccadilly* (London: Collins, 1947), 5; hereafter cited in text as *GP*.

Chapter Five

1. *Harlequinade* (London: Chatto & Windus, 1943), 4; hereafter cited in text as *H*.
2. *Theater Shoes* (New York: Random House, 1945), 42; hereafter cited in text as *TS*.
3. See Michele Barrett and Mary McIntosh, *The Anti-Social Family* (London: Verso, 1982).
4. *Party Shoes* (New York: Random House, 1947); hereafter cited in text as *PS*.
5. *Movie Shoes* (New York: Random House, 1949), 261.
6. Henry Pelling, *Modern Britain, 1885–1955*, vol. 8 of *A History of England*, ed. Christopher Brooks and Denis Mack Smith (Edinburgh: Thomas Nelson & Sons, 1960), 180–90.
7. *Skating Shoes* (New York: Random House, 1951), 6; hereafter cited in text as *SS*.
8. *Osbert* (Chicago: Rand McNally, 1950).

Chapter Six

1. Marjory Stoneman Douglas, "Fiction Notes: *Mothering Sunday*," *Saturday Review of Literature*, 11 March 1950, 34.

Chapter Seven

1. David Thomson, *England in the Twentieth Century* (Baltimore: Penguin Books), 261.
2. *Family Shoes* (New York: Random House, 1958), 110; hereafter cited in text as *FS*.

3. *New Shoes* (New York: Random House, 1954), 14; hereafter cited in text as *NS*.

4. *The Magic Summer* (New York: Random House, 1967), 55; hereafter cited in text as *MS*.

5. *Thursday's Child* (New York: Random House, 1970), 132; hereafter cited in text as *TC*.

6. Benny Green, "Analogies" (review of *Meet the Maitlands*), *Spectator*, 16 December 1978, 23–24.

Chapter Eight

1. *The Royal Ballet School* (New York: Collins, 1959), 131.

2. *The First Book of the Opera* (New York: Franklin Watts, 1966), 1; hereafter cited in text *FBO*.

3. *A Young Person's Guide to the Ballet* (New York: Warne, 1975).

4. *The Years of Grace* (London: Evans: 1956), 12.

5. *The Christmas Holiday Book* (London: Dent, 1973).

6. *The Boy Pharaoh, Tutankhamen* (London: Michael Joseph, 1972); hereafter cited in text.

7. Maureen A. Mahoney and Barbara Yngvesson, "The Construction of Subjectivity and the Paradox of Resistance: Reintegrating Feminist Anthropology and Psychology," *Signs* 18, no. 1 (Autumn 1992): 63.

8. *On Tour* (New York: Franklin Watts, 1965), 158; hereafter cited in text as *OT*.

9. Emily Hancock, *The Girl Within* (New York: Dutton, 1989), 8; hereafter cited in text.

10. Belle Gale Chevigny, cited in Susan Groag Bell and Marilyn Yalom, ed., *Revealing Lives* (Albany: State University of New York Press, 1990), 3.

11. *Gran-Nannie* (London: Michael Joseph, 1975), 9; hereafter cited in text as *GN*.

Chapter Nine

1. John Stephens, *Language and Ideology in Children's Fiction* (New York: Longmans, 1992), 227.

2. Karen Offen, "Defining Feminism: A Comparative Historical Approach," *Signs* 14, no. 1 (Autumn 1988).

3. Fred Inglis, *The Promise of Happiness* (Cambridge: Cambridge University Press, 1981), 34.

4. Myra Marx Ferree, "Beyond Separate Spheres: Feminism and Family Research," in *Feminist Frontiers III*, ed. Laurel Richardson and Verta Taylor (New York: McGraw-Hill, 1993), 237; hereafter cited in text.

Selected Bibliography

PRIMARY WORKS FOR CHILDREN

Fiction

Ballet Shoes: A Story of Three Children on the Stage. Illustrated by Ruth Gervis. London: Dent, 1936. Published in the United States as *Ballet Shoes.* Illustrated by Richard Floethe. New York: Random House, 1937, 1965, 1979. Illustrated by Diane Goode. New York: Random House, 1991.

Tennis Shoes. Illustrated by D. L. Mays. London: Dent, 1937. Published in the United States as *Tennis Shoes.* New York: Random House, 1938. New York: Dell, 1956, 1984.

The Circus Is Coming. Illustrated by Steven Spurrier. London: Dent, 1938. Published in the United States as *Circus Shoes.* Illustrated by Richard Floethe. Random House, 1939. New York: Dell, 1938, 1985.

The House in Cornwall. Illustrated by D. L. Mays. London: Dent, 1940. Published in the United States as *The Secret of the Lodge.* New York: Random House, 1940.

The Children in Primrose Lane. Illustrated by Marcia Lane Foster. London: Dent, 1941. Published in the United States as *The Stranger in Primrose Lane.* New York: Random House, 1941.

Harlequinade. Illustrated by Clarke Hutton. London: Chatto & Windus, 1943.

Curtain Up. Illustrated by D. L. Mays. London: Dent, 1944. Published in the United States as *Theatre Shoes; or, Other People's Shoes.* New York: Random House, 1945. New York: Dell, 1945, 1983. New York: Delacorte Press, 1985.

Party Frock. Illustrated by Anna Zinkiesen. London: Collins, 1945. Published in the United States as *Party Shoes.* New York: Random House, 1947.

The Painted Garden. Illustrated by Len Kenyon. London: Collins, 1949. Published in the United States as *Movie Shoes.* New York: Random House, 1949. New York: Dell, 1949, 1984.

Osbert. Illustrated by Susanne Suba. Chicago: Rand McNally, 1950.

The Theater Cat. Illustrated by Susanne Suba. Chicago: Rand McNally, 1951.

White Boots. Illustrated by Milain Cosman. London: Collins, 1951. Published in the United States as *Skating Shoes.* New York: Random House, 1951. New York: Dell, 1982.

The Fearless Treasure. Illustrated by Dorothy Braby. London: Michael Joseph, 1952.

The Bell Family. Illustrated by Shirley Hughes. London: Collins, 1954. Published in the United States as *Family Shoes*. New York: Random House, 1954, 1958. New York: Dell, 1954, 1985.

The Grey Family. Illustrated by Pat Marriott. London: Hamish Hamilton, 1956.

Wintle's Wonders. Illustrated by Richard Kennedy. London: Collins, 1957. Published in the United States as *Dancing Shoes*. Illustrated by Richard Floethe. New York: Random House, 1958, 1980.

Bertram. Illustrated by Margery Gill. London: Hamish Hamilton, 1959.

New Town. Illustrated by Shirley Hughes. London: Collins, 1960. Published in the United States as *New Shoes*. New York: Random House, 1960. New York: Dell, 1960, 1985.

Apple Bough. Illustrated by Margery Gill. London: Collins, 1962. Published in the United States as *Traveling Shoes*. New York: Random House, 1962. New York: Dell Yearling, 1962, 1984.

Lisa Goes to Russia. Illustrated by Geraldine Spence. London: Collins, 1963.

The Children on the Top Floor. Illustrated by Jillian Willett. London: Collins, 1964. New York: Random House, 1964. New York: Dell, 1964, 1985.

Let's Go Coaching. Illustrated by Peter Warner. London: Hamish Hamilton, 1965.

The Growing Summer. Illustrated by Edward Ardizzone. London: Collins, 1966. Published in the United States as *The Magic Summer*. New York: Random House, 1967. New York: Dell, 1967, 1987.

Old Chairs to Mend. Illustrated by Barry Wilkinson. London: Hamish Hamilton, 1966.

Caldicott Place. Illustrated by Betty Maxey. London: Collins, 1967. Published in the United States as *The Family at Caldicott Place*. New York: Random House, 1968.

Gemma. Illustrated by Betty Maxey. London: Armada, 1968. New York: Dell, 1968, 1986.

Gemma and Sisters. Illustrated by Betty Maxey. London: Armada, 1968. New York: Dell, 1968, 1987.

The Barrow Lane Gang. London: BBC Publications, 1968.

Gemma Alone. London: Armada, 1969. New York: Dell, 1969, 1987.

Good-Bye, Gemma! London: Armada, 1969. New York: Dell, 1969, 1987.

Thursday's Child. Illustrated by Peggy Fortnum. London: Collins, 1970. New York: Random House, 1970. New York: Dell, 1970, 1986.

Ballet Shoes for Anna. Illustrated by Mary Dinsdale. London: Collins, 1972.

When the Siren Wailed. Illustrated by Margery Gill. London: Collins, 1974. Published in the United States as *When the Sirens Wailed*. New York: Random House, 1977.

Far to Go. Illustrated by Charles Mozley. London: Collins. New York: Dell, 1976, 1986.

Meet the Maitlands. Illustrated by Anthony Maitland. London: W. H. Allen, 1978.

The Maitlands: All Change at Cuckly Place. Illustrated by Antony Maitland. London: W. H. Maitland, 1979.

Verse

Dennis the Dragon. Illustrated by Ruth Gervis. London: Dent, 1939.

Play

The Children's Matinee. Illustrated by Ruth Gervis. London: Heinemann, 1934. Contains *The Fourum, Me-ow, Olympus, The Princess and the Pea, The Cats, The Lily, Gentlemen of the Road, The Thirteenth Fairy.*

Nonfiction

The Picture Story Book of Britain. Illustrated by Ursula Koering. New York: Franklin Watts, 1951.
The First Book of Ballet. New York: Franklin Watts, 1953. London: Bailey Brothers & Swinfen, 1956.
The First Book of England. Illustrated by Gioia Fiammenghi. New York: Franklin Watts, 1958. London: Bailey Brothers & Swinfen, 1958.
Queen Victoria. Illustrated by Robert Frankenberg. New York: Random House, 1958. London: W. H. Allen, 1961.
The Royal Ballet School. Photographs by Gabor Denes. London: Collins, 1959.
Ballet Annual. London: Collins, 1959.
The January Baby, The February Baby, The March Baby, The April Baby, The May Baby, The June Baby, The July Baby, The August Baby, The September Baby, The October Baby, The November Baby, The December Baby. 12 volumes. London: Barker, 1959.
Look at the Circus. Illustrated by Constance Marshall. London: Hamish Hamilton, 1960.
The Thames: London's Royal River. Champaign, Ill.: Garrard, 1964. London: Muller, 1966.
Enjoying Opera. Illustrated by Hilary Abrahams. London: Dobson, 1966. Published in the United States as *The First Book of the Opera.* New York: Franklin Watts, 1966.
Before Confirmation. London: Heinemann, 1967.
The First Book of Shoes. Illustrated by Jacqueline Tomes. New York: Franklin Watts, 1967. London: Franklin Watts, 1971.
Red Riding Hood. Illustrated Svend Otto. London: Benn, 1970.
The Boy Pharaoh, Tutankhamen. London: Michael Joseph, 1972.
A Young Person's Guide to Ballet. Illustrated by Georgette Borbier. London and New York: Warne, 1975.

Anthologies

The Years of Grace (editor). London: Evans, 1950. Essays.
By Special Request: New Stories for Girls (editor). London: Collins, 1953.
Growing up Gracefully (editor). Illustrated by John Dugan. London: Barker, 1955.
Confirmation and After (editor). London: Heinemann, 1963.
Priska, by Merja Otava (editor). Translated by Elizabeth Portch. London: Benn, 1964.
Nicholas, by Marlie Brande (editor). Translated by Elisabeth Boas. London: Benn, 1968. Chicago: Follett, 1968.
Sleepy Nicholas, by Marlie Brande (editor). Translated by Elisabeth Boas. London: Benn, 1970. Chicago: Follett, 1970.
The Christmas Holiday Book, The Summer Holiday Book, The Easter Holiday Book, The Birthday Story Book, The Weekend Story Book (editor). Illustrated by Sara Silcock. London: Dent, 1973–77.

PRIMARY WORKS FOR ADULTS

Autobiographies and Memoir

A Vicarage Family. London: Collins, 1963. New York: Franklin Watts, 1963.
Away from the Vicarage. London: Collins, 1965. Published in the United States as *On Tour: An Autobiographical Novel of the Twenties*. New York: Franklin Watts, 1965.
Beyond the Vicarage. London: Collins, 1971. New York: Franklin Watts, 1972.
Gran-Nannie. London: Michael Joseph, 1976.

Fiction

The Whicharts. London: Heinemann, 1931. New York: Coward McCann, 1932.
Parson's Nine. London: Heinemann, 1932. New York: Doubleday, 1933.
Tops and Bottoms. London: Heinemann, 1933. New York: Doubleday, 1933.
A Shepherdess of Sheep. London: Heinemann, 1934. New York: Reynal and Hitchcock, 1935.
It Pays to Be Good. London: Heinemann, 1936.
Caroline England. London: Heinemann, 1937. New York: Reynal and Hitchcock, 1938.
Luke. London: Heinemann, 1939.
The Winter Is Past. London: Collins, 1940.
I Ordered a Table for Six. London: Collins, 1942.
Myra Carroll. London: Collins, 1944.
Saplings. London: Collins, 1945.
Grass in Piccadilly. London: Collins, 1947.

Mothering Sunday. London: Collins, 1950. New York: Coward McCann, 1950.
Aunt Clara. London: Collins, 1952.
Judith. London: Collins, 1956.
The Silent Speaker. London: Collins, 1961.

Romances (as Susan Scarlett)

Clothes-Pegs. London: Hodder & Stoughton, 1939.
Sally-Ann. London: Hodder & Stoughton, 1939.
Peter and Paul. London: Hodder & Stoughton, 1940.
Ten-Way Street. London: Hodder & Stoughton, 1940.
The Man in the Dark. London: Hodder & Stoughton, 1941.
Baddacombe's. London: Hodder & Stoughton, 1941.
Under the Rainbow. London: Hodder & Stoughton, 1942.
Summer Pudding. London: Hodder & Stoughton, 1943.
Murder While You Work. London: Hodder & Stoughton, 1944.
Poppies for England. London: Hodder & Stoughton, 1948.
Pirouette. London: Hodder & Stoughton, 1948.
Love in a Mist. London: Hodder & Stoughton, 1951.

Plays

Them Wings. Produced in London, 1933.
Wisdom Teeth. Produced in London, 1936. London: French, 1936.
Many Happy Returns (with Roland Pertwee). Produced at Windsor, 1950.
    London: English Theatre Guild, 1953.

Nonfiction

The Day before Yesterday: Firsthand Stories of Fifty Years Ago (editor). London:
    Collins, 1956.
Magic and the Magician: E. Nesbit and Her Children's Books. London: Benn, 1958.
    New York: Abelard Schuman, 1958.
Introduction to *Long Ago When I Was Young*, by E. Nesbit. London: Whiting
    and Wheaton, 1966. New York: Franklin Watts, 1966.

SECONDARY WORKS

Books

Armstrong, Nancy. *Desire and Domestic Fiction: A Political History of the Novel*.
    New York: Oxford University Press, 1987. Cultural history of the
    English novel, linking novels to the creation of domestic ideals of the
    middle class.

Bakhtin, M. M. *The Dialogic Imagination*, edited by Michael Holquist. Austin:
    University of Texas Press, 1981. Theorizes the novel as a genre structured
    within developing reality and able to depict social structures through the
    observation of linguistic difference.
Bull, Angela. *Noel Streatfeild: A Biography*. London: Collins, 1984. The most
    complete biography, drawn from a study of Streatfeild's personal papers.
    Discusses in detail the family background and her interest in the arts and
    in reviewing children's books; includes several photos. Depicts Streatfeild
    as unreflective and rather compulsive about writing but brave and ener-
    getic, especially during the blitz. Generally presents the writer as an
    attractive, albeit somewhat reserved, personality.
Cadogan, Mary, and Patricia Craig. *Women and Children First: The Fiction of Two
    World Wars*. London: Victor Gollancz, 1978. Describes fictional represen-
    tations of women and girls in wartime era and in retrospective fiction,
    giving social background and development of literary forms.
_____. *You're a Brick, Angela!: The Girls' Story, 1839–1985*. London: Victor
    Gollancz, 1986. Traces history of magazines and books in relation to the
    genre girls' fiction; 15 of Streatfeild's novels are discussed under the head-
    ing "New Vistas." Provides an extensive bibliography.
Cawelti, John G. *Adventure, Mystery, and Romance: Formula Stories as Art and
    Popular Culture*. Chicago: University of Chicago Press, 1976. Lays out a
    theory of formulaic literature, addressing intersection of aesthetic and
    social experience. Suggests formulaic literature assists in assimilation of
    change into traditional mores; accounts for differences among authors by
    applying the auteur concept from film theory.
Crouch, Marcus. *The Nesbit Tradition: The Children's Novel in England,
    1945–1970*. Totowa, N.J.: Rowman & Littlefield, 1972. Sees Streatfeild
    as participant in a cycle of children's literature moving from Britain to
    North America and back. Notes her as beginning career books and pio-
    neering the modern children's novel as an integral and well-researched
    whole; sees novels that convey information a product of postwar era.
Eagleton, Terry. *Literary Theory: An Introduction*. Minneapolis: University of
    Minnesota Press, 1983. Overview of contemporary literary theory, using
    class issues as primary focus; suggests cultural studies as appropriate to
    and needed in the education of children, not only to observe ideological
    patterns but to enhance linguistic range of readers from all social groups.
Ellis, Anne W. *The Family Story in the 1960s*. London: Clive Bingley, 1970.
    Examines children's novels from the perspectives of human relations,
    everyday life, and problems of characters, with a history dating back to
    Maria Edgeworth. Mimetic approach criticizes trends in the family novel,
    such as the skillful disposing of parents.
Elshtain, Jean Bethke. *The Family in Political Thought*. Amherst: University of
    Massachusetts Press, 1982. Collection of essays, including a review essay
    by Jane Flax, dealing with political theory in relation to the family as

institution. Stresses importance of studying family as depicted in classic texts of philosophy and literature.

Eyre, Frank. *British Children's Books in the Twentieth Century*. New York: Dutton, 1973. Cites Streatfeild following lead of Arthur Ransome in depicting the "adventure of living."

Fisher, Margery. *Intent upon Reading*. New York: Franklin Watts, 1964. Study of modern fiction for children; sees Streatfeild as showing real life's connection with the exotic.

Frye, Joanne S. *Living Stories, Telling Lies: Women and the Novel in Contemporary Experience*. Ann Arbor: University of Michigan Press, 1986. Analyzes narrative forms in relation to social milieu and readers' participation in cultural change.

Gilbert, Sandra, and Susan Gubar. *No Man's Land: The Place of the Woman Writer in the Twentieth Century*. Vol. 1, *The War of the Words*. New Haven: Yale University Press, 1988. Describes differences for male and female writers in the experience and construction of modernism in the context of the rise of feminism and the decline of Victorian ideals of femininity; calls institutions of marriage, family, and education "a vexed terrain" of male/female conflict.

Heilbrun, Carolyn. *Writing a Woman's Life*. New York: W. W. Norton, 1988. Argues for study of biography and autobiography of women in relation to questions of power, friendships, and narrative strategies. Gives a useful bibliography of scholarly sources.

Ruddick, Sara. *Maternal Thinking: Toward a Politics of Peace*. Boston: Beacon Press, 1989. Philosophical perspective on the work mothers do; includes concept of male mothers. Practices chosen by mothers can lead to reimagining of a peaceful world; emphasis on maternal nonviolence and concepts of the body deemphasizes attractiveness of violent sacrifice and transcendence of warrior ethos.

Wilson, Barbara Ker. *Noel Streatfeild*. London: Bodley Head, 1961. New York: Walck, 1964. Early monograph, based in part on personal acquaintance with Streatfeild. Cites family solidarity as key to Streatfeild's children's books; draws on Streatfeild's deliberate self-construction as public person.

Articles

Kuznets, Lois R. "Family as Formula: Cawelti's Formulaic Theory and Streatfeild's 'Shoe' Books." *Children's Literature Association Quarterly* 9 (Winter 1984–85): 147–49, 201. Posits Cawelti's work as a basis for analyzing the family novel, using Streatfeild as an example. Links formulaic works to developmental stages of readers and discusses the need to examine microlinguistic variations of the novels.

McDonnell, Carol. "A Second Look: *Ballet Shoes*." *Horn Book Magazine*, April 1978, 191–93. Points out the literary qualities of the book.

Tucker, Nicholas. "Two English Worthies." *Children's Literature in Education* 17, no. 3 (Fall 1986): 191–97. Praises Streatfeild for an advanced social outlook for her time but sees her silence about sexuality as a sign of immaturity.

Index

The Author

Nancy Huse is professor of English and director of Women's Studies at Augustana College (Illinois). She received her B.A. from Caldwell College, Caldwell, New Jersey, her M.A. from Duquesne University, and her Ph.D. from the University of Chicago. She has published essays on Tove Jansson, Katherine Paterson, Meridel LeSueur, L. M. Montgomery, and Padraic Colum, as well as on children's literature and literary theory. In 1983–84 she received an American Council of Learned Societies grant to investigate the aesthetics of children's literature in Germany and Sweden. She is currently president of the Children's Literature Association.